THE
SERPENT'S
FURY

KELLEY ARMSTRONG

PUFFIN CANADA

an imprint of Penguin Random House Canada Young Readers,
a division of Penguin Random House of Canada Limited

First published 2021

1 2 3 4 5 6 7 8 9 10

Jacket design: Kelly Hill
Jacket art: © Cory Godbey

Manufactured in Canada

Library and Archives Canada Cataloguing in Publication

Title: The serpent's fury / Kelley Armstrong.
Names: Armstrong, Kelley, author. | Daumarie, Xavière, illustrator.
Series: Armstrong, Kelley. Royal guide to monster slaying (Series)
Description: Series statement: Royal guide to monster slaying |
Illustrated by Xavière Daumarie.
Identifiers: Canadiana (print) 20200368958 | Canadiana (ebook) 20200368974 |
ISBN 9780735270152 (hardcover) | ISBN 9780735270169 (EPUB)
Classification: LCC PS8551.R7637 S47 2021 | DDC jC813/.6—dc23

Library of Congress Control Number: 2020948566

www.penguinrandomhouse.ca

Penguin
Random House
PUFFIN CANADA

THE
SERPENT'S
FURY

CHAPTER ONE

"So, tell me about the dropbears," my brother, Rhydd, says as we ride toward the Dunnian Woods.

"They're bears," Alianor says. "And they drop."

At a look from me, she throws up her hands. "Fine, they're marsupials. Happy? They still drop."

"More like plummet," I say. "Dive-bomb, maybe? *Drop* implies a slower—"

"Stop, Rowan. Just because you're the royal monster hunter doesn't mean you need to be so particular about monsters."

"Um, I think the fact that I'm the royal monster hunter *does* mean I need to be particular. False information leads to—"

"La-la-la," she says, hands pressed to her ears.

I turn to Rhydd. "Just wait until a dropbear falls on us. Alianor's dying words will be 'That monster moved *so* much faster than I expected.'"

Rhydd grins. In front of me, my jackalope's nose rises, twitching, as he scans the sky for marsupial monsters plummeting from the clouds.

Dain rolls his eyes. "Trees, Jacko. They need trees to drop from. Remember?"

"Plummet."

"Yes, princess." Another eye roll for me, and he spurs his horse to catch up with the other hunters ahead.

The four of us are joking, keeping things light, trying to forget we're heading into the monster-filled Dunnian Woods to deal with a dropbear-filled cabin. As for why there are dropbears in a cabin . . . The week before, they'd attacked us, and we'd lured them into the cabin to keep them contained until we could figure out what to do with them. We'd left food and water, as well as a couple of guards to ensure they survived their imprisonment.

Dropbears never used to come this close to Tamarel. Given the choice between a single gryphon and a swarm of dropbears, I'd rather face the former. Yes, a gryphon is as big as a small house, with a beak that can snap a person in two. But dropbears only come in swarms, attacking at night with claws and fangs, and a viciousness I haven't encountered in any other beast.

Still, I never considered *not* joining this expedition. I *am* the royal monster hunter. Well, technically, I need to complete my trials first, but until then I carry the ebony sword and do my duty.

I'm also a princess. Mom's the queen, and Rhydd will succeed her on the ivory throne. That's how it works in our kingdom. The oldest child gets the throne, and the next one takes the sword. I'm two minutes older than Rhydd, but after my aunt died—killed by the gryphon that injured Rhydd's leg—we switched roles, which is what we always wanted.

Our kingdom is Tamarel, and it's separated from other kingdoms by the Dunnian Woods and the mountains, both infested with monsters, just like the ocean along our other borders. That's why our clan—Clan Dacre—is in charge.

We have a gift for monsters, and not just hunting them. I'm riding a ceffyl-dwr—a carnivorous river horse—with a jackalope sitting in front of me. A pegasus filly flies overhead. A warg—which is like a giant wolf—runs at my side. Rhydd rides our late aunt's unicorn, Courtois.

There's another monster who is very much on my mind these days. Tiera, a young gryphon I raised from birth. Last week, I left her in a gryphon aerie with others her age. It was the right thing to do, but it still hurts so much.

As happy as I am to have the monsters around, I'm thrilled to have so many of my favorite fellow humans on this mission. Riding beside Rhydd is Alianor, daughter of the Clan Bellamy bandit warlord. She's also a healer in training who has declared she wants to be Tamarel's first monster doctor. And then there's Dain, who's training alongside me to be a hunter. As for grown-ups, we have our trainer, Wilmot, plus my guard, Kaylein, and six monster hunters, not to mention a few members of my father's clan, including my great-great-aunt Yvain. Her family had been tracking the dropbears when we found them, and we left a couple of her granddaughters to watch the cabin.

That's a huge group for an expedition into the Dunnian Woods. Proof of just how dangerous dropbears can be. It's also large because Mom agreed to let Rhydd join us. All Tamarel's kings and queens must be fully trained monster hunters, so he argued that he should come along. He isn't allowed to actually get near the cabin, though. This is why I happily gave up the ivory throne to wield the ebony sword: One of these things is a whole lot more exciting than the other.

We took the back roads through Tamarel. That's a must if we want to get anywhere fast. We're the country's prince and princess riding with an entourage of monsters. For local villagers, it's like the best parade ever. This trip isn't about meeting our subjects, though. It isn't even just about handling a cabin full of dropbears. It's about figuring out why the drop-bears are here—what's bringing them and other monsters to our border.

Wilmot and Yvain mapped out a route to minimize our path through the woods. At the edge, we need to leave the horses and the equine monsters behind. The forest is too thick for them to pass through easily, and if we're attacked by predators, it's also too thick for them to defend themselves properly.

We overnight there, and then two of the hunters remain with our mounts while we head into the forest. One problem with that is that equine monsters aren't horses, and we don't treat them as such. Courtois wears a saddle but no bridle. I've been riding Doscach—the ceffyl-dwr—bareback. Monsters are never under our control, and they always stay with us by choice. Courtois has no interest in venturing into the woods and happily stays behind. The pegasus filly, Sunniva, takes off flying, doing as she pleases. Doscach, though, insists on following me, and I have to ask him, very politely, to stay behind. When that fails, Courtois keeps him out by herding him away.

Once inside the forest, we need to move quickly. It's a long hike to Dropbear Cabin, and with the marsupials being nocturnal, it'll be easier to deal with them during the day. We're off at the crack of dawn, and we eat our midday meal as we walk, reaching our destination by mid-afternoon.

That's where my adventure comes to a screeching halt.

"Rhydd?" Wilmot says as our hunters check their weapons. "You'll be staying here with Kaylein."

"What?" Rhydd and I say in unison.

"Your mother said you could come as long as you didn't get within a hundred feet of the cabin."

"A hundred *feet*?" I say. "I know he can't go to the cabin, but he can't even *see* it from here." I sweep my hand across the view, which consists of trees, trees and more trees.

"Rhydd and Kaylein will stay here and watch for stragglers," Wilmot says. "We'll surround the cabin and then close in on it. A couple of dropbears may escape."

"And run in this exact direction?"

Wilmot skewers me with a look, but I only shoot the same look back.

"Remember that time when we were little?" Rhydd says to me. "We wanted to help Jannah and Dad drive off a pack of wargs, and they left us in the next town, standing on the inn steps with our practice swords, in case a warg came our way . . . while they chased them in the other direction." He lifts his gaze to Wilmot's. "I have no idea why this plan would remind me of that, since I'm no longer a child. Coincidence, I presume."

Wilmot grunts and says nothing.

"I will be thirteen next month," Rhydd says, his voice even. "I am a young man and a future king, and I would like to be treated as both. That doesn't mean I insist on being allowed to join the hunt. It means I insist on being told the truth."

Yvain walks over. "Your mother doesn't want you within a hundred feet of that cabin, your highness, because you *are* the future king, and because your leg still causes you trouble, and because dropbears are a match for a fully trained hunter, which you are not yet. She's allowed you on this excursion but drawn the line at actually allowing you to deal with the dropbears. If you feel that treats you as a child, I won't say I blame you. It's something you need to discuss with her, though."

I open my mouth to protest, but Rhydd cuts me off with, "Understood. Thank you for telling me the truth." He shoots a quick glance at Wilmot.

Wilmot grunts again, but this time there's apology in it. I still want to argue, which is why my brother is better suited for the throne. We shouldn't argue with those who are simply carrying out the queen's orders.

And this is where I need to make a difficult decision. Where I need to remember who I am and my own responsibilities.

If I were the full-fledged royal monster hunter, I'd be leading this expedition. But the reason Alianor, Dain and I trapped the dropbears was because we couldn't deal with them in any other way.

I'm not fully trained. I haven't passed my trials. While I'm a good fighter, Kaylein is better, and she shouldn't be left behind.

"I will stay with Rhydd," I say. "Kaylein should take my place in the attack." I turn to Alianor and Dain. "Alianor? Would you stay with me? Dain—"

"No," Dain says, crossing his arms. "Don't ask, princess. I'm not staying behind."

"If Rowan asks, you *will* stay," Wilmot says. "As long as you're training as a hunter, you are part of her troop."

Dain's scowl should be aimed at Wilmot. Of course, it isn't. Wilmot is the foster father who rescued Dain from a life of servitude. The one who gets his scowls is me, as usual.

"I was going to give you the option," I say, channeling my brother with my calm voice. "You may go with the hunters or stay with us. I was also going to suggest to Wilmot that whoever does stay behind should patrol at a hundred-foot perimeter and deal with any dropbears who escape the hunters." I look at Wilmot. "Would that fulfill my mother's requirements?"

Wilmot lifts one shoulder. "I believe so."

Yvain smiles as she pats my arm. "Well done, child. That is a fine plan."

"All right, then," Wilmot says. "Dain, you'll help Rowan."

"What happened to me getting a choice?" Dain squawks.

"That was your royal monster hunter talking. This is your guardian. Now come along, and I'll show you the boundary line."

CHAPTER TWO

We're patrolling at a *two*-hundred-foot perimeter. That's what Wilmot insisted on, to be absolutely certain we don't come within a hundred feet. I can grumble, but I understand his point. It's not as if we can accurately measure distance out here, and if we wander too close to the cabin and get hurt, Mom will blame him. Put us at two hundred feet, and we're definitely far enough away.

I still feel like a child again, standing on that inn front step with my practice sword. Maybe I made the wrong choice here. I thought I was being mature, giving up the adventure to protect my brother and allow Kaylein to fight. I also thought we could provide a valuable service. But this far from the cabin, in the thick woods, we might as well be a mile away. We can't even overhear the others.

"I can go see what's happening," Dain says. "Report back."

I hesitate and then shake my head. "We should stick together. I'm sorry."

"Leaders don't apologize," Alianor says.

I disagree, but in this case, she has a point. I should reserve my apologies for real mistakes, not toss them out like flower petals at a spring festival.

"The fact that we're not hearing anything suggests nothing is happening," I say. "Either the hunters are still planning or the dropbears are gone. Let's keep patrolling."

At my wave, Jacko leaps into the lead, his head high, nose higher, like a leporine army general. The warg, Malric, stays at the back of our group. I could say he's guarding the rear, but the way he's dragging himself along—while casting glances toward the cabin—tells me he's feeling like a babysitter put in charge of the children while everyone else goes to the party.

"You can join them if you want," I say.

I get a baleful, yellow-eyed stare for that. When Jannah died, she asked Malric to look after me. Kaylein might be assigned as my guard on expeditions, but the warg is my bodyguard, at my side nearly every moment of the day, whether he likes it or not.

I fall back beside him and murmur, "I know how you feel. This is boring, isn't it?"

He chuffs. Monsters are smarter than regular animals, but they can't talk or understand human speech. What they understand is body language and facial expression and vocal tone.

When Jacko lets out his alert cry, I swear all five of us—Malric included—perk up. Everyone reaches for their weapons, and Malric presses against my leg as he looks about. Jacko zooms to sit on my feet, which I appreciate. In his jackalope mind, he's protecting me, but I just want him close so I can protect *him*.

Around us, the forest is silent, and I'm about to declare it a false alarm when a growl ripples Malric's flanks.

I follow his gaze to see the undergrowth quivering. Something's coming, fast, but it's small, hidden beneath the ferns that tremble, the only sign of its passage.

Snake? There are several dangerous snake-monsters.

A shape bursts from the undergrowth, racing straight for us only to notice us at the last moment and nearly bowl itself over tumbling to a halt. The creature rises onto its hind legs, swaying from side to side as it surveys our group. Its gaze lands on Jacko, and it lets out a shriek and topples over backward in its panic to escape.

As it runs, I sputter a laugh. "Well, Jacko. That's a first. Apparently, you're scarier than Malric. At least to a colocolo."

We watch the tiny monster run off. From the back, it looks like a lizard with weirdly long legs. Instead of scales, though, it has mottled brown feathers that blend with the autumn undergrowth. When it glances back, we see its feathered rodent head and furry ears.

I bend down to Jacko. "You do know that's supposed to be your dinner, right?"

He squeaks, gaze fixed on the undergrowth, his entire body tense, as if expecting the rat-sized monster to wheel in attack.

"That's what happens when you coddle a jackalope," Dain grumbles. "He's scared of his food."

I shoot Dain a look. That's all it takes to make him shift and glance away. Dain is cranky about being kept out of the cabin attack, and so he's taking it out on us, and my look warns him I won't put up with that. I used to make allowances for his horrible childhood, but I've learned that isn't really what he needs or even wants. He's given me permission to tell him when he's being a jerk, and I will, if only in a look.

He knows he's wrong here, too. Jacko is only half-grown, but he's already able to hunt for himself. I can only guess that the colocolo makes him nervous because he's never seen one. While we do get them in the barns during winter, they're rare, being mostly from the mountains, where they live in colonies.

I scratch behind Jacko's antlers. "Thank you for the warning."

Dain snorts, and I expect Malric to do the same, but when I look over, the warg is staring after the colocolo. I frown. Wargs generally just ignore colocolos—too small to be a threat and too small to eat unless they're starving.

So why—

The answer hits a heartbeat before the ground vibrates under my feet. I leap up and reach for my sword.

"Rowan?" Alianor and Dain say at the same time, as Rhydd pulls his own blade.

"Fleeing," I blurt. "What was the colocolo flee—?"

Before I can get my sword out, the undergrowth erupts. At first, I see nothing. I'm looking overtop of the bushes, watching for what is coming, my gaze swinging between the treetops and the mid-view, expecting a predator at least the size of a warakin.

Instead, I only hear the thunder of running paws and then shrieks of panic and alarm, shrieks that come from both monster and human, as the foliage explodes and a wave of colocolos washes over us.

I'm not sure what's happening even as my feet fly out from under me. Jacko screams, and then I'm falling, feeling cold bodies running over me, tiny claws digging in.

I flail as my brain screams that this is ridiculous—they're *colocolos*, barely bigger than mice. Yet I am trapped under this wave of creatures, drowning under it, fighting, clawing at the air, nothing but black above as a writhing blanket of darkness suffocates me.

Another scream, and that cry pierces the panic. That cry is both a goal and a fresh source of terror.

Jacko. He's here somewhere, buried under this wave of colocolos. I fight the horde, my arms and legs churning, knocking tiny bodies aside as I focus on the muffled cries of my jackalope. It's like battling the tide, relentless and unceasing, as tiny reptilian bodies pour over me, too panicked to care about my blows.

Whatever they're fleeing is scarier than a jackalope. Scarier than a twelve-year-old human girl. Scarier even than a warg.

I push down the thought. What matters is that Jacko is suffocating.

One final cry. A horrible, gurgling cry, and I manage to rise, colocolos hanging off me. Then I throw myself in the direction of the sound. One hand touches fur. Soft rabbit fur. I grab as hard as I can, sending up a silent apology as my fingers dig in, knowing if I lose him, he'll be carried away on this tide. I clasp Jacko tight with one hand and then the other, and I hoist him over the bodies.

Something hits me. Something moving against the tide. I'm propelled up as a beast the size of a small pony flips me onto its back. A flash of black fur. A growl.

"Malric," I say, the name coming on an exhale of breath.

Before I can react, I'm swept from the stampede of colocolos, awkwardly half riding Malric, one leg over him, the other bent under me. Clutching Jacko to my chest, I manage to grab a handful of Malric's fur and stay on as he fights through the tide. At first, I can't see anything. The colocolos keep climbing me, as if I'm a tree stump in their path, their claws needling my skin.

Finally, my head is clear of the river. I see them then, and it is a sight my brain can't quite comprehend. It truly looks like a river, a roiling torrent of brown, the colocolo shapes lost in the flow. There must be hundreds of them. No, *thousands*, forming a deep current.

"Rhydd!" I scream.

I twist, panic lighting anew, imagining him under that sea of bodies.

"Rowan! Here!"

I follow the voice and see him on the "shore." He's with Alianor, and he's holding onto a thick tree branch as she grips his free hand and stretches toward me.

Malric leaps. One massive bound and he's free of the tide, hitting the ground hard enough that I roll off, still clutching Jacko.

I scramble up, stray colocolos running over my feet, and look about wildly. "Where's Dain?"

No answer.

I spin on Alianor and Rhydd. "Where is Dain?"

They're both scanning the colocolo river now. We all are. Jacko climbs onto my head and sounds his alert cry. Malric

— 13 —

lopes alongside the colocolo onslaught as he hunts for any sign of Dain.

I break into a run, following the flow, my gaze skimming over it as I shout, "Dain!" Jacko scrambles down onto my shoulders and clings there for dear life.

Thousands of colocolos. *Thousands.* Colonies of them streaming in a panicked rush, trampling everything in their path. I twist to look behind me and see Rhydd and Alianor, now jogging beside the stampede, shouting for Dain.

I keep running, searching in vain for anything among those feathered brown bodies. There's nothing. Nothing at all and—

A figure half rises, on all fours, pushing up for no more than a heartbeat before being engulfed again.

"There!" I scream. "He's there!"

I run as fast as I can. Malric overtakes me, but the river of bodies shifts, colocolos swarming over the warg's paws. He tumbles to the side, and I race past even as he snarls and snaps at me.

Dain rises on all fours again, only to topple backward and be carried along by the flow. I keep running until I'm ahead of him. Malric lunges into my path, but I only snarl back at the warg. A two-heartbeat standoff between us. Then Alianor is there, Rhydd behind her, his bad leg dragging slightly.

"Form a chain!" I shout. "Like you were doing before!"

I point at a tree. Rhydd makes it there, one arm wrapping tightly around it as he reaches for Alianor. She clutches his hand. I tug Jacko from my shoulders, and he doesn't like that, but he only chatters his disapproval as I shove him toward Malric. Then Alianor grabs my ankle, and I leap into the stampede.

CHAPTER THREE

I hit that roiling mass of tiny bodies, and there is a moment of absolute panic as something inside me screams.

What am I doing? Didn't I just get free of this? What if Alianor can't hold me? What if Rhydd loses his grip? I'll be as lost as Dain, suffocated under a river of colocolos.

I grit my teeth as the tiny lizard monsters scrabble over me and the sunlit forest disappears into darkness. Alianor's fingers dig into my ankle, and I am safe. She won't let anything happen to me.

Dimly, I hear Alianor and Rhydd shouting to Dain. The last I saw him, he was being carried down this side of the river. Any moment now, he'll hit me or hit Alianor, and we'll catch him.

Something warm brushes my outstretched fingertips. In a sea of cold-blooded bodies, that can only be Dain. I throw myself sideways, hands grasping as I reach. My fingers close on Dain's arm. It's thinner than I expect, but it's warm, and so I grasp it and pull.

Dain screams. It's a spine-chilling scream, and I imagine him being ripped apart by colocolos. I yank with all my might, and my hands rise above the colocolo tide, gripping Dain's wrist, his skin darker than I remember—

That isn't skin. Nor is it Dain's hand. I'm holding the leg of some black-furred beast, with a paw as big as my palm. A webbed paw. Claws shoot out, four dagger-like claws, and my brain whispers that this is the point at which I should release my hold. I don't. I'm holding some creature—some monster—and if I let it go, it will die.

When those razor claws spring out, I only release my hold with one hand to keep feeling around for Dain, because he is my priority. I will let go of this beast if I can't hold it and save him, but—

Dain slams into me. There's no doubt it's him—the cursing gives it away. He rams into my side, and I twist and grab him even as his own hands find my tunic and hold tight. A shout from the shore and we are being pulled in, scrabbling and gripping with all our strength until Alianor gives a tremendous heave and we fly free of the stampede, Dain still clutching my tunic and me holding his arm. We tumble to the ground, and Rhydd lets out a shout, and then there is a scream.

Something rips at my hand sharply enough to make me howl. There's a moment where I think it's Dain clawing at me. Then the scream and the pain merge, and I remember Dain wasn't the only one I was holding. Which may explain why my brother is running at me with his sword out.

I leap to my feet and lift both hands to stop Rhydd. Dain jumps up and pulls his dagger, and then Malric is there snarling and snapping at . . .

A black cat. That's all I see at first, everything happening so fast that my brain is reeling. I blink, and the shape comes into focus. It is a cat . . . sort of. It's the size of a hunting dog, low and lean and rippling with muscle. A sleek black-furred wildcat with webbed feet and gills that flutter as it breathes. What looks like dark stripes at first becomes strips of jet-black scales, glittering in the sunlight that pierces the forest canopy.

"Cath palug," I whisper.

"I can see that, princess," Dain growls, brandishing his dagger. "Now back away from it before it skewers you with those claws."

"But it's . . . it's a cath palug. I've never seen one. It must have gotten swept up in the colocolos and—"

"And it is now crouched in front of you, trying to decide whether you're too big to eat. The answer is no, princess. You are not too big for a cath palug. It's already scratched you, and it can smell the blood, which is dripping from your arm, in case you can't feel that."

I wave off his concern and absently wipe the blood away. It's a small wound, not even worth bandaging. The monster feline keeps staring at me, its tail swishing. That tail ends in a barb— or it should, but I can't quite make it out while it's moving.

I glance over at the colocolo river, but it's only a trickle now, the main body of rodent monsters disappearing through the forest.

"I want a better look at it," I say.

"Great," Dain says. "Just let me kill it first."

I give him a look for that.

Dain turns to Rhydd. "Please, your highness, could you talk some sense into your sister?"

"Having known Rowan from birth, I can tell you that dissuading her from this is a fool's task. One does not come between Rowan and her monster studies. Would you like me to restrain it, Ro?"

Both Dain and Alianor squawk in alarm.

"Oh, come now," Rhydd says, moving forward. "I'm sure I could wrestle it to the ground and—"

I lift a hand to stop him. "You're giving Dain heart failure. He doesn't realize you're joking."

Rhydd's lips twitch. "Perhaps I'm serious. We are nearly thirteen. Filled with the madness that overtakes young men, I shall throw myself upon the beast and pin it down, surviving with the scars to prove my—"

"Utter stupidity," Alianor says.

"I was going to say warrior blood, but that works, too."

Rhydd takes a strip of dried meat from his pocket and passes it to me.

I peel off a piece and toss it to the beast. It sniffs first, and then snatches up the meat and swallows it whole. The cath palug regards me then, golden eyes fixed on mine. I take a closer look at the creature while tossing it bits of meat. A cath palug is an aquatic feline, like the ceffyl-dwr is an aquatic equine. Many monsters seem to be a mash-up of two or more regular animals. That leads to stories about their origins, usually some variation of "animal *x* fell in love with animal *y* and had a baby." Romantic, but as any scientist knows, impossible.

The truth is evolution, with the monsters being a later version of the animals.

At first glance, the cath palug just looks like a black wildcat. Then you notice the adaptations: the webbed feet, the scaled stripes and those glorious gills. I don't manage to get around its backside to get a close look at its tail, but it is indeed barbed, almost like a fishhook. I've seen pictures of cath palugs "fishing" with their tails, which is nonsense, of course. The barb is for fighting. Its claws and teeth do the hunting work.

When I run out of meat scraps, I try giving it a dead colocolo, who'd been trampled by its brethren. I toss the lizard-rat at the cat monster's feet, and the cath palug only fixes me with a baleful stare.

Dain chuckles. "I think it's saying it never wants to see another one of those, much less eat one."

"No doubt," I murmur.

I back away then and wave everyone else to follow. The cath palug stretches, as if it had decided to rest here and hadn't been "trapped" by humans and their companion beasts. Then it saunters off with a flick of its tail.

"Bye, kitty!" Alianor calls. "No need to thank us for rescuing you!"

"It already did," I say. "By not shredding my face."

The colocolo river is long gone, leaving a swath of destruction, as if it truly had been a rushing current diverted from its course. Grass, undergrowth, brush, even saplings have been flattened.

"That was . . ." Rhydd mutters.

"Unexpected?"

He sputters a laugh. "I was going to say terrifying. But definitely unexpected."

"Fascinating, too." I walk to the flattened ground and crouch to flip over the body of another dead colocolo. "Fascinating and terrible. Something panicked them enough to make them flee, entire colonies of them, running as fast as they could, trampling everything in their path, even each other."

Alianor shivers. "I'm with Rhydd on this. *Terrifying* is the right word, because all I can think of is . . . what would make them do that?" She peers into the forest. "While I'm always right behind you for an adventure, Rowan, I'm not sure we should hang around to see what they were fleeing from."

When I hesitate, she steps toward me. "I'm serious, Rowan. This isn't the time for scientific curiosity."

"Agreed, but it's not the time to flee for *our* lives either. That was a panic stampede. I've heard of it with colocolos, though it's usually only one colony. Animals like cows do it, too. Even humans will, if they're frightened enough. But with colocolos, once they start, they don't stop. The panic is infectious. For that many colonies to come together, the root cause is likely miles away."

Rhydd nods. "One colony panics and then 'infects' another as it passes."

"That would be my theory. The only thing killing them right now is each other."

A moment of silence, respect with a touch of grief, for the monsters so frightened they would crush one another to escape a threat that they've long outrun.

"Now the problem is where they're going," I say. "Not where they've been."

With that, Rhydd straightens so fast his bad leg falters. He wheels to the east—to Tamarel.

"We need to get home," he says. "Before they do."

I nod. On their own, colocolos are no more dangerous than lizards or mice. A colony can destroy a crop, but they're mostly just pests. Thousands, though? They would destroy everything in their wake. Crops, livestock, even humans, suffocated beneath them, as we almost were.

"We need to get Wilmot," Dain says. "Forget the drop-bears for now. Warn him . . ."

He trails off with a whispered curse as he realizes what I already know—that we delayed too long with the cath palug. That was my fault. I thought the danger had passed. I didn't stop to think it through. Now that I have, it's too late to go get the others.

The moment I realize the problem, I start moving and the others follow.

"Someone needs to tell Wilmot," Dain says again.

"I will," Rhydd offers.

Dain shakes his head. "That's a messenger's job, not a prince's. Alianor—"

"Alianor has two legs that work at full capacity," Rhydd says. "She can run. I cannot."

"But you shouldn't go alone," I say. "This is still the Dunnian Woods. No one should be alone. Alianor, would you please—"

"On it," she says, and then to Rhydd, "Let's go, your highness."

As Dain and I run, I try not to worry about Alianor and Rhydd. I also try not to worry about Wilmot and the expedition. Shouldn't they have heard us cry out when we were being trampled? They were only a couple hundred feet away, weren't they?

What if something happened to the expedition? What if they'd been fighting for their lives . . . and I just sent Rhydd and Alianor into danger?

Or what if they'd left the dropbears in the cabin and come to find us? Rhydd and Alianor might walk in thinking it was empty, since the hunters were gone.

These are baseless worries. If my hunters had been fighting for their lives, we'd have heard it. If Rhydd and Alianor found the hunters gone, they'd check before entering the cabin.

What's really bothering me is the fact that I'd been too preoccupied with the cath palug to realize the colocolo stampede was bearing down on Tamarel. Having failed there, I'm going to second-guess every impulse now. I suppose that's a good thing in the sense that I'm taking time to work through all possibilities—which I didn't do earlier.

While I do question whether I've made the right choice, I don't turn around. I've already lost enough time. Dain and I run full-out for as long as we can, racing after the colocolo swarm, seeing where they're heading so we can warn the hunters waiting at the forest's edge.

Jacko tires first, and I go to scoop him up, but Malric grabs the jackalope and swings him over his head. Jacko lands on the warg's broad back and latches on, his semi-retractable claws digging in. Then we're running again.

I'd wondered how the cath palug got caught up in the stampede. Of course, we'd been caught off guard, too, but we aren't creatures of the forest. Even Malric and Jacko grew up in the castle. Yet a forest monster should have had time to get out of the way.

Soon I see what probably happened to the cath palug. Earlier, I'd reflected that colocolos were too small for bigger predators. But the stampede has left dead ones trampled everywhere, and few predators will ignore an easy dinner.

As we run, we see other carnivores. A lone wolf crunches through a small pile of colocolos. A wildcat snatches a dead one from the trail right before we pass. Two warakins spar over the right to colocolos still on the path.

I see more animals and monsters on that run than I saw on our entire walk through the forest. Not one does more than glance our way. After a river of colocolos, two human children fleeing a warg-riding jackalope is simply another sign that the world is ending and they should eat while they still can.

And then we hear the screaming.

At first, my heart stops, imagining Rhydd and Alianor and the others being swallowed by a sea of colocolos. Of course, that makes no sense. We must have gone at least two miles, and the sound comes from in front of us.

As we pause, Dain doubles over to catch his breath. I focus on the source of the screaming. How far away is it? *What* is it?

"It's the colocolos," Dain says between heaving breaths. "That's what they sound like when . . . when they're being attacked."

He means being killed. He's just putting a gentler face on it, and I bristle, thinking he's sparing my feelings. Killing is a part of my job. A last resort, but even when I regret it, I know it's the right thing to do.

Then I realize this isn't about me.

It's about Dain.

When he was only five—a time when my own parents were giving me a colocolo hunt in our barn—Dain's family sold him into indentured servitude as a ratcatcher. *Killing* rats, because there was no chance that anyone cruel enough to use child labor was going to release the pests, as my parents did after my "hunt." Dain grew up killing these rodents and, undoubtedly, killing colocolos, too. What he's saying here is that he knows what they sound like when they're dying. He stopped himself because he didn't want me thinking of him killing them.

He didn't want me judging him for a choice that was never his to make.

I peer in the direction of the squealing and screaming. "What could do that? A cath palug didn't faze the colocolos. Nor a wolf, a wildcat, warakins . . ."

"Exactly. What could be bad enough to scare the colocolos when none of those other predators did? A terrible, terrible monster that we absolutely, positively should not get closer to. We should just count ourselves lucky—princess? Get back here, princess. We . . ."

I don't hear the rest. I'm already jogging toward the screams.

Dain is still grumbling. Grumbling, but following. When I point this out, he shoots back that he's just keeping an eye on me, because if I die on his watch, my mother will throw him to a pack of wargs. Ludicrous, of course. We've never had capital punishment in Tamarel. Also, like Rhydd, my mother knows that when I put my mind to something, nothing can stop me. That's why I'm in the Dunnian Woods with my ebony sword in hand. Believe me, if she had her way, I'd be safe inside the castle walls with my history book instead.

Dropbears and colocolos live in and near the mountains to our west. Something has them—and other monsters—migrating east. That's a problem for the country that lies in the east: ours. Now something has the colocolos screaming loud enough to be heard a quarter mile away. I wouldn't be doing my job if I ran in the other direction.

I'm walking now and assessing with each step, listening and peering into the forest. The shrieks have died down to the occasional squeal. When Malric stops and snorts, I nod.

"Time to get off the trail."

I'm looking for a good route when Dain taps my arm. He motions for me to follow him. When I hesitate, we exchange a series of looks that communicate as well as words. It helps that Dain expresses as much with body language as any beast—in his case, mostly scowls and glowers and grunts and eye rolls. It's really amazing how many different things you can say with an eye roll, each little nuance giving it a whole new meaning.

In those looks and gestures, I let him know that I'm hesitating because he doesn't want to investigate, so I suspect he's leading me astray. He responds—via a hard stare—that he wouldn't do that. He's taking the lead because he's the one who has spent a third of his life in this forest. If I want to sneak up, he's better at doing that. True.

With a nod and a wave, I tell him to carry on. He cuts wider around the noise than I'd have, farther from the epicenter of the situation.

"*Epicenter?*" he whispers, face screwing up, when I tell him so.

"It means—"

He waves his hand. "I can figure it out, princess. Smaller words work just as well."

"Words are like tools. Another might do the job, but there's usually one that's exactly right."

He mutters about show-off princesses. Three more steps, and I grab him around the shoulders so fast, he stumbles against me and then shoots me a glower.

"Was that necessary?" he whispers.

"Hugs are always necessary."

The look on his face makes me sputter a laugh and then slap a hand over my mouth to keep quiet. Malric moves up against me. On his back, Jacko strains forward, nose wriggling. I nod ahead, where the forest has gone silent.

"Something's wrong," I say.

"There are many things wrong today, princess. You'll need to be more specific."

I bend and place one hand on the ground. Jacko hops down to sniff beside me. "I could feel the earth vibrating. Even before the colocolos. It's stopped. Maybe you're right. We should head back."

"Come on, princess," he says. "Let's go solve your mystery."

"If you insist."

CHAPTER FOUR

We've solved the mystery. And our problem has been solved at the same time. There is no longer a colocolo stampede, and I don't feel one heartbeat of relief at that.

We're standing at the edge of what was once a riverbank. Below used to flow a tributary of the Michty River, which mysteriously dried up years ago. Over the centuries, the tributary had worn away the soil and bedrock, leaving a cliff taller than our castle. That is what the colocolos reached.

They weren't attacked. They ran over the edge. Those shrieks were the tiny rat-lizards realizing what had happened. Shrieking to warn the others. To warn those who were too panicked to pay attention.

Some heard. Some understood. There's trampled undergrowth all around the embankment from streams of colocolos breaking off and scattering. They've disappeared into the forest. Scores—maybe even hundreds—of survivors, rattled from their terrified rush, now running off to lead ordinary lives, no threat to Tamarel.

Some who fell over the edge also survived. I spot colocolos perched on every ledge and jutting stone, all finding ways to climb down the cliffside. They will be fine. Like the others, they'll disperse, and the Dunnian Woods will have many more colocolos than it did yesterday, which could upset the ecosystem, but it's not an imminent danger.

The rest, though? The rest went over the edge and perished at the bottom. One look at the heap and I quickly back away. I want to believe many are just stunned or unconscious. Some will be. But most are dead.

I remind myself that this is nature. Some animals are known to walk off cliffs or into bodies of water, and people think that makes them stupid. It doesn't. While I've never been part of a true crowd—princes and princesses are always kept clear for safety—I've seen tightly packed throngs at festivals. Imagine if the earth opened up in front of them. They wouldn't be able to see what was happening because they're moving together as one body. That's what happens occasionally in nature and even then, as with the colocolos, some at the back will realize the problem in time to stop.

This is nature, wonderful and terrible. When Dain glances over the cliff edge, I peek down to see hawks swooping in to grab dead colocolos. Weasels drag off more. Soon larger predators will come, and then the scavengers. It's like the carnivores clearing away dead colocolos from the path—one good thing coming of the deaths. With the autumn days growing colder, this food will be welcomed by every predator anxious to gain winter weight.

When I say this to Dain, he nods. He seems to relax, too, as if he'd been worried about how I'd react. I love monsters. I hate to see them suffer. I hate to see them die. But I'm not a child who sees only cute and cuddly creatures coexisting in peace. I understand the cycle of life, and that is where I must find solace from the grief. What happened here was horrible for the colocolos, but a boon for predators and scavengers.

Malric nudges me. When I glance down, he looks in the direction of the distant cabin. Time to get back to Rhydd and the others. There's no threat to Tamarel here.

The trail left by the stampede allows us to find our way back easily. The trouble might come in knowing where to stop, but I think I'll recognize the landscape there. Dain says he definitely will.

We've been walking for maybe a half mile when I'm so lost in my thoughts that I almost wander off the trail. Malric has to grab my tunic and yank me back. Jacko starts to topple off my head and then jumps down to chatter at the warg.

"You should be walking anyway," Dain says to the jack-alope. "You aren't a baby."

"It's all right," I say as I hoist Jacko up. I cradle him in my arms, and he snuggles against me, careful to keep his antlers from bashing my face.

"I don't know how I walked off the path." I laugh, but it comes out ragged. "Silly, huh?"

"Sun's dropping." He waves at the shadowy forest in front of us.

"We need to move, then. We can't be out after dark."

"It'll be a long time before that." He pauses. "Except that doesn't help much, does it? Twilight's more dangerous than night, because most predators hunt at dawn and dusk. What's the word for it?"

I don't answer.

"Cre-crep—" he says.

"Crepuscular."

He snaps his fingers. "That's it."

He's humoring me. I want to say I'm fine. It's a lie. He can tell that by the way I'm lost in my thoughts, by the way I'm clutching Jacko, who's nuzzling me, offering comfort. Even Malric trots at my side instead of hanging back like usual.

"You couldn't have stopped the colocolos from going over that cliff, Rowan."

"I know. I'm actually thinking of what made them panic in the first place. Of what drove the dropbears east. Something is . . ."

"Pushing them out," he says. "Not drawing them in. Yes, I've joked about you being a monster magnet, but don't go taking all the credit for this."

I manage a half smile. I do have nightmares that all of Tamarel discovers they're being invaded by monsters attracted by their new royal monster hunter's overly strong clan blood. That isn't true. If I seem to be a monster magnet, that's because I'm always looking for them.

My "clan gift" is an affinity for monsters and an understanding of them. Even if there's more to it, if I could possibly be giving off something, like a pheromone that draws them to me, there's no way it'd attract monsters fifty miles away. That would be magic. There is no magic here, just science.

Science says there's something else driving the monsters down. Something is happening in the mountains.

"What if I can't fix it?" I blurt.

He glances over. "Fix . . . ?"

I wave my arms. "This. Gryphons were bad enough, and I was pleased with myself for resolving that problem, so it's like . . . it's like the universe threw this one at me. Something I can't fix."

"You're afraid of failing," Dain says as I pet Jacko. "Afraid you can't stop this problem, and Heward will use it as proof you aren't fit to carry the ebony sword."

Heward is my mother's cousin. If I fail as royal monster hunter, his children—who are a few years older than us—will take our spots. Not just mine, but Rhydd's. They'll rule Tamarel, but really it'll be Heward, who's horrible and greedy and power-hungry.

I don't answer for a few more steps. Then I say, my voice barely above a whisper, "But that's never going to stop, is it? The problems will just keep getting bigger, and Heward will keep using them as a reason to take the throne and the sword. I think I've finally proven myself . . . and then there's another task. Another challenge. It won't ever end."

Dain doesn't answer.

My cheeks heat. "Sorry. This is politics. Boring politics."

"Not boring. Just . . ." He flails. "I don't understand it. I mean, I do, in a way. The mayor I worked for, he was all about politics. Whatever it took to get more money and power. He's like a miniature Heward. But when I worked for him, he was my boss. My master, even. You don't work for Heward. You're a princess. You're above him. You don't work for anyone but yourself. Except maybe your mother."

I shake my head. "I work for the people. Just like my mom."

"But if that's true, then Heward *really* isn't your boss. He's one of thousands of bosses, and it's their opinions that matter, right? The more good things you do, the less people will want a royal monster hunter who *hasn't* stopped gryphons and a colocolo stampede."

"I didn't stop—"

"But we could say you did."

"That's—"

Malric leaps into my path. He blocks us, growling and looking up into the trees. As soon as I see the direction of his gaze, I fall back, my arm going out to push Dain along with me.

Trees. Twilight. Dropbears.

Bright-red eyes glow high in a treetop. I crouch, one knee going to the ground as I keep my gaze fixed on that tree. I lower Jacko and pull my sword. Dain's hand goes for his bow—his weapon of choice—but then moves to pull his dagger instead. His hand flexes on it as we continue to back away while scanning the trees.

"I see one," he says.

"In a white birch?" I say. "Twenty feet ahead to our left?"

"Yes."

"Me, too. Any others?"

"No," he says.

"Will you keep your eyes on that one while I look around?"

"Of course."

I do that, pivoting to scan the treetops. The sun has barely begun to sink, bringing just enough shadow to show those glinting red eyes.

"Do you know of any other tree-climbing forest animals with red eyes?" I ask.

A sound cuts Dain off. A soft cry, like a child or a wounded animal. I tense, but I stop myself before running forward.

Dropbears use that sound to draw in good and decent people. Which proves that dropbears are kind of evil.

"I'm not falling for it this time, tiny monster bear!" I call.

"Monster marsupial, you mean."

I stick out my tongue at Dain. Then I square my shoulders and march forward.

"Uh, Rowan?" he says.

Malric blocks me again, growling. Only Jacko marches along at my side, ready to do battle.

"It's one dropbear," I say. "We need to get back to Rhydd and the others before dark."

"What if it's a trap?"

"Then the only way to spring it is to walk in."

"That makes no sense, princess," Dain says as he comes up behind me.

"If it's a trap, we could retreat, only to discover that is what the dropbears wanted. If we continue on, they'll reveal themselves."

"And kill us both."

"Probably."

He snorts at that but stays in step behind me. When we reach Malric, the warg digs in, his head lowered, fur bristling in warning.

"Do you see or smell others?" I say, gesturing at the one dropbear and then at the woods.

He looks about, and his nose samples the air. It's a discreet movement, as if he doesn't want to admit he understands what I'm asking. When he glowers, I know the answer is no. He doesn't detect anything except that one dropbear.

"You may lead if you like," I say, waving. "But I *am* going past it. I must."

Malric tosses his head, fangs flashing, but then stalks toward the dropbear's tree. I follow.

Five feet from it, he plants his furry rump, a clear sign that this is as far as we're going. We aren't passing until we're sure there's only one dropbear.

From here, I can see its outline.

"It's small," I say. "Really small."

"That's what they want you to think," Dain says. "Because it's the bait."

"Cover me, please."

I sheathe my sword and take out a fire stick box. I ignite one and hold it up. Between the stick and the remaining sunlight, I can see well enough. The dropbear lets out that same wounded-beast cry.

"Yeah, that's not working anymore," I say. "We can see you, and you're not . . ."

I trail off as the flame reflects off wet blood down the beast's chest.

"That'd be from its dinner," Dain says. "Don't be fooled, princess."

"The blood comes from its shoulder," I say. "You can see the gash from here. It's injured."

"No."

"No what?"

"We are not rescuing a dropbear."

"Baby dropbear."

"Even worse. You have a weakness for baby monsters."

I lift the fire stick. "Isn't that . . . take a look at its left ear. It's ragged, like the one that accidentally followed us into the cabin when the dropbears first attacked." I step forward, earning myself a growl from Malric. "I think it's the same juvenile. It stayed up in the rafters and didn't hurt us."

"Not for lack of trying."

I shake my head. "It never actually tried. It correctly assessed the situation and realized it was no match for us, and it stayed in the rafters. Now it's out and injured and—"

"No."

"—and alone. Whatever happened to the others, this little one is alone and—"

Dain throws up his hands. "Fine." He shoves the dagger into its sheath. "If I die in the next few minutes, you'd better make sure I get a bard song."

"You're not going to die. The dropbear is safely in that . . ."

I trail off as he starts stalking toward the birch. "Dain?"

"A bard song, celebrating my deeds as your companion. The gryphon, the jba-fofi, the dropbears and ceffyl-dwrs. Saving your blasted bunny from certain death. I want it all in there. And sending the colocolos over the cliff? That was my idea. Afterward, I perished at the claws of a huge dropbear while defending you from certain death."

He stops under the tree.

I start toward him, Malric only watching and following. "The only death you're going to get is falling from the tree if you try to climb it. You can't—"

He whistles, the sound slicing through the silent forest. Then he lifts his arms. "All right, baby dropbear. Do your thing. Drop."

I barely get a squawk out as I race forward to knock Dain out of the way. The dropbear is already plunging, paws extended, and I cannot see its claws in that blur, but I know they're out as it drops straight onto Dain's—

Straight *into* Dain's arms.

CHAPTER FIVE

Dain staggers back in surprise and tries to throw the dropbear off, but it clings to his tunic. It does not slash him with its claws. Does not dive for his neck with its razor teeth. It just clings and whimpers.

At that whimper, Dain's arms reflexively cradle the beast, even as his horrified expression says he wants to throw it to the ground and run.

"Rowan?" he says in a strangled voice. "It . . . it's . . ."

"*So* cute. You're both just so cute."

His look cuts me off. That look tries for outrage, but it's tinged with fear and worry.

"Could you please . . . take it?" he says.

I reach out, but the dropbear hisses at me and snuggles against Dain. Jacko bumps my leg with his antlers, and when I look down, he rears onto his haunches, telling me he would also like to be picked up. When I do, I think he wants a closer look at the dropbear, but he only cuddles into my arms and then gives a haughty sniff to the wounded creature.

I chuckle. "Yes, you are the royal monster hunter's snuggle-beast. Dain now has one of his own, the lucky boy."

"I didn't want—I *don't* want . . ." Dain manages, in a strangled tone.

"You rescued it."

"For you. I was getting it to drop out of the tree so you could examine it. Could you please . . . take it?"

As much fun as this is, we *do* need to get back to the others. I set Jacko down and try to take the dropbear again, but neither small monster likes that. Jacko chitters with jealousy, and the dropbear hisses with annoyance. I get Dain to drop to his knees as I settle onto the ground. The small beast still won't budge. It's staying with its rescuer, and that's not me. So I examine it on Dain's lap.

"It's a she," I say.

"Not really my main question right now."

"I know. Well, you'll be pleased to know she doesn't seem too badly wounded."

"Also not my main question. How do I get rid of her?"

I look at him. "So you *aren't* concerned about her injuries?"

He shifts, one arm tightening around the dropbear when she starts to fall. "Fine. I am, of course. Just . . . examine her, and let's get going."

"She's torn the skin at her shoulder. A bite, I think. It isn't deep, but it would likely become infected because she can't clean it—she'd need another dropbear to do that, and she seems to have lost the others."

"Or they drove her out. Maybe they blame her for the trap."

I consider that. "I don't think so, but they might have rejected her because she'd been inside with us. With humans. Whatever happened, she's alone and she needs this shoulder stitched. We'll bring her along. Alianor can fix her up, and then we'll let her go. Unless you want a baby dropbear."

"No."

My lips twitch. "I'm teasing. She's old enough to be on her own. We'll get her fixed up and then—"

Malric twists suddenly. He's been standing guard, watching the treetops. Now, when he turns, his gaze fixed up there, I think he's overreacting. I don't see a thing. Yes, it's a little darker now, but there are no telltale red eyes.

I'm about to joke about Malric's nerves when something moves overhead. A shape perched high in a massive oak. Another shape moves beside it. Both are the size of full-grown dropbears.

Dain leaps up, and the juvenile lets out a squawk and digs in her claws. He grabs her and holds her at arm's length. "None of that. You *did* lay a trap."

"Not necessarily," I say. "She could have been separated, and they've come for her. Either way, though, we need to give her back. Let me set her on the ground."

I reach out, and the marsupial monster's head swivels as she snaps at my hand. Malric growls, and Jacko chatters, but the dropbear just glares at them and clings to Dain.

"Maybe if you take off your tunic," I say to Dain.

"Ha, ha."

"I'm serious. Slide it over your head, and then we'll run. Malric can make sure she doesn't follow."

"This is silly." He grabs the dropbear. "You need to go—"

The dropbear yowls, a most piteous sound as she throws back her tiny head. Dain ignores her cries and tries to wrestle her free of his tunic.

I gesture for Malric to guard the dropbear as we make our escape. Dain crouches, holding her at arm's length while he wriggles himself out of his tunic. Then he gives the dropbear a little toss, very gently, onto the ground. The moment she releases her grip on the tunic, he snatches it up. Then we run. A snarl behind us as Malric leaps into her path. Shrieks— furious shrieks—as the dropbear tries to follow. When we're about twenty feet away, I turn.

Malric still blocks the dropbear's path. And she's still on her hind legs, screeching at him. Dain looks from me to the monsters, and then squares his shoulders.

"It's for the best," he says as he puts his tunic back on.

"It is."

"She'll be fine."

"She will."

Jacko chitters at us. When I glance down, he looks between Dain and the dropbear and chitters again, in obvious concern.

"She will be fine," I say firmly. "Her pack is right there."

Jacko rises on his hind legs and sniffs the air. Then he looks at me and chitters.

"Yes," I say. "We know there are dropbears, and we're going to make a run for it as soon as they come for her."

He eyes the treetops. Malric is still facing off with the dropbear, growling and snapping and sounding exasperated. She's screaming at him, equally frustrated.

"Come on, dropbears," I murmur. "Come get your—"

Jacko sounds his alert cry and races back toward Malric. He jumps over the warg, thumping Malric with his hind legs and earning a snap. But Jacko doesn't seem to notice. He's leaping at the dropbear.

"Jacko!" I scream. "No!"

The dropbear pulls back one paw, claws seeming to glitter in the near-darkness. I run at them, shouting. Malric lunges, his black form nearly invisible against the dark. Two more dark forms drop from the tree.

No, they don't drop.

They *swoop*.

It's two large, winged shapes, bigger than owls or hawks. I shout and draw my sword as Malric leaps overtop of Jacko and the dropbear, sheltering them. Dain must have already had his bow out when I ran to protect Jacko. He fires an arrow. It's one with firebird-feather fletching, and it glows like flame through the dark sky.

The arrow hits, and a swooping shape lets out a scream— a *human* scream. It plummets, and the second one keeps diving. It's aiming straight for Malric. He doesn't move. Doesn't try to go after it. He's protecting the smaller monsters and trusting us to handle the threat.

I'm there in a flash, sword swinging through the air. It hits the creature at the same time as another arrow. Droplets of blood spray. The beast lets out one of those chillingly human screams, but we are not for one moment fooled into thinking we've injured actual people. Every monster hunter knows which flying beast screams like a person.

A harpy.

The injured beast flaps its long wings and disappears into the darkness overhead.

"There will be more," I say. "They only travel in flocks."

"I know."

"Have you ever dealt with them?" I ask, gaze still fixed on the sky.

"Once. A woman came through the forest saying her child had been carried off by harpies. Wilmot thought she was lying. He still went, but he said that harpies don't ever leave the mountains, and sometimes people say flying monsters made off with their children if there was an accident. That's what he expected had happened."

"But it was actually harpies?"

"Yes. The family lived too close to the mountains. They were trappers."

"And their child . . ."

"Yes."

That's all he says. All he needs to say. I still shiver.

Dain continues. "Wilmot said if he'd known it really was a harpy nest, he'd never have taken me. I was about nine at the time. I was fine, but . . ."

I don't say anything. I understand what he means. Harpies are bigger than eagles and, like dropbears, they always hunt in groups. They've been known to carry off adults. When I first heard that, I'd scoffed to Jannah, expecting her to join in.

She hated misinformation about monsters, especially the kind that incited fear.

Instead, she'd told me that years ago, on a manticore hunt with Wilmot and my father, she'd watched harpies carry off a hunter. Then last year, when we studied harpies, she told me the part she'd left out. My father had wanted to shoot down those harpies. Jannah had feared they'd drop the woman, but Dad knew that was a risk. And he'd said it was better than the alternative. So they'd all tried to shoot the creatures down, because a quick death from a fall would be better than what would happen to the woman when they got her to their nest.

I look at the dead harpy and try not to shudder. Even last year, Jannah refused to tell me exactly what would have happened to that hunter. She didn't need to. My imagination worked just fine.

The escaping harpy has gone silent, and so has the forest. We keep our guard up, though, watching and waiting. Then I kneel beside the dead harpy, tensed and half watching the sky.

Legend says that the harpy is half bird and half woman. When I'd first seen a picture of a harpy, I'd been offended. Half woman? Half *ugly* is what they were. Maybe it's because the scream sounds like a woman's and the top half is simian.

I find most monkeys adorable. Yes, some are jerks, but they're all cute. Harpies are a nightmare version, their skin stretched taut over the bone, making their heads skull-like, with beady eyes and tiny ears and protruding fangs. They have four legs, plus wings, and the back legs are birdlike with talons. The front legs are a monkey's, with five fingers, including opposable thumbs. The tail is prehensile—long, slender and capable of grasping.

"Would you like to examine it?" I say as I rise.

"I did that the last time. It was enough."

I hand him back his firebird arrow. "Good shot. A clean kill."

He only mutters about his second shot not doing the same. I ignore that. He's ducking my compliment, but secretly, he's pleased.

"We should get moving," I say. "Does anyone see any more? Malric?"

The warg sniffs the air. He's been scanning it, and I'm sure he's been sniffing, too, but now he makes a show of it. A grunt says he doesn't detect more harpies.

"Dain?"

He shakes his head. "This is a long way from their territory. Even more than the dropbears and the colocolos. It must have been just these two."

"It could be they were the only survivors, or they split off from the flock to hunt. Either way, we really need to get to the others before dark. Jacko?"

The jackalope pops his head out from under Malric. I praise him for staying there. He's been getting better—understanding that he can't fight *all* the monsters. It's a lesson we've both needed to learn.

I'm reaching out to give Jacko a cuddle when another head pops from the shadows under the big warg. I'd forgotten about the juvenile dropbear.

When Jacko hops out, he glances back at the dropbear. Then at me. Then at her.

"I know," I murmur. I look at Dain. "We definitely need to take her now. She was the one the harpies were going for."

He puts his bow on his back and drops to one knee. "Come on, then."

She zooms out, and he tumbles backward, hand falling to his dagger. But the dropbear only leaps onto his chest and clings there, making little mewling noises, as if she'd been abandoned by her only friend.

"Hug her," I say as he stands there, arms at his sides, the dropbear hanging from his tunic.

He gives me such a look you'd think I'd ordered him to kill the poor beast.

"Put your arms around her so she doesn't fall," I say.

He gingerly wraps his arms around her, and I try not to roll my eyes. I scoop up Jacko and settle him onto my shoulders. The dropbear eyes him, her head tilted.

"No," Dain says. "Absolutely not."

She puts one tentative paw on his shoulder and hoists herself up. He tugs her back down.

"No," he says firmly. "Keep that up and you're walking, injured shoulder or not. If you wanted the nice human, you should have picked Rowan."

As he talks, she watches him intently. Then she snuggles against his chest, and we continue on.

CHAPTER SIX

"Did you see that?" I ask as we make our way through the dark forest.

"See what?"

I stare up into the treetops and then shake my head. "I thought something moved."

He squints. "Maybe the wind rustling the leaves?"

I glance at Malric, who waits patiently for us to continue, having detected nothing. We get another ten steps before the warg is the one slowing and looking up.

"Malric?" I say.

He grunts and continues on. Next, it's Jacko, who arches up on my head and sniffs the air. Then he settles again.

"Are we all just paranoid?" I murmur.

"We have reason to be," Dain says. "The trees could be full of harpies, and we'd never see them."

"That is *not* helpful."

He passes me a small smile. "Usually you're the one saying things like that, so I thought I'd beat you to it."

"Thanks."

Dain and I squint into the trees. I even lift a fire stick. Malric and Jacko sniff the air. The dropbear raises her head, saucer ears swiveling, but she doesn't seem to understand what we're doing.

After a few moments, I say, "Let's move a little faster. We can't be more than a half mile from the cabin."

We walk quickly along the path left by the colocolo stampede. I glance up just as a shape glides from treetop to treetop. It's clearly bigger than any owl.

"At least one harpy," I whisper.

I take Jacko from my head, and Dain and I continue moving as each of us clutches a smaller companion to our chests. A single harpy isn't going to take on a human or a warg.

We keep moving, our eyes on the sky, weapons in hand. When something lands in a tree ahead of us, I nearly bash into my own sword.

I stop and flex my grip. My palms are sweaty, and I swallow hard.

"You saw that," he says.

"Five trees ahead on the left. About halfway up. I can still make it out."

A long, thin tail flicks under the branch. Definitely a harpy.

Dain looses an arrow, and at the same moment that the bowstring twangs, the harpy drops. It plummets from the branch and then swings toward us, only to sheer out of the way as Dain fires a second arrow. Before he can string a third, the harpy disappears into the darkness.

Dain lets out a growl, making the dropbear yip in alarm. He wraps one arm around the beast, cradling it. "How did I hit both times before, and now I missed twice?"

"Because you surprised them the first time. We just need to keep the smaller beasts safe and keep our eyes and ears open."

Malric grunts. Jacko leans forward in my arms, straining to sniff, his long ears swiveling. The dropbear watches our exchange with obvious fascination. Then she looks up at Dain and makes a clicking noise.

"No, I can't understand you," he says.

"But you just did. You knew she was making noise to see if you could understand her. I—"

A shape swoops between two trees. Dain lifts his bow.

"Don't," I say. "Unless we have a clear shot, we're wasting time and arrows. Just keep—"

Malric growls. He's looking up into the trees . . . on the opposite side of where I just saw the harpy. When I squint, I can make out another shape on a branch over there.

"There are two—" I begin.

Jacko sounds his alert and scrambles up to nudge my face with his antlers. He looks to the right and up . . . and there is a third harpy. Even as I'm watching that one, a fourth silently lands in the same tree.

"They're surrounding us," Dain whispers. "I count four— no, five. They're stalking us."

Two harpies fly from a tree behind us. We don't hear them until they're right there. I spin, and talons come right at me.

No, right at *Jacko*. One brushes him before a swing of my sword sends the harpy screaming. The other's talons scrape the top of my head.

"Run!" I say.

I want to stop and fight. I have my sword. I have Malric, and I have Dain. But I also have Jacko and a young dropbear . . . and no idea how many harpies are surrounding us.

"Wilmot!" I shout. "Kaylein!"

I am not ashamed to call for help. I've learned my lesson on that. I'm not *the* monster hunter. I'm the *royal* monster hunter, part of a team.

The forest stays silent except for the pound of our boots.

Malric runs behind us. Every now and then a harpy swoops, but it's almost like they're intentionally trying to scare us. When they dive, they snatch at my head or Dain's, or they skim Malric's back. Talons scrape my scalp and pull out hair. Tails lash hard enough to make me yelp. The more they taunt and hurt us, the more I'm tempted to stop and fight.

They want to panic us until we lash out blindly, and then we'll be easy prey. Maybe that's just a hunting strategy, but it feels cruel.

"What if no one's at the cabin?" Dain yells.

"Then we go inside."

"What if they couldn't clear the dropbears?"

"Then we fight."

I'm not sure there is any other plan. We can't climb trees to escape them. We can't duck into a cave or dive into a river. I rack my brain for alternatives, but nothing comes.

When Malric imitates a dog's bark, I know he's trying to get our attention, fast.

I turn just as a harpy dives at my legs. Malric lunges at it and catches one huge wing. He whips his head, and the harpy comes free, but blood sprays as the beast takes off screaming. Then another one dives at my legs, and Malric sends it off with a snap. A third one doesn't even get close before Malric's snarl makes the beast change its mind.

Why are they aiming for my legs? At least when they're diving at my head and shoulders, they're too high for Malric to catch.

Does it matter?

Something tells me it does.

Dain lets out an oath, the word carried on a yelp of surprise. I lunge for him, but Malric grabs me, and I see Dain has only tripped. He's about to right himself when a harpy dives and knocks him off balance.

That's what they were doing. Trying to trip me. Only Malric wasn't going to let them, so they attacked Dain instead.

When the second harpy plows into Dain, he's already wobbly, and he falls. I lunge at the same time as Malric, and we collide. I spin out of the way as Malric twists.

A harpy dives at my face. All I see are talons, each as long as my finger. I swing my sword up. It cleaves into the beast, and the harpy screams.

Another grabs my hair. I swing again, wilder now, even as Jannah's voice whispers for me to slow down. My blow hits broadside, and the vibration almost makes me lose my grip.

Jacko drops from where he'd been clinging to my chest. "Jacko!"

I catch a glimpse of him rearing up, antlers and teeth and claws flashing. One harpy veers away, but when another flies for him, I shout, "Hide, Jacko! Hide!"

Please hide. Please get out of here.

The harpy I'd hit broadside isn't even dazed. It's already diving at me again, darting and dodging, easily avoiding my sword swings.

Two harpies swoop at Jacko. One manages to grab him, and I let out a scream, running and swinging. My sword hits the beast, and it drops Jacko.

"Hide!" I shout again. "Now! Please!"

The jackalope gives me one look, and then his tail flashes as he starts to run . . . down the open trail.

"Jacko!" I shriek.

His white tail is a clear target for the two harpies that chase him. As soon as one dives, though, he tears into the forest. When they pull away, he veers back. He's leading them away. He's fast, and he has antlers and teeth and claws. I need to trust he'll be all right.

At a muffled cry behind me, I spin to see Dain on the ground, with three harpies going at him. Two more taunt Malric. They dive in and out of range, keeping the warg from getting to me or Dain.

Dain is on his stomach. The dropbear must be sheltered beneath him, and at that angle, all the harpies can do is strike at his back. I run and slash one. Then another grabs my foot. I don't see it. All I know is that one moment

I'm upright and running, and then my foot is flying from under me.

I swing my sword . . . and nearly fall again with the momentum. The ebony sword is too big for this fight. I knew that when I nearly lost my grip the first time. The harpies might be big, but they dart and dive like swallows.

I sheathe my sword and pull my dagger instead. Then I sprint toward Dain, but only get two paces when a harpy grabs my hair again. Before I can swing my dagger, a second harpy digs its talons into my long curls and yanks me off the ground.

Pain rips through me. Instinct takes over, my training forgotten. I claw upward with my left hand, my right stabbing the dagger uselessly.

Memory flashes. Tiera's gryphon mother snatching me in her talons and carrying me into the air. Yet as terrifying as that had been, it hadn't hurt. This is sheer agony, every hair feeling as if it's being pulled from my scalp, pain stabbing through my neck as my entire body is suspended from it.

I'm only a few feet off the ground. However much it hurts, I am alive, and the harpies aren't strong enough to get me higher. They're screeching at their flock for help, but none come. Beneath me, something grabs hold of my foot, and I have a horrible image of being carried up by my legs and my hair. Then strong jaws clamp around my boot.

Malric.

He tugs, and at the same moment, I slash my dagger upward. I hit my hair—I feel that—but I also strike something hard, and one of the harpies screams. I hit again. Blood rains down, and the beast surges off, shrieking.

My feet smack into the ground, but the other harpy doesn't let go. It's screaming and pulling, and I think it's trying to get me into the air by itself. Then I realize it's caught in my hair.

I drop to my knees and slam my head toward the ground. The beast hits with a thud. Before Malric can attack, a brown blur flies from the forest.

Jacko launches himself at the harpy. He bites its chest and claws at it as it continues to shriek and struggle. Each flail rends at my scalp, and I grit my teeth as I reach up to untangle my hair.

Wings slap my hand, and talons scratch me, but they're blind strikes as the harpy tries to fight while trapped in my hair.

Finally, the beast is free, and I grip its leg and drag it down to me. Its monkey mouth chatters and shrieks. Blood stains its sharp teeth, and it snaps at me, but I have it by both rear legs now, and it can't get at me with teeth or talons. I look into its eyes, and they blaze a hatred that takes my breath away.

When I was trapped by Tiera's mother, I never stopped to ask why. Jannah had done her best to teach me about monsters, but part of me was still like every villager who kills a trespassing animal without asking *why* it's trespassing. There had been a reason that gryphon attacked—she'd been pregnant with Tiera when I'd injured her. She'd come after me knowing I would eventually come after *her*.

The hate that radiates from this harpy is different. That hate in that monkey face looks human, and it chills me to the bone.

Wings beat at me as the harpy flails for a hold with those human-like furred hands. I kill the beast as humanely as I can. Then I run for Dain.

He's still on his stomach, protecting the dropbear. Two harpies have the back of his tunic and are trying to lift him. Malric is already fighting two more, who block him from getting to Dain.

I'm only a few strides away when the two who are blocking Malric suddenly swoop at Dain instead. I let out a scream of rage and lunge for him just as all four harpies grab his tunic and hoist him into the air.

CHAPTER SEVEN

My fingers scrabble at Dain's back but don't find a hold. I wrap my arms around his leg instead. As the harpies falter, I let out a grim chuckle. Four can lift Dain, but they can't lift both of us. We're—

A screech and then we're sailing up, and I manage to look up to see two others have joined in. Six harpies, their talons wrapped in Dain's hair and gripping his tunic and clenched around one arm.

Malric leaps for my leg, but his teeth slide off.

The harpies struggle to lift us, squawking and screaming. One lets go, as if it's giving up, and we jolt toward the ground.

Except that's not what the harpy is doing at all. It flies straight at me. I brace for the blows of those wings and talons, pulling into myself, eyes squeezed shut. I still have my dagger, held flat against Dain's leg. I can use it, but that risks losing my grip. Better to just withstand the pain.

Fingers touch my own, and I flinch so hard I nearly release Dain. I open my eyes to see the harpy hovering as it tries to pry my fingers from Dain's leg. I shudder as my brain feels human fingers while my eyes show me that pale simian face, with fangs jutting over its gray lips, wide brow scrunched up in concentration. Then the harpy turns my way, and I recoil, because that look is human, filled with hatred and cunning.

The harpy sneers at me. I swear it does. Its lip curls up, and its eyes fix on mine, and it sneers. Meanwhile its fingers are working to peel mine from Dain, and its tail is working with them. For a split second, I marvel at that. The beast is flying . . . while working at my hand *and* getting its tail in there to help.

Of course, that fascination—and grudging admiration— lasts only a blink before I see the ground about ten feet below. Dain must have let go of the dropbear when he was wrenched upward. She's down there, with Jacko standing guard over her, the jackalope on his hind legs, screeching his alarm cry as he watches me clinging to Dain. Malric runs back and forth, leaping with every few steps, trying to grab my leg, but the harpies keep us just out of reach.

Just out of reach.

That's the key here. They're very careful not to let us dip low enough for Malric to grab me, but that's taking all their energy, and they can't get higher until their flock-mate pries me off Dain.

The harpy is working on my right hand. The one pressed against my dagger handle. It's smart. Get that hand free, and I'll lose both my grip and my weapon.

I clasp Dain's trousers with my left hand, fingers digging in for a better hold. I wrap my arm around his leg, too. Then I clench my right hand, and the harpy lets out a shriek of victory, feeling my fingers move and thinking it has achieved its goal.

Keeping my right arm around Dain's leg, I slash using my wrist. It's awkward, but the harpy isn't expecting attack, and the dagger slices its chest. It howls and strikes out blindly. A flick of my wrist, and blood wells on the beast's forearm. It screams and flaps down to get out of my reach . . . and it swoops right into Malric's range. The warg grabs it.

The other harpies are all screeching now, those terrible human cries, underscored by the thump of their wings as they valiantly try to stay in flight.

If the harpies were hawks, they'd just keep trying to fly off with us. Being monsters, they see the futility of it. They lost their one chance to unburden themselves of the extra human, and if another harpy releases Dain to dislodge me, the remaining four will drop us both. They're screaming for the rest of their flock. And no one is coming.

As the five remaining harpies screech in vain, Malric doesn't even bother jumping for my feet. He's just tracking me and waiting, knowing they'll tire any moment now.

But then, a shriek. And an answering one. Two more harpies appear, dark forms against the dusk. They're winging straight for us and—

One falls. It barely emits a gurgling cry as it drops. I twist to look, still clinging to Dain's leg. I'd heard a sound before the harpy fell, one I know well, but it doesn't make sense.

It comes again.

The twang of a bowstring. Then the thwack of an arrow hitting its target.

The second harpy drops.

Wilmot. It must be. No one else is that good with a bow.

Hope surges and spurs me on with a rush of adrenaline. I twist and—renewing my left arm's hold on Dain's leg—dare to release my right and slash at the harpy leg closest to me. My blade sinks in, and with a screech, the beast drops Dain.

That's all it takes—one set of talons releasing their grip as one harpy is distracted. The weight is too much and, in a blink, we're low enough for Malric to grab my leg.

As Malric keeps hold of me, another harpy falls, an arrow through its breast. Then Dain writhes and clutches the leg of the harpy gripping him.

I loosen my grasp on Dain. That's scary—I envision Dain hoisted into the air, out of reach—but I know that there aren't enough left to carry Dain off.

As I let go, I slash at the one I already injured. My dagger barely makes contact before it flees, screaming. Another lies on the ground, arrow-shot, and the one Dain grabbed has wrenched free and is flapping its great wings, escaping as fast as it can, as Dain falls safely to the earth.

I land on my feet and spin, dagger ready. The harpies are gone. Five lie dead on the ground. The others have fled, one of them badly wounded.

"Wilmot?" I shout.

No answer. He must be busy watching for those two harpies to return. I stagger over to Dain on wobbly legs.

"You okay?" I ask. He's rising gingerly to his feet.

I take his arm to steady him, and he makes a move to brush me off. I let go before he can, but he pauses and then claps an awkward hand against my back.

"I'm fine," he says. "Thank you for not letting go."

"I never would," I say, meeting his eyes.

He ducks my gaze and nods. I glance over at Malric. He's making the rounds of the downed harpies, ensuring they're dead.

Jacko stands watch over the dropbear. The jackalope's whole body vibrates, his gaze on me, clearly wanting to hop over. He's declared the dropbear his responsibility, though, so he's staying there. The dropbear seems fine. She's eyeing the sky nervously, but there's no sign of fresh blood or injury.

As I make my way over, I call again, "Wilmot? We're okay. We—"

Dain lunges and grabs my arm. "Those aren't Wilmot's arrows," he whispers.

Before I can react, Malric is in front of us, pushing us back and placing himself between us and whoever shot those arrows.

These arrows are homemade and as distinctive as Wilmot's or Dain's, but definitely not theirs. The shafts are fashioned from two types of wood, with striped feather fletchings. As Dain peers into the oncoming night, he sneaks a peek at the arrow nearest us, as if itching to study it.

"We should retreat into the forest," I whisper. "We're easy targets here."

Dain nods, and as we back past Jacko and the dropbear, he scoops up the latter. I reach for Jacko, but the jackalope shoots to my feet instead, guarding them as we move swiftly into the woods.

Malric waits until we're clear, and then he lopes to us.

"Hello!" I shout.

Dain frantically motions me to silence.

"They know we're here," I whisper. "And they saved us from the harpies."

He shakes his head. "We were fine. You and Malric had it under control."

I realize he hadn't seen the other two coming—he couldn't from his vantage point. For now, I just whisper, "Whoever it is *did* help us."

"So why aren't they coming out?"

"Because they don't know us. They're making sure we aren't dangerous."

He opens his mouth, and I lift a hand.

"We're bickering," I say, "and this really isn't the time. We're trapped, and I'd rather not wait for the harpies to return with reinforcements." I take a deep breath. "My name is Rowan of Clan—"

Dain's hand slaps over my mouth. "If you don't know who's out there, you certainly shouldn't tell them you're a princess."

I glare, but he has a point. The last time I identified myself, I wasn't believed. The time before that, my assailants were kidnapping me *because* I am the princess. So far, saying, "Greetings, I am Rowan of Clan Dacre, royal monster hunter and princess of Tamarel," has only ever made things worse.

"I'm Rowan of Clan Hadleigh," I call. "I'm here with my great-aunt, Yvain, and others from her clan."

That isn't a lie. Hadleigh is my father's clan, and Yvain is my great-aunt. Or maybe it's great-great-aunt . . .

When no answer comes, I say, "I am with Dain of . . ." I trail off. I don't know Dain's clan. I've never asked, and my cheeks burn with that.

"It doesn't matter," he mutters. "Just Dain is fine."

"But I should know—"

"Just Dain." He raises his voice. "I'm Dain, apprentice to the hunter Wilmot of Clan Kendral."

No answer. Whoever's out there is listening, though. They must be.

I continue, voice louder now. "We are here investigating the migration. There is a cabin nearby, filled with dropbears and—"

"And what might you know of that?" a woman's voice says, winding around me like a soft breeze. There's an odd note to it, one that raises my hackles. "Did you have anything to do with it, Rowan of Clan *Dacre?*"

I tense. Dain has his dagger out, and he hefts it as Malric growls and Jacko chitters. I squint into the forest, but it's dark and silent. When I glance at Malric, he's sniffing and his expression says he can't find a smell, which means she's downwind.

I turn in that direction and straighten. "Yes, I am Rowan of Clan Dacre. Royal monster hunter–elect and princess of Tamarel. And I am responsible for the dropbears. I am happy to discuss that. To whom do I have the pleasure of speaking?"

"Such pretty manners," the voice says.

I realize the "odd note" in her voice is nothing but an accent. I roll my shoulders, trying to calm my nerves. Then I strike a fire stick and hold it aloft.

"I'm a princess," I say. "I was supposed to sit on the throne. Do you expect me to speak like a farm worker?"

"I have met farm workers with very fine manners."

"True enough," I say. "So why mock me for mine?"

"Am I mocking you?"

Beside me, Malric's growl echoes my own frustration.

Dain rocks forward. "We don't have time for this," he says to the disembodied voice. "It's almost night, and we're in the Dunnian Woods, and we've already been attacked by harpies."

"So why are you here, children? This is not the place to play."

Dain waves at the sword on my back. "Does that look like a toy?"

"It does on her. She's far too small to wield such a weapon."

"Agreed," I say. "I would far rather it was still on my aunt's back. But since she is no longer here, I have taken on the responsibility."

"It would fit far better on *my* back. Perhaps I should take it." The voice moves to the left. "Yes, I think I would like it, as payment for my help."

Dain squawks, but I put a hand on his arm.

"Would you also like the responsibilities that come with it?" I ask. "Whoever wields this sword must devote their life to keeping Tamarel free of monsters. Is that what you're asking for?"

Her chuckle ripples through the forest. "You are far too bold for such a little monster hunter, lost in the woods."

"I'm not lost. I know exactly where I'm going."

"My mistake. Then you are far too bold for a girl at the mercy of a witch."

"Witch?" Then it clicks. "Oh, you're the healer. Cedany, isn't it? That's your cabin I filled with dropbears. I am sorry about that. We didn't have a choice, and we returned as soon as we could to fix the problem. I'm glad to get the chance to meet you. I have a friend who might be out here, and she really wanted to make your acquaintance. I hope she's still around."

The healer's sigh wends around us. "That is not the proper reaction to hearing I'm a witch, little girl. Do you even know what that is?"

"Don't get her started," Dain mutters.

"There's no such things as witches," I say. "Not in the folklore sense, as women with magical powers. What people commonly call witches are healers, usually women, who live outside of villages and cities, and make their living collecting herbs and creating medicines. While villagers are happy for their help, they also fear them because they live outside traditional society. And because medicine can be used as poison. While the healers don't hurt anyone, people fear their power to do so. There is also the problem of physicians spreading stories out of professional jealousy, which is terribly unfair."

I purse my lips. "It's all terribly unfair, and if you've had to endure any of that, I'm sorry for it. I'm also sorry about the dropbears."

Silence. Then, "That was a very complete answer."

"I warned you," Dain mutters.

"What if I told you I *do* have magical powers?" she says.

"Then I'd have to tell you there is no such thing as magic, and what you're experiencing is more likely the power of suggestion and coincidence."

"Did I tell you not to get her started?" Dain says. "Rowan has very firm opinions on magic and witches."

"Oh, I suspect Rowan has very firm opinions on most things." The voice draws closer. "And she is delightful for it." A figure steps from the forest, hand extended. "Cedany of Havendale."

I knew she was young—Yvain called her a "young woman of twenty"—but I'm still surprised to see she doesn't look much older than Kaylein. She's tall for a woman. Maybe six feet. Broad in her hips and her shoulders, with a pale-skinned face. People in Tamarel have skin tones mostly ranging from light to dark brown. There are people from countries over the mountains who have lighter skin and hair, like Wilmot. Cedany's is even paler, though that may be because she lives in a forest, without much sunshine. Her hair is even more different, red-gold, like bronze coins.

"Havendale," I say. "That is very far away." It's one of the farthest countries from Tamarel, not only across the mountains but with several more countries between us. "I have heard they have good monster hunters there."

"They do," she says. "Also very good witches. Oh, I'm sorry. *Healers.*" Her lips twitch. "So you don't want to see me perform magic?"

"If you actually could, yes, I would love to see it. I'm not opposed to the concept. But what people call magic is usually just science they don't understand."

Another twitch of her lips. "You are a very bright child, with very strong opinions."

"*Can* you perform magic?" Dain asks hesitantly.

She smiles at him. "Sorry. I am teasing. Though some do say my knowledge of herbs and plants is quite magical."

"As is your skill with a bow," I say. "Dain's an archer, and he'd love to know more about your arrows, even if he won't ask."

"I would have asked," Dain grumbles as he shifts the dropbear in his arms.

"Do I even want to know why you're carrying that?" Cedany asks. "The warg, I have heard, belonged to Princess Jannah, so he makes sense. As for the jackalope?" She glances down at Jacko, who's watching her warily from my feet. "Well, being quite fond of jackalopes myself, I find myself envious and unable to question the princess's choice of companion. The dropbear, though?"

"She's injured," I say. "We're taking her to my friend, the one who'd like to meet you. She's training to be a healer and hopes to specialize in monsters."

"You're taking the dropbear . . . to be healed. So it may live long enough to drop on an unsuspecting human. I thought you were the royal monster *hunter*."

"Actually—" I begin.

"Please," Dain says, raising his free hand. "Do *not* get her started again, unless you want another lecture."

"I would happily hear another informed and informative speech from our princess. However, this is not the time. We need to get you out of this forest. I would suggest my cabin." She gives me a mock-stern look. "Had someone not stuffed it full of dropbears."

"It should be clear now," I say. "Or so I hope. We were heading there. I—"

Running footsteps pound along the colocolo path, and we all reach for our weapons.

"Uh, guys?" a voice calls. "I think Rowan must be close by. Just follow the trail of dead harpies."

I grin and jog from the trees to see Alianor crouched over a harpy body.

"You're still here," I say.

"So are you," she says, coming over to hug me. "And only slightly worse for wear, despite all the harpy screaming. Hey, Dain." She squints. "Are you cuddling a dropbear?"

He quickly adjusts his grip on the beast.

I grin. "It's a long story."

"And we will look forward to hearing it." Yvain approaches. She sees the young healer, and her wrinkled face beams. "Hello, Cedany. Wondering what happened to your cabin, I'll bet."

"We were just about to explain," I say. "As soon as we got someplace safer."

"An excellent idea," says Wilmot, approaching with Rhydd. "Cedany's cabin isn't in the best of shape yet, but we can take shelter there."

CHAPTER EIGHT

The hunters had managed to clear the cabin. Some of the dropbears had already escaped by breaking a hole between the rafters. Those were the smallest, like Dain's. So the hunters had enlarged the hole and sedated the others as they came through. Then Yvain's family put the sleeping dropbears on their river raft. They'll release them farther from habitation when they leave.

Had Dain and I made it to the cabin, we'd have found the others camping there with plans to return home in the morning. Wilmot and Rhydd had decided it was best to wait for light, and they'd presumed Dain and I were safely in Tamarel with our guards.

As for the damage to Cedany's cabin, Rhydd assures her it will be fully repaired, with extra payment for the inconvenience. She's satisfied with that.

The bigger concern is the monster migration. The

dropbears, the harpies, the colocolos . . . why are they on the move and heading east?

Wilmot doesn't want to discuss that tonight.

"We'll never get any sleep if we start," he grumbles.

He has a point. It's getting late, and I'm starving, and I have companion monsters to look after. Cedany and Alianor have been tending to the dropbear, who only needed wound cleaning and stitching. I watch them work while I eat my dinner—shared with Jacko—and Malric hunts for his. Then I gather around the fire outside with the others to tell the full story of the colocolo stampede and harpy attack.

The hunters and Yvain's family sleep out of doors. I wanted to join them—the royal monster hunter's place is with her troop. Yet Wilmot insisted I sleep inside Cedany's cabin, and both Alianor and Cedany agreed on account of my injuries. I griped that my injuries were mild—a sore scalp, a wrenched neck and various cuts—but no one listened to me.

Wilmot also insisted that Dain sleep indoors. He was badly bruised from the harpies, and his objections were also ignored. So were Rhydd's when he was told to sleep inside, the excuse there being that he was the future king. Alianor stayed with us, though in her case, the only person who insisted on that was Alianor herself. She claimed she needed to help Cedany tend to our injuries, but really, she just wanted to be more comfortable.

Comfortable isn't quite the word for Cedany's cabin. It *had* been, before the dropbear infestation. The beasts had made a royal mess, breaking the furniture and ripping apart the bed. While the hunters did clean up the more noxious signs of habitation—the urine and feces—the smell still lingers, both from that and from the dropbears themselves. Fortunately, Cedany has plenty of herbs to combat the stench, and we all sleep with sachets of lavender near our noses.

I wake once during the night. Jacko is cuddled against me, making his odd little purr of contentment. That isn't the noise that woke me, though. It comes from Dain's direction. We'd made the dropbear a bed in the rafters, and she'd settled in there, but now she's curled in Dain's arms, both of them snoring softly. I smile, pat Jacko and drift back to sleep.

The next morning, the hunters hunt and Yvain's family fish. Kaylein—whose family are fishers—goes with them once Wilmot assures her I don't require her bodyguard services. While they're gone, Wilmot and Yvain make breakfast. I offer to help but . . . I possess many skills, having had the luxury of teachers and trainers, but there are some things I haven't learned because, well, I'm unlikely to ever need them. Cooking is one of those and, let's be honest, no one wants their breakfast made by a princess who decides today's the day she wants to try her hand at cooking.

Rhydd sits at the fire to talk to Yvain. He wants more information on our father's clan, and they'd begun discussing the topic yesterday. I'd like to know more, too, but they're deep in a conversation about waterway rights, a subject guaranteed to put me back to sleep.

I'm more interested in Cedany and Dain's discussion about the arrows she makes. Alianor listens, too, mostly because she got kicked out of Rhydd and Yvain's conversation. The biggest feud of waterway rights is between Clan Hadleigh and Clan Bellamy. Rhydd wanted to hear Yvain's side of the story without Alianor jumping in. She'll certainly give her opinion later.

While Wilmot and Yvain cook over one fire, we huddle around another, stoked to stave off the dawn chill. I'm on the ground, with Malric behind me, pretending to offer back support while, I suspect, really just enjoying my body heat. Jacko is curled up on my lap. Across the fire, Dain sits with the dropbear on his lap as she eats strips of dried meat, holding them in her prehensile hands and nibbling on them, her red eyes fixed on Cedany, as if she's listening as intently as Dain. I can't help taking a closer look at her front paws. I've never seen a dropbear's hand this close, and only now realize she has three fingers and *two* opposable thumbs. That must be how dropbears climb so well.

When breakfast is ready, we can finally talk about "the problem." The number of monsters in Tamarel and the Dunnian Woods has been on the increase for months.

Numbers always fluctuate, with seasonal changes and prey migration. A long and hard winter will bring wolves and wargs to Tamarel livestock pastures. A summer drought brings deer into Tamarel crops, with predators following close behind. There can be human causes, too, such as when people dam a waterway or overfish a river or overhunt a forest or start a new settlement.

While the monster hunters always pay attention to increased activity, they hadn't been overly worried until recently—when our expedition to return Tiera had ventured into the woods and found dropbears where there'd never been dropbears before. There, we met Yvain and her daughter and grand-daughters, who were tracking the dropbears and concerned about their movement eastward.

Yvain's village is the farthest western settlement in Tamarel, and they'd been the first to notice the migration of both animals and monsters. It hadn't worried them until the dropbears appeared. And now we've had the colocolo stampede and the harpies, which Wilmot and Yvain and Cedany all agree have rarely been seen this far east.

"So we have a problem in Tamarel because the monsters are heading that way," I say. "But we also have a problem at the root, wherever this is happening. We need to tackle both."

Rhydd nods. "The logical solution is that I return to Tamarel with the hunters, and Rowan continues on with Wilmot to investigate."

Wilmot shakes his head. "Your mother would pin my hide on her wall if I waltzed off into the mountains with Rowan."

"So *you're* the one who's been scaring Dain with tales of what my mother will do," I say.

"Fine," Wilmot says. "She wouldn't nail my hide to her wall. She'd just very nicely ask me to go look after some tiny monster problem in the deepest, darkest part of the woods ... where I'd conveniently stumble into a jba-fofi burrow."

"That's not so bad," I say. "I dove right into one, and I'm fine."

Cedany looks over. "You dove—?"

"Don't ask," Dain says. "Please."

"I believe Wilmot's concern is that he's acting as your

guardian," Yvain says. "I agree that separating would be the most efficient solution, but not if it will upset the queen. We can get to the horses by nightfall, and someone can ride ahead to speak to Mariela. That way, she is notified, and we'll lose no more than a couple of days before she sends back her agreement."

Rhydd and I look at each other and burst out laughing. Alianor snickers. Even Wilmot's and Dain's lips twitch.

"You haven't spent enough time around our queen," Alianor says. "There is no way she's going to tell a messenger it's fine to let Rowan continue on to the mountains."

"She'll refuse," Rhydd says. "Then we'll need to argue our case. Eventually she'll see the point. As much as she'll hate sending Rowan into the mountains, she trusts Wilmot and she knows this is right for the kingdom."

"However," I say, "by that time, Heward will have heard. He'll insist on a council vote, which means we'll have to start the whole thing again, stating and arguing our case to them."

"And he'll stall," Alianor says. "That way, if the migrating monsters do cause trouble, he can say Rowan didn't do her job."

Cedany's face screws up. "Why would he—? Oh yes, if Princess Rowan fails, his children take the sword and throne. What a terrible little man."

"He's not that little," Alianor says. "Quite tall, actually."

"I mean that his spirit is little. He needs to *feel* bigger, which he would if his children ruled."

"We can debate this all we want," Rhydd says. "But . . ."

"The monsters are migrating," I say. "We need to move."

My brother nods. "As the heir to the throne, I believe I outrank everyone on this expedition, and while I hate to point that out, it comes in handy here. Rowan will continue on with Wilmot. The hunters will return to deal with any monsters who cross our borders. I'll go with them and tell my mother. If she is absolutely against Rowan's expedition, she can send a fast rider to catch up. Kaylein should stay with Rowan, as her guard. Everyone else is free to make their own choices."

"I stay with Wilmot," Dain says.

"I'll go with Rowan," Alianor says.

"And I will say my goodbyes here," Yvain says.

I sit upright. "So soon?"

Her face creases in a smile. "I would have thought you'd be happy to be rid of a cranky old lady."

"You aren't cranky. Not in a bad way, at least."

She chuckles. "I take that as a compliment."

"It is," Rhydd says. "You're also family, and while we understand you need to leave, we hope to see you again soon. We had little contact with our father's clan growing up."

Her eyes shadow. "That would be our fault. When his parents died and Clan Dacre offered fostering, his clan thought it was best to let him go. He was clearly destined for great things, and we did not wish to interfere. He never forgot us, though. When we sent delegates to the castle, he made sure to host them himself. When he died, we held our own clan funeral, as we did not wish to interfere with yours."

"It wouldn't have been interfering," Rhydd says softly.

"I see that now. So while I will take my leave here, we will see you again soon. Your sister's group will travel faster if it remains small, attracting as little notice as possible. Meanwhile, we will release those dropbears and then return home and keep a watch on the rivers."

Rhydd nods. "Thank you." He turns to Cedany. "We will send builders to repair your cottage and compensate you. In the meantime—"

"I'll be with your sister."

Everyone pauses. Rhydd says slowly, "That is a very kind offer—"

"It's not an offer. It's a statement of fact. Your sister is off on a lovely adventure, and I am in great need of one."

"I don't think . . ." Rhydd begins, even slower now.

"I am an expert archer and healer, and I know these woods. Besides, your mother won't send builders during a monster infestation, and I can hardly live in my house as it is. I'll join the expedition." She rises. "That's settled. Let's get ready before we lose any more daylight."

Dain's dropbear is gone.

I'd been with Rhydd, saying a private goodbye while making sure he was okay going back and leaving me to my adventure.

"I like adventures just fine," he said. "But I'm beginning to think I prefer them in smaller doses. The colocolo stampede was enough for me. Fixing this with Mom is the kind of challenge I prefer."

Then I saw him off with the hunters. Yvain and her family had already left. Now Alianor is with Cedany, putting together a medical kit. Wilmot and Kaylein are discussing the trip. And so I'm the only one to notice Dain standing on the forest's edge, staring into it.

I walk over, and he doesn't even seem to hear me. Then he says, "She's gone."

I almost ask who. That's when I realize he's alone, and I haven't seen him that way since we returned from the forest yesterday.

"Did something happen?" I say, hurrying to him. "If she's disappeared, we need to look for her, in case—"

"She left," he says, his voice monotone.

"Are you sure? Maybe—"

"I let her go, and she went." He turns to head back to the clearing, his gaze averted, hands deep in his pockets. "Her shoulder will be fine, and it was time for her to go. That's the right thing to do."

"It is, but . . ."

When I try to see his expression, he keeps his face averted and squares his shoulders. "I brought her out here and told her she'd be fine. I gave her a little push, so she'd understand. When she didn't, I put her on a branch. Then she took off." He points into the forest. "That way."

"I'm sorry."

He glances over then, and his eyes are glistening, just a little. "It was the right thing to do."

"It was, but that doesn't make it easy."

He shoves his hands down farther into his pockets.

"If you were Rhydd or Alianor, I'd give you a hug," I say.

"But I know you don't want that, so I'm just going to tell you that I would. Consider it a verbal hug."

One corner of his mouth twitches. Then he puts out his arm for an awkward back pat, and I lay my head on his shoulder, very lightly, waiting for him to pull away. Instead, he just keeps his hand against my back.

"I am sorry," I say. "I know she liked you, though. It wasn't about that."

He nods. He doesn't say he liked her, too. He did, of course. For some of us, though, admitting things like that is hard. It'd taken him a very long time to admit we were friends, and even now, he's more likely to refer to himself as my companion.

We stand there, my head on his shoulder, his arm against my back. Then he takes a deep breath, and when he speaks, he's as tense as if he's about to admit some terrible secret.

"I . . . I kind of . . . kind of hoped . . ."

"I know," I say, when he doesn't finish. "You did the right thing, but you were hoping she'd give you an excuse to keep her."

He nods and relaxes. Then he turns his head and murmurs, "Thank you."

As I look up to smile, I catch sight of Wilmot. He's standing about ten feet away, watching us with an odd look. When Dain notices, he jumps away so fast you'd think we'd been caught kissing.

I glare at Wilmot. Dain had actually relaxed and confessed his feelings about something, and now Wilmot is making him feel like he's done something wrong. Yet the look isn't really like that. It's just . . . wistful? Sad?

Is Wilmot thinking of Jannah? I know I look like her, and they were friends when they were our age. I realize that's it—seeing Dain and me together, quietly talking, reminded Wilmot of Jannah. Maybe it was something in my expression or in the forest backdrop. Whatever it was, it made him miss her, and I regret my glare. So I replace it with a smile and walk over and quietly tell him what happened.

"It's for the best," he says, his gruff tone exactly like Dain's. The look in his eyes is the same, too, as if he's telling himself that when he doesn't really believe it.

Yes, the dropbear belongs in the forest. She's old enough to be on her own, and if there's no excuse for interfering, we shouldn't. Staying with us has to be her choice. I just can't help wishing, for Dain's sake, that he *had* been her choice. But she'd chosen to return to the forest, and that isn't his fault or hers.

After yesterday, I expect we'll have a full day of monster encounters. I'm wrong. Very wrong. We don't have a single one, and while that should be a relief—proof that we've over-estimated the problem, even—it worries me. I don't tell the others. They might think my "worry" is actually disappoint-ment, and I'm not in the mood to be teased.

I'm not sure what kind of mood I *am* in. I'm sad for Dain, losing a possible monster companion. I'm concerned about what Mom will say and whether Wilmot will get into any trouble. I miss my brother—until this year, we'd never been apart for long, and now it's one separation after another.

My mood, then, is "not good." Not bad, but not good, either. I'm distracted now and then, when Cedany points out a healing plant or when Wilmot points out animal tracks. I talk to Kaylein for a while, and that's always good, but she's careful to remember she's my bodyguard, too, and by afternoon, she's walking behind us with Cedany.

Alianor tries carrying on a conversation with me, and I try to reciprocate, but my mood seems to match the sun today. It starts low, with Dain and the dropbear, and then rises briefly midday before dropping again.

By late afternoon, I'm walking in silence with Dain. It's a comfortable silence, though— the kind I don't find with anyone else. He walks beside me, and Malric guards my back, and Jacko alternates between hopping ahead and riding on my shoulders.

"There should be more monsters," Dain murmurs after at least an hour of silence.

I glance over. Wilmot is in the lead, and everyone else is too far behind to hear him.

"We haven't seen a single one," Dain says. "You've noticed that, right?"

I lift one shoulder. "Maybe the migration isn't as bad as we thought."

He peers at me, dark eyes boring into mine. When he doesn't say anything, I squirm and shrug again.

"It's never this quiet," he says. "Especially when you're around."

I tense.

"I'm not blaming you, Rowan," he says, sounding exasperated. "I'm stating a fact. It's also a fact that I've lived in this forest for years, and I can't remember ever walking a full day and not catching at least a fleeting glimpse of a monster."

When I don't answer, he says, "You have noticed. I know you have. So why aren't you talking about it?"

"Because she doesn't want you to mock her," Wilmot says without turning.

Now it's Dain's turn to tense. "I—"

"Mock her. Tease her. She isn't in the mood for that, from you or anyone else. She isn't in the mood for any of it. The silence is bothering her too much." Wilmot glances back. "Am I right, Rowan?"

I don't answer.

He lets us catch up and then resumes walking, leading us as he talks. "Your aunt used to get that. It's the Clan Dacre blood. Something isn't right here, and it's putting you on edge."

Alianor jogs up beside me. "Should we stop, then? Figure out what's wrong?"

Wilmot shakes his head. "Not unless Rowan senses danger. When Jannah got that way, it was just a sense of unease. The balance is off. First there were too many monsters, and now there are none." He glances back. "Is that what you're feeling, Rowan?"

I nod.

"Then we'll continue on. Just let me know if it changes."

CHAPTER NINE

The next two days continue to pass with far too few monster sightings for the Dunnian Woods. The forest is overly quiet, empty of both monsters and animals. The more I think about it, though, the more it makes sense. We've encountered colocolos and dropbears and harpies, all not usually found in this region. As they passed through, they'd upset the balance. The colocolo stampede would have unnerved every creature in its path. The dropbears and harpies have been hunting, frightening prey animals and prey monsters alike.

While it's possible this is happening all across the forest, I feel as if we're walking a migration corridor. To our left, rivers flow from the mountains. A few miles to our right is the empty riverbed left by the Michty River.

We seem to have encountered the dropbears on the path the monsters are taking east. Then we returned to that region and found the colocolos and harpies. According to Cedany, there's been increased monster activity near her cabin for weeks.

It's been three days since we left Rhydd and the others. No one has caught up to turn us back. We're walking and talking. Well, the female part of our entourage is. I know people say that women talk more than men, but Mom always said anyone who said that hadn't met our father. On this trip, though, the stereotype holds, because the male contingent is Dain and Wilmot.

I often wonder what it was like when the two of them lived alone together. Did entire days pass without a word exchanged?

I'm in front with Alianor while Cedany and Kaylein bring up the rear, deep in conversation. They have been talking more and more since we left the others. They're close to the same age, and while it might seem that a healer and a bodyguard wouldn't have much in common, they find plenty to discuss. They do have something in common—they both take care of others—but they also just like each other. You don't need to have much in common for that.

Cedany has been teaching Kaylein about plants, and Kaylein has been teaching her fighting techniques. Sometimes they're talking about that and other times they're just talking.

As for me and Alianor, we aren't so much talking as goofing off. My mood has lightened in the last couple of days. I've forced it to lighten. I get annoyed with Dain when his moods affect everyone else. I can't let my own unease infect the expedition.

When that mood feels like it's going to drag me under, I let myself give in to it. That's what Mom taught us. Find a quiet place and allow yourself to feel down for a while. I do that with Jacko and Malric, and then I rejoin the group. While my time alone seems to confuse Alianor—who wants to cheer me up—Wilmot convinces her it's best to leave me be, and I appreciate that.

My mood is better today, and Alianor and I are passing the time making up imaginary monsters—what if you put the head of a wildcat on the body of a horse and stuff like that.

Earlier we'd been planning our dresses for the winter festival. I remember the first time Dain heard us talking about clothing. He'd said we didn't seem like the sort of girls who'd care about such things. We'd both retorted that a girl could swing a sword or stitch a wound and still like pretty dresses.

There isn't a "sort" of girl any more than there is a "sort" of boy. Rhydd likes dressing up as much as I do. Our dad did, too. Our mom does not, which we always thought was funny because she wears gorgeous dresses almost every day. Or maybe that's *why* she doesn't like dressing up for parties—for her, it's everyday wear, while for us, it's special.

The dress conversation scared Dain away. He claimed it was boring, but we both noticed he fled once we asked his opinion about which colors suited us best. Now that we're talking about imaginary monsters, he stays away. I'm sure he thinks it's silly. Such creatures don't exist, so why are we discussing them?

This is why I like having more than one friend. For most of my life, it was just me and Rhydd. With Dain and Alianor, plus Rhydd, I have friends I can talk to about anything. If one doesn't understand, another will. Only Rhydd can truly understand what it's like to be royal. Only Dain truly understands monsters and monster hunting. Alianor is the one I can be silly with, be imaginative with, and yes, talk about things like dresses and jewels with. That's far from the extent of our conversations. There is, however, a companion best suited for each of my interests, someone who really *gets* me on that subject, and that is a wonderful feeling.

"What if Sunniva and Doscach had a baby?" Alianor says as we walk. "That'd be a new kind of monster horse. One with wings *and* gills. It could fly in the air *and* swim in the ocean."

"Or it might not be able to do either," I say. "It could just be a green horse with a red mane and hooves." I wrinkle my nose. "Not sure if that'd look good or not. Probably not."

When she glances at me, I shrug. "Science, right? You don't inherit all your parents' traits. I don't even know if a pegasus and a ceffyl-dwr could mate. They're both equine monsters, but that doesn't necessarily mean it would work."

"Doesn't mean what would work?" Dain says as he catches up.

"Sunniva and Doscach having a baby," Alianor says.

"W-what?" Dain sputters. "They're not even old enough to . . . to . . ."

"Hypothetically," I say.

"Because they're in *looove*," Alianor says. "At least, Doscach is."

Dain sputters some more as Alianor giggles and shoots me a look. Alianor is fascinated by romance, maybe because she's a half-year older than me.

"We aren't making marriage plans," I say. "We're theorizing. That's what happens when you put the future royal monster hunter with the future royal monster healer. We start talking science."

"But *scientifically*, how does cross-species reproduction work?" Alianor says. "I know dogs can mate with wolves. We've had a few of those. My brother—the idiot—always bugged Dad for a half-wolf dog. Dad said there was a reason people keep domesticated dogs instead. So, a few years ago, Lanslet got himself a half-wolf dog, and it escaped as soon as he let it off the chain."

"Because true domestication takes many, many generations," I say. "Your dad was right. Now, if a wolf-dog was more strongly dog, it would be fine, but there's no way of knowing that, so it's best just to find a dog you like. As for cross-species between monsters—"

Wilmot raises a hand, and I stop mid-sentence. He's spotted something, and we need to be quiet and stop moving.

I creep up beside him, which would be a lot more of a "creep" if I didn't have a giant canine lumbering at my heels. Wilmot's gaze swings from side to side.

After a moment, a bird squawks. A raven's croak. Wilmot motions for the others to stay back and for me to follow. I ask Malric to wait. He grumbles but plants his furry rump. Then he looks at Jacko as if to say, "He'd better not be allowed to go if I'm not."

I bend and ask Jacko to stay with Malric. He pretends not to understand until Malric raises a massive paw, threatening to pin the jackalope. Jacko lets out a grumble of his own and settles in.

Wilmot is already two steps away, and I hurry to catch up. The raven's caw came from the left of the path, and Wilmot waits for me there. He doesn't say a word or even gesture, but I know he wants me to choose a path that will least risk disturbing the raven. I check the wind direction, though that's more important with mammals. Then I check the ground. It's autumn, and crunching leaves underfoot are a giveaway, but this particular area is mostly coniferous forest.

I ease in. The raven has gone silent, but when I strain, I pick up a sound I can't quite place, from roughly the same direction. Then there's another croak, this one loud and angry, accompanied by a flap of wings. I stop short, thinking I've disturbed the bird. Then I see it. Them, actually. Two ravens. One is perched on an animal thigh that's nearly bone. The other wants to share the first's feast.

Wilmot peers over my shoulder and grunts. He motions for us to retreat. As we do, one of the ravens must spot a movement in the trees. It lets out an alert cry, and they both take wing.

"Nothing," Wilmot calls to the others. "Just ravens scavenging."

"May I quickly check what they were eating?" I say. "I think it was a mountain goat, and I want to see whether I'm right."

He nods. Dain joins me. Alianor follows. This is one interest we all have in common.

The bone is from an average-sized mammal, almost certainly genus *Capra*. In other words, a goat. We're close enough to the foothills for mountain goats. This one was probably killed by a larger predator and dragged here. It's only the haunch, with teeth marks on the bone. Alianor and I are examining it when Dain says, "The rest's over here," from a dozen steps to the south.

"It's not a wild goat," he says as we approach. "It's domestic."

We're at least a two-day walk from the nearest settlement.

So how did the goat get here? It could escape, of course, but that's a long way for a domesticated animal to survive in the Dunnian Woods.

I say this, and then add that it's probably a dropped kill. No predator is going to drag a goat haunch for two days.

"Gryphon would be the obvious answer," I say. "A manticore could carry it, but I don't think they'd bother. Or perhaps a large wyvern? We know gryphons will return food to their den, especially if they have young ones. I'm not as sure about wyverns."

I bend to take a closer look at the teeth marks. When Wilmot appears, I rise. "Sorry. We don't have time to satisfy this much curiosity."

He shakes his head. "We have time. And we're at least a half-day's walk from Tiera's den—in the wrong direction for a gryphon to be flying there from a farmer's field. If there's another gryphon den in these foothills, we need to be aware of that."

Even if I can determine that a gryphon killed this goat, that won't tell us where its lair might be. Wilmot is humoring me. If we really did need to get moving, though, he'd say so. I'll take this brief break to practice my detection skills.

After months of studying Tiera, I know what gryphon bite marks look like. They're actually beak marks, a gryphon having the head of an eagle. These don't match. I ask Dain to confirm, and he does. Wilmot does, too. These are bites, from teeth.

Manticores have lion bodies, wings and simian heads which—like harpies—have been mistaken for human. Their teeth are simian. That's what I see here. Teeth marks that look human.

"Could they *be* human?" Alianor asks.

"That would mean tool marks and I don't . . ." I turn the bone over, and Alianor crows, pointing to an obvious slice, like one made with a knife.

"It's been butchered."

Someone cut meat off this bone. And also chewed it? With raw meat still attached?

"It's a folklore remedy for nausea caused by dietary issues," Cedany says, as if she read my mind. "You chew the bone of a hoofed mammal."

Alianor wrinkles her nose. "I've never heard of that one."

"It's from Roiva."

"So someone from Roiva—with stomach upset—butchered a domestic goat in the middle of the Dunnian Woods?" Dain says.

"The fact that the tradition is from Roiva doesn't mean the person is. Folk remedies travel." She walks over to where there's more of the goat. "In this case, though, you are correct, Dain. Or that is a reasonable assumption, given that the goat is also from Roiva."

I follow and see what looks like the top half of a regular domestic goat. She points out the bridle markings and the long tufts on what remains of its ears. When I don't comment, she chuckles, "I suppose a princess doesn't see many goats."

"Not really."

"Well, I studied in Roiva, and I've only seen these goats there."

"An expedition from across the mountains," Wilmot murmurs as he bends beside the carcass. "Look here. See these worn patches on the goat's hide? Those are from saddlebags.

It's a common practice to use goats for carrying supplies on long journeys and then, when the supplies run out . . ."

"They butcher the goat for meat." I examine both pieces of the goat. "There's a lot left, though. Wouldn't they dry it all?"

"They would. Otherwise, they'd let the goat keep walking and grazing until they needed the meat." Wilmot rises from his place beside the carcass. "Something happened to either make them butcher it early or to force them to stop before they'd finished."

He rises. "Look for a clearing. If we find the remains of their camp, we might get some answers."

I'm walking with Kaylein. Alianor and Cedany stayed behind to take a closer look at the goat. Dain is searching with Wilmot.

I catch the smell of wood-fire smoke first. We've been walking off the path, hunting for a clearing, when the wind brings the faint smell our way. We follow it until we spot the clearing. It doesn't hold the remains of a camp, though. It holds an actual camp—tents circling a smoldering fire.

When I start forward, Kaylein grabs me at the same moment Malric snags my tunic.

"They're traders and travelers," I say. "That's what Wilmot said. An expedition from Roiva."

Kaylein shakes her head. "He just meant that the travelers seem to have come from Roiva. There's no way of knowing their intentions."

"It won't be a war party, though. No one's going to make the trek through the mountains and the forest for that."

"True. Their purpose is likely legitimate. But that doesn't mean they're safe. This is the Dunnian Woods, your highness. Many miles from any settlement. There is no law out here." Before I can speak, she says, "Yes, the forest is technically under Tamarel's rule, but it's impossible to enforce. Just ask Alianor's clan."

She has a point.

"Caution is always warranted, your highness. Particularly for you."

"How ought we to proceed, then?"

"Allow me to make first contact, your highness. I'm dressed in the royal colors, and my sword proclaims me a member of the guard. That should make them think twice if they have any thoughts of robbery."

"Take Malric," I say.

She hesitates, but I ask the warg to go with her, and when he doesn't grumble, I know it's the right choice.

As they walk into the clearing, I survey the camp. Three very basic tents. A fire, which is snuffed out and likely has been since dawn, leaving only a thin stream of smoke perfuming the air. It was a big fire. Too big, I think, with a spark of superiority, as if I am already an expert on forest travel.

That's all I can see from where I sit. Tents and the smoldering remains of a large fire.

"Hello," Kaylein calls as she marches into the camp.

It's not a question but a statement, and she has one hand on her sword, her dark eyes flint hard, muscles tight as she looks around. In that moment, I'm awed by how strong she looks. Of course, she must be strong—she's the youngest royal guard. But I'm accustomed to seeing her as a companion, sometimes laughing, sometimes silent, always relaxed and easygoing. Here, she looks like a warrior striding into camp, and I know she must be nervous, but I don't see it, and that is a true skill.

"Hello," she says, louder. "My name is Kaylein of Clan Montag. Royal guard of Tamarel. Cousin to Berinon of Clan Montag, captain of the royal guard and bodyguard to Queen Mariela."

I'm surprised by the last sentence. She has said her clan takes great pride in Berinon, who went from blacksmith's apprentice to a noble's guard to personal guard of the queen herself. Yet this is more than pride. It is protection. People outside the kingdom know who Berinon is—because of both his position and his deep friendship with my parents. He is a man of importance. Attacking his cousin would be worse than striking at an unknown palace guard.

As Kaylein strides through the camp, her voice rings out. When no one answers, her face hardens.

"You are on Tamarel land," she says. "While our country welcomes all visitors, we do have the right to ask the purpose of anyone crossing our border. Please show yourselves immediately."

No answer, and as she stalks to a tent, I know what she's going to find even before she yanks open the flap.

Nothing.

The tent is empty.

The camp is empty.

CHAPTER TEN

Kaylein has gone to get the others, and I stand in the
middle of the empty camp, listening to the wind.
The unfastened flap on one tent flutters in the breeze.
I walk to it and peer in.

There are two packs inside. One is open, one cinched
tight. I discover that another tent contains three packs, the
third holds none.

Wilmot walks over as I'm backing out from the second tent.
"Could they be hunting?" I ask.

He shakes his head. That fire is almost out, and I'd already
speculated it has been that way since morning. What I hadn't
considered was *why*. Not why the fire was out, but why the camp
was still here long after the night's fire had been extinguished.

Wilmot called this an expedition. While people do travel
into the forest to hunt, that is extremely rare this deep in the
Dunnian Woods. People are here for one reason—they're

moving *through* in one direction or the other. These people butchered a goat because they needed the food to continue moving. If they felt safe stopping to hunt, they'd have done that instead.

Something happened here.

That's what we're all thinking as we stand in that empty camp, listening to the tents flapping in the breeze. Empty tents. Forgotten fire. Abandoned packs.

There's the half-butchered goat, too.

"Is there any reason they'd start cutting it up last night and leave the rest for morning?" I ask.

Wilmot shakes his head. "It isn't like chopping wood, where they might tire and decide to finish later. A half-butchered goat will attract unwanted attention."

Scavengers. Predators. Even monsters.

Is that what happened here? As I stand at the edge of camp, I imagine night falling. It's time for bed, but someone is still working on the goat. Everyone else is . . . in their tents? No. It's dark but not late, and they've built a huge fire. The tents are too small for anything more than sleep, so they're sitting around the fire talking. And then . . .

In my mind, a huge shape swoops down from the sky. A gryphon. The vision only lasts a moment before I dismiss it. The clearing isn't big enough for a gryphon to land without knocking down the tents.

Wyverns aren't big enough to carry off people. Harpies can, obviously. Is that what happened?

I look around. Three tents. Four packs, one tent without any. I'm going to guess that means six or seven people. It took four harpies to lift Dain. At least twenty-four harpies would have been needed to carry off six people.

The bigger problem here is the lack of damage. When people are attacked—presumably civilians, mostly unarmed—they're going to run for shelter. Or run to their packs to grab a weapon. I can't imagine at least six people being attacked and leaving behind a camp so tidy it looks as if they've just stepped away to wash.

"Rowan?" Wilmot calls, yanking me from my thoughts.

He motions me to where the others stand in a knot, talking. I'm still on the edge of camp, with Jacko sniffing around my feet and Malric lying beside me. I walk over to the others.

"As the royal monster hunter, you are the leader of our expedition," Wilmot says. "Tell us what you think happened here."

"No pressure," Alianor mutters.

Wilmot turns an even look on her. "Rowan is learning how to lead . . . and accept constructive criticism without embarrassment. Rowan?"

I take a deep breath. Then I tell them what I've worked out.

"I was just going to start looking closer," I say when I'm done. "Searching for clues that aren't obvious. Footprints or blood or signs of a struggle."

"And Malric?" Wilmot says.

I frown at the warg, seated beside me.

"Malric is your companion," Wilmot says. "Like all companions, he has skills you lack. One of them would be useful here."

"Oh!" I say. "His nose. I hadn't thought of that."

"You can do that in a moment. For now, your theory seems sound. I agree it's highly unlikely that this many people were carried off by monsters of any kind, leaving a camp so tidy. So what could force people from their camp without leaving the mess of an attack?"

I mentally run through lists of monsters.

"Two legs," Wilmot prompts.

A monster on two legs? There's nothing . . .

"You think people did this," I say.

Once I consider it, that answer seems so obvious that my cheeks heat. As the royal monster hunter, I naturally saw this scene in terms of monsters. Yet however intelligent monsters might be, they cannot do the one thing that stops humans from fighting back: issue threats. What we're seeing here is a group of people who seem to have just walked away.

They were sitting around the campfire, on guard against animals and monsters, but what comes from the forest is very different. Maybe the intruders take a couple of hostages to force the others to leave the camp.

"Which means this doesn't fall under the princess's area of expertise." Cedany turns to Alianor. "It falls under yours."

Alianor's gaze cools. "What does that mean?"

"That these people have been attacked by bandits. Your clan."

"Are you saying my clan—?" Alianor begins.

"No one is accusing Clan Bellamy of this," I say quickly. "However, Cedany has a point. You would know more about this sort of thing than we do."

"This sort of thing?" Alianor enunciates each word, her gaze locked on mine. "Is this what you think we do, Rowan? Fall on innocent travelers and march them away at knifepoint?

Yes, we have been known to relieve travelers of their belongings when they fail to pay us—"

"Is that what you call it?" Cedany says.

"Stop, Alianor," Dain says. "We're tired of hearing you defend your clan. If Rowan doesn't argue with your excuses, it's because she doesn't want to argue with *you*. You're her friend. She doesn't want to insult your family. But this?" He waves at the camp. "People are missing. You can't keep pretending your clan aren't *bandits*."

I want to leap to her defense. To soften the blow. My breath comes quicker as I watch her gaze swing my way, and it's like there's a wall hovering over the space between us. Say the wrong thing—or fail to say the right thing—and that wall will slam down. I'll lose a friend.

But sometimes, saying the *right* thing is actually the wrong thing, if it's a lie meant to make someone feel better when they need to face the truth. Or when it's a leader who treats someone differently because they're a friend.

"I . . . I'd like to speak to Alianor privately," I say.

She crosses her arms. "No, Rowan. Whatever you have to say, say it right here. In front of everyone."

I shift my weight and look around. Kaylein seems as if she wants to jump in and help. Wilmot's face is blank. He's staying out of this. Dain and Cedany watch me with guarded expressions, and I know if I say the wrong thing, they will judge me for it. They will judge my ability to lead.

"Clan Bellamy has overcharged travelers for guide service," I say. "In the past, the clan was known for raiding and banditry, and so travelers presume part of that charge is for protection—that if they don't pay it, they might be subject to thievery on their journey." I look at Alianor. "Is that incorrect?"

Her jaw tightens. "It is not our fault if they believe that. The fact is that they pay the fee and we provide the service."

"Or they don't pay it, and they're set on by bandits," Cedany says.

Alianor spins on her. "We do not—"

"Then explain this," Cedany says. She tugs down the collar of her tunic and points to a small scar on her collarbone. "I have been keeping silent until now. I know all too well that we should not be held responsible for the actions of our families, so I would not have mentioned it. I received this the first time I crossed the mountains. Being from Havendale and not understanding the customs, my group hired a guide who wasn't Clan Bellamy. We were stopped by your people, who demanded a toll for passing. My guide expected me to pay it. I refused. I was seventeen and very certain I was in the right. This forest belonged to the Queen of Tamarel. Those people were not collecting money on her behalf, therefore, I did not need to pay. One of the men held a knife to my throat, and when I remained stubborn, he gave me this." She points at the scar. "Another in our party paid my toll. Otherwise, I'm quite certain I would not be here today."

"No!" Alianor says. "That's a lie."

"Which part?" Cedany steps toward her. "Exactly which part is a lie, little girl?"

Alianor's jaw stays tense, but there's just the slightest wobble in it. When I step forward, Kaylein speaks before I can.

"You were right earlier, Cedany," Kaylein says, her voice soft but firm. "Alianor isn't responsible for her clan's actions.

I understand we need to consider all possibilities, but perhaps we can do it with less . . . vigor."

While it's a gentle rebuke, I still expect Cedany to defend herself. Like Alianor, she has a temper. Instead, Cedany's pale skin reddens, and she mumbles something before withdrawing.

"It's true that we sometimes demand tolls," Alianor says. "We use the roads for travel and for guiding, and we keep them as safe as possible. It wouldn't be fair to allow just anyone to benefit from our work." She sneaks a glance my way. "But yes, our right to collect those tolls has been questioned by the queen, and my father has been negotiating the matter."

Alianor looks at Cedany and straightens. "I would appreciate a description of those who injured you. My father allows his people to be firm in their requests, but he would draw the line at violence. I'm not doubting that you were hurt. I'm just saying it isn't sanctioned. What upset me was the suggestion that my clan would have committed murder for an unpaid toll."

"Yes," Kaylein says, her voice still soft. "But Cedany *felt* as if her life was at risk. That's what matters. She was threatened, and she believed the threat."

Alianor dips her gaze. "I understand. But what happened here—a kidnapping—that wouldn't be Clan Bellamy. We don't take hostages."

I clear my throat, just a little, and she flushes. "Fine," she says. "But not like that. Not grabbing random travelers."

"We have no way of knowing they were *random*," Kaylein says. "The party may have included someone of importance. Or an enemy of your clan."

"I still don't think —" Alianor stops short and shakes her head. "All right. I cannot say beyond all doubt that it wasn't Clan Bellamy."

"Either way," Wilmot says. "It's no concern of ours."

I bristle. "The woods are our land. If travelers were kidnapped—"

He raises a hand. "I mean that it cannot be our concern right now, Rowan. A brief stop to investigate a possible monster attack is an acceptable diversion. But there is no sign that monsters did this, and so we must continue on and advise the authorities upon our return."

"May we at least check the packs?" I ask. "Attempt to identify those who went missing, so I may pass that information to my mother?"

He nods. "Quickly."

CHAPTER ELEVEN

We find nothing identifying in the tents, but as we search one of them, Alianor becomes agitated. No one else notices. It's just me and her and Kaylein in the tent with three packs, and Kaylein is too preoccupied to see how quickly Alianor closes the pack she's searching.

"Anything?" I ask.

She shakes her head and busies herself adjusting her bootlace. "Nothing of note."

I hesitate. "May I have a look?"

"Of course."

She helps Kaylein while I check the pack. It contains women's clothing and several books. I pull out two science texts. Geology, far above my level. I put them away and keep digging, finding only personal items.

When I leave the tent, the others are already waiting to go.

"Did anyone find any valuables?" I ask.

"No," Cedany says, "but when you travel across the mountains, you'd be advised to hide valuables on your person, in case of bandits."

"Did we find anything that suggests this wasn't *bandits?*" I ask. "Either Tamarelian or foreign?" I add the last so Alianor won't feel targeted again.

Everyone says no. The packs contained only personal items, nothing that could be resold. I'm not sure whether to be relieved or not. I hoped to find something to prove it wasn't bandits, and therefore Alianor's clan couldn't be responsible.

This has always been the awkward part of our friendship. Other people go to prison for the things her family does. It's only their name that keeps them safe. Our country was formed through a union between the clans. Taking away Clan Bellamy's livelihood would be like taking away Clan Hadleigh's right to guide on the rivers or Clan Montag's right to fish the seas.

Dad always grumbled that we should just give Clan Bellamy land and tell them to start farming. Mom would ask where we'd find this land for them to farm. Force people off theirs so Clan Bellamy could have it?

No, the only solution is infuriating, endless, excruciatingly slow negotiation. Currently, it's around the tolls. Mom wants the clan to be clear why they're demanding money for passage and request it as soon as travelers start on the trails, rather than intercepting them after several days, which is kind of like charging someone after they've eaten three-quarters of the food you left out.

The fact remains that my best friend is a bandit warlord's daughter. Mostly, Alianor and I just don't talk about that. I'm not sure that's the right answer. Especially after watching her going through that pack. I suspect that whatever she saw confirmed that her family did this.

I can't worry about that now. Wilmot is right that we need to get moving. I ask him to allow me to quickly comb the surrounding woods with Malric, to get an idea of where the hostages may have been taken. He hesitates, but again only tells me to be quick. Unless Malric finds that the trail heads in the same direction we're going, we can't follow it.

The problem is that the travelers left scent trails every time they headed to the water or ventured out to forage for nuts and berries. Their attackers also would have left trails as they skulked about preparing to strike. That means a whole web of scents.

I've been following Malric, while Jacko hops along, madly sniffing the ground. I'm wondering whether he has any idea what we're looking for when he lets out an alert cry, and I dive into the brush to see . . . goat tracks. Jacko prances around, head high, clearly pleased with himself.

I step back toward the clearing, only to spot someone in the forest. I stop short and duck to peek. Malric sighs and shakes his head, telling me I've made a mistake that is, to him, as foolish as Jacko's.

The figure in the forest is one of our own party. Alianor. I realize that when she crouches and the fading sun winks off her jeweled hair clip. I'd given that clip to what I thought was a poor flower girl. It'd been Alianor spying on me outside the castle. She's since offered to return the clip—one of my favorites—but I told her to keep it, and she wears it all the time. Because we're friends. Best friends. I wanted her to have something special of mine that she obviously admires, and she wants me to know she treasures it.

I need to speak to her about what she found in that tent. The subject must be approached with care so I don't damage our friendship.

I step toward her. That's when the sun winks off something silver. Not the clip this time, but something in Alianor's hand. A necklace? A bracelet? It's a silver chain caught on a bush, and she's bent to untangle it. Once it's free, she holds it up.

"Alianor?" I say.

She jumps and deftly tucks the chain into her pocket as she rises, making a show of brushing off her leggings.

"Hey," she says. "Find anything?"

"No. You?"

"Nope."

She walks toward me, and I duck past to where she'd found the chain. She grabs at my arm saying, "We should go," but I keep moving. Once at the spot, I survey it.

"Broken twigs," I say. "Someone came through here."

"Someone or something. I found goat tracks over there."

"So did I, but there's a boot impression here."

She bends to examine it, and I expect her to claim it's something else, but she says, "That's definitely a boot print. Can Malric follow the trail from here?"

I ask him. He sniffs around, and then looks from me to Alianor and back.

"What?" Alianor says.

He senses something's up. He eyes her for a moment and then lumbers in the other direction, nose to the ground. The person's trail merges with the path, and it's clear they walked along it, in the same direction we did.

Wilmot catches up, and I tell him Malric followed this trail from camp.

"Yes," he says. "But that's also the direction they *came* from."

Cedany nods as she approaches. "Which means it might be an old trail."

"Their trail *to* the camp." I exhale. "All right. I hate leaving people who could be in trouble, but I guess we can't . . . we can't do anything about it."

I drag out the last words, hoping someone will jump in to say we must investigate.

"They're hostages, presumably valuable," Kaylein says. "That's a diplomatic matter for your mother."

"And if we follow them," Alianor says, "we may end up spooking their captors into hurting them."

I cut a look her way, but she avoids my gaze.

"I'm being impulsive," I murmur. "Not thinking it through. Not doing what's best for Tamarel."

"No," Kaylein says. "You're being kind and considerate, and we want that in our rulers."

"Unless being kind and considerate to a few people means endangering the lives of a hundred times that many." I sigh. "Have I mentioned how glad I am that I'll never be queen?"

"Once or twice," Alianor says, and she enfolds me in a hug, which doesn't help as much as it should.

I know what I saw her do. And I'm not sure how to handle it.

I am, however, sure how to handle *this*.

"We need to keep moving," I say. "Whether this was kid-nappers or wild animals or monsters, we don't want to be here come nightfall."

It starts raining before we've gone more than a mile. It isn't a light mist, either. It's pouring, and we're close enough to a rocky foothill that it makes sense to run there for shelter rather than push on.

At the hill, we find a rock overhang big enough to cover all of us. We still hope to get farther that day, but when the storm breaks, the sky doesn't lighten—we've lost the sun as it drops behind the mountains. We split into pairs and go in search of a better camping spot. Dain finds a cavern, and Kaylein starts a fire.

After dinner, Alianor wants to explore the cavern, which stretches into what looks like a crawlspace in the back, pos-sibly a cave system. I decline, and that earns me a piercing look from both Dain and Wilmot.

"I'm just really tired," I say.

Alianor slips off with a shrug, as if she doesn't care, but shortly after, she returns.

"There are bones in there," she says. "Some really old ones. You should come see if we can identify them."

"I'm fine," I say. "But thank you for thinking of me."

The way she hesitates, as if trying to think of something to entice me, makes me feel as if she's trying too hard to get my attention. Trying too hard to convince herself I didn't see anything, and everything is fine.

I should go and check out the bones to reassure her, but I'm afraid if we're alone together, I'll confront her.

I glance at Dain. Having him along would help because I'd never confront Alianor in front of someone else.

When I look over, though, he's busy working on an arrow.

"I'll just . . . go look at these bones on my own," Alianor says.

I nod, and she disappears through the tunnel. I glance at Dain again. He looks up with a "Hmmm?" but I wave for him to return to his work. Then I settle near the fire with Jacko and scratch behind his antlers.

I know what I saw. Something in that one pack got Alianor's attention, and then she pocketed the silver chain and pretended she hadn't found anything.

I see two possible reasons for her behavior, and I don't like either.

One, she took something from the pack and then also took the chain. I won't say "stole," because they'd been left behind, though I guess that's splitting hairs. If she'd found a necklace in the forest and asked what I thought, I'd have said to keep it. Same as if she'd found a pack just lying around. But these people were victims of something, and the fact that she hid what she took proves she knows it's wrong. Yet that's what bandits do, right? If they came across that camp in the forest, they'd take whatever they could, knowing anything left behind would be lost or scattered by animals. Still, I'd be uncomfortable taking things from there myself.

Maybe that's why she hid it. So I wouldn't judge her upbringing.

The other possibility is that Alianor took the items because they proved that her clan was responsible for attacking the travelers. Again, she didn't want to be judged. I can't blame her for that.

I need to talk to someone. As I brood, Jacko snuggles in with little chitters. Even Malric, lying between my feet and the fire, casts concerned looks my way. I'd happily talk to either of them, but sadly I need someone who can talk back.

Dain is the wrong person entirely. I'd be sharing a secret I'm not sure I should share, and I'd be asking him for advice he won't feel comfortable giving.

I turn my gaze on Wilmot, drying his boots by the fire. I can't guess how he'll react, and I also don't know him well enough to feel as if I can confide in him.

My answer is Kaylein. I like her. I respect and admire her, and I think she's thoughtful and kind. But she's also my bodyguard. Does that mean I shouldn't ask her for personal advice? Mom confides in Berinon, though. He's her bodyguard, friend and advisor. I can at least approach Kaylein and see what she says.

CHAPTER TWELVE

Wilmot says Kaylein is gathering wood, but when I step into the forest, Cedany's laugh floats over, followed by Kaylein's. They must both be getting wood, which is wise—no one should be alone out here. Even though I'm with Malric, Wilmot warned me against going more than fifty paces from the cave. I'm at twenty-five when I round a stand of trees to see Cedany and Kaylein.

They aren't still gathering wood. There's a pile by their feet, but they're sitting on a fallen log, heads together as they giggle over something. I keep struggling to remember Cedany is only twenty—she acts so much older. Right now, though, she looks her age, her face relaxed, eyes dancing with some shared joke.

I start to back away, not wanting to interrupt. Cedany leans over to whisper something, and Kaylein taps Cedany's arm as if in mock-outrage at whatever she said, and—

I trip over Malric, who is right behind me. As I stumble, arms windmilling, the two young women leap up.

"I'm fine," I say, getting my balance. "I saw you were talking, so I was leaving and someone"—I glare at the warg—"was guarding my back a little too closely. I'll go back to camp. Sorry to interrupt."

"Were you looking for us?" Kaylein says as I start to leave.

"Yes, but it wasn't important."

"Perhaps not," Cedany says. "But we shouldn't linger in the forest at night, nor allow you to do the same. I found yarrow, and we stopped to pick some in case anyone gets foot sores from damp boots. I'm guessing Wilmot sent you to shoo us back to camp."

"No, I just . . . I'll take some wood, but you don't need to hurry back."

"A princess ought not to be carrying firewood," Cedany says with a smile. "If I were a princess, I certainly wouldn't."

"Then how would you know what it was like to be someone who did? What it was like to need to chop your own wood to stay warm?"

"Your mother taught you that, didn't she," she says with an eye roll. "Queens are supposed to be evil. Every fairy tale I've read says so. If they seem nice, they're secretly evil." She squints at me. "Queen Mariela is actually stockpiling all those monsters you hunt, isn't she? Then, one day, she'll threaten to unleash them on Tamarel unless we pay her a hundred bushels of gold."

"Mmm, that's actually possible," Kaylein says. "You haven't seen Rowan's monster collection. It's not exactly a stockpile yet, but she's working on it." She turns to me. "What did you wish to see us about, your highness?"

"I just wanted to speak to you for a moment. But—"

"I can take a hint," Cedany says, throwing up her hands. "Let me gather some more yarrow, and I'll be gone."

I tell Kaylein my predicament as we sit on the fallen log, while Malric rests at my feet and Jacko hunts a mouse. When I finish, she's quiet. Too quiet. I glance over to see uncertainty and discomfort on her face.

I stand quickly. "I'm sorry. I shouldn't have brought you into this. It isn't your job. I just—" I swallow and straighten. "I'll figure it out. That's *my* job."

"But it shouldn't need to be. I forget how young you are. At your age, I could barely lift a sword, let alone be expected to wield it against monsters."

I eye her skeptically. "Berinon said he gave you a tin sword at the age of five, and Berinon never exaggerates. He always used to say he left the stories to my father."

She smiles. "Fair enough. Let me think a moment on this."

I lower myself onto the log again and watch Jacko hunt as Kaylein thinks.

Finally, she says, "When my brother was fifteen, and I was twelve, he was sneaking out at night to cause trouble with other boys. I knew it, and I had no idea what to do. It wasn't terribly bad trouble—just the sort of mischief young people do at that age—but my parents would talk about what was happening and say they couldn't believe anyone let their children out at that time of night."

She shrugs. "How heartbreaking would it be to discover their own son was one of them? Everyone was talking about the mischief the boys caused, and if it was discovered, my family would have lost business. But telling them felt like tattling. I realized I had to talk to my brother myself. Tell him that I knew and ask him to stop or I'd need to tell our parents."

"And he was all right with that?"

She throws back her head and laughs. "How would you feel if Rhydd said that to you?"

I consider it. "Angry. Hurt, but mostly angry. At first. Then I'd think about it and realize he had a point."

"Which is exactly what Asher did. He cursed and ranted and called me a little sneak and a spoilsport. He was only having fun, after all. For a whole day, he wouldn't speak to me. Then he confessed to our parents, and they came up with a plan. The boys could sneak out and pull harmless pranks, but they had to do good things, too, like magically mending an old fisher's net. So if their mischief was caught, people wouldn't be as upset." She straightens. "That part doesn't apply to your story, of course, but my point is that you should speak to Alianor alone and let her tell the others, but be prepared for her to be angry at first."

I nod.

She continues. "Next, I believe the question you need to ask is what harm you do by waiting."

I glance up, brow furrowed.

"Either she looted the camp because that's how she was raised," Kaylein says, "or she's covering up her family's involvement. The latter is more troubling, but is it an issue *now*? That is the question."

I consider what she's saying. "Even if we knew her clan took the travelers hostage, it isn't an issue until Tamarel investigates. That's what you mean—that there's no reason I need the truth now."

"But you will need it soon, if only for the sake of your friendship. She can't keep secrets like that, and she can't keep worrying that you're judging her clan."

"We need to talk. Just not while we're focused on our mission."

She glances at me. "Does that work?"

"It does. Thank you."

Kaylein exhales dramatically. "Good. This looks so much easier when Berinon does it. But you can always ask me for advice. I might not be able to help, but the more I practice, the better I'll get at it."

"May I ask you something else?" I say.

"Of course, your highness."

"Could you call me Rowan? Please?"

She laughs. "That might be even more difficult than giving you advice. But I'll certainly try."

I sleep amazingly well. Whatever anxiety I might still feel from abandoning the travelers has been drowned out by the relief of coming up with a plan for the Alianor problem. At one point, I wake to Jacko nudging my face and chattering. I'm so tired all I can do is lift my head and mutter something before falling back to sleep. I wake again to him doing the same, but this time, Malric silences him with a growl, and I'm too groggy to even wonder what's the matter. It isn't until dawn, as I'm slowly waking, that Jacko's nighttime chattering comes back and I bolt upright, terrified that he needed a toilet trip outside, and I ignored him, and he went alone and has been devoured by monsters.

He's right there, though, awake and watching me.

"I'm so sorry," I say as I rise, whispering so I don't wake the others.

I shake off sleep as Jacko hops over my legs, telling me to hurry. Then I blink hard. There's a fire burning outside the cave entrance and Kaylein is sitting at it.

That makes me wonder why Jacko is in such a hurry. He could have gone out at any time last night and done his business under the careful watch of whoever was on guard duty.

I shake off the question. He wants me to go with him; it *is* dawn, and I'm fine with getting up a little early.

The cavern isn't quite tall enough for me to stand up in, though I'm the shortest in the party. Head ducked, I walk outside and yawn as I greet Kaylein.

"You're up early," she says.

"Early bird gets first pick of breakfast," I say. "And by this point, we don't have many options."

"Of course we do. There's dried meat, dried meat or dried meat. It might even be three different *kinds* of meat if you're lucky."

I smile and reach for the food pack. As I do, Jacko slams his antlers into my knee.

"Hey!" I say, jumping back. "It's a little early for ramming, don't you think?"

He chatters up at me.

"You don't need me to escort you into the forest," I say. "And if you insist, give me a moment. I think there's still some hard bread down here, and I—"

He whacks me again, and his chatters turn angry. I frown. Rhydd jokes that the jackalope is spoiled, but that just means Jacko gets his own plate of food and his own bed by the fire. He's never demanding.

"What's wrong?" I ask.

He zooms back into the cave.

"Better see what he wants," Kaylein says. "Before he wakes everyone, and they blame you."

I snort my agreement and march back into the cave, ducking my head. The firelight outside actually makes it darker in here, as if the darkness swallows all light beyond the first step or two. I'm guessing that's just because my eyes had accustomed to the bright flames.

Jacko chatters louder, and Kaylein's right that I'll be blamed if he wakes everyone. That is not how I wish to start my day.

I hurry to hush him. He's at the back of the cave, by the tunnel Alianor explored. He zips in and out again, and chatters at me.

I struggle to remember what Alianor said about the tunnel. I glance over to see whether she's awake, but they're all silent lumps under sleeping blankets. My concern is whether something could be living in there. Or if the tunnel could connect to the outside, giving predators a way to sneak in. That doesn't matter much now—I'm awake and alert for trouble—but it's clearly bothering Jacko.

I sigh and jog back to tell Kaylein where I'll be. I look longingly at the food pack, with that one piece of hard bread in the bottom. Then I take a bite of the dried meat in my hand, stuff the rest into my pocket and enter the tunnel.

Once in the tunnel, I wish I'd explored it last night with Alianor. Not just to check for danger but to enjoy an adventure together. This is exactly the sort of thing I love, and the fact that I skipped it shows just how upset I'd been. Now I creep through on all fours and marvel at the tunnel system.

We don't have anything like this at home. There are a few mines, for digging up stone, iron and other resources, but they aren't like this, rocky tunnels and corridors spreading out like a maze of unexplored possibilities.

I let Jacko lead, and I'm careful to leave marks so I can find my way back. While I don't know if this system is big enough to get lost in, any delay on my part would annoy the others.

I don't think the jackalope knows exactly where he's going. He's following a trail, sniffing every now and then, and pausing at branching paths to be sure he's heading the right way.

It reminds me a bit of the jba-fofi tunnels. Those had been dirt, though, and roots, and while I see some of that, these are mostly rock. For the first hundred feet or so, I can see where I'm going. There must be vents to the surface, with faint light coming in. After a while, that fades, and I need to light a fire stick.

I find the bones Alianor was talking about, but when I pick one up, admiring its smoothness, how it's been worn by age, Jacko chitters at me to stop dawdling. He's right. I want to see what's bothering him, and the others will wake soon.

A lot of the passages are too small for me, and luckily, those aren't the ones Jacko wants, which makes me worry about the size of the creature that's concerning him. As we pass one dark side tunnel, something inside moves. I freeze, but Jacko only chatters, prodding me along. When a sound comes from that tunnel—a high-pitched whistle—I back up, peek around the corner and shine my fire stick. At first, it looks like a nest of snakes. But then I see legs. Lizards? One lifts its head from the nest. A cat's head. Its mouth opens and it squeals.

I slap my hand over my mouth before I squeal myself. I tap Jacko.

"Tatzelwurms," I whisper. "A nest of baby tatzelwurms."

He's not nearly as impressed as my fellow monster hunters would be. Tatzelwurms are rarely seen outside the mountains. They have cats' heads and bodies that look half snake, half lizard—serpentine torsos with clawed legs. Legend says they don't have rear legs, but that's just because their back ones are smaller than their front, and they fight by rearing up like snakes.

I don't see a momma tatzelwurm, but I doubt that would be what concerned Jacko. Full-grown, they're no more than two feet long. After another look, I reluctantly leave the nest and continue along. The tunnel lightens after that, and I snuff out my fire stick. We turn one last corner, and the rising sun hits so bright, I blink and draw up short.

We're in another cavern, one that faces east. Also, apparently I'd been crawling upward because I'm looking down on the scrubby treetops surrounding the foothill.

This cavern is smaller than the one we slept in, and I stand on the ledge, looking out at the dawn.

"It's beautiful, isn't it?" I say, scooping up Jacko.

The jackalope chatters and squirms and shakes his antlers in obvious annoyance.

I chuckle. "Sorry, I know you didn't bring me here to admire the view. You were pointing out that there's another entrance, which a monster—or a person—could use to sneak up on us. Thank you. Guess we got lucky."

I'm not sure it's good fortune as much as ordinary odds. I can't imagine a monster being hungry enough to crawl through all those tunnels after us. A human could sneak in, but after we found the camp, Wilmot had been particularly careful about looking for signs of others.

Of course there's no way for Jacko to know this, and the fact he realized the "back door" could be dangerous is impressive. He must have gone exploring after we were asleep. I'm just glad nothing bad happened, and I need to heed his warnings more carefully in the future.

I look around and consider my options. While the cave is about thirty feet off the ground, there's an easy slope down, and I can smell our fire from here. It'll be quicker going around rather than back through the tunnels. I don't have my sword, but I'm armed with my dagger and my jackalope, and I'll move fast and keep to the upper ground.

I do that, and I'm close enough to hear voices when Malric comes at a run. That's almost as impressive as Jacko finding the back entrance. Running really isn't the warg's style.

Malric bounds up and snaps his teeth at me, growling his displeasure.

"I went through the tunnels," I say. "I just came back this way because it was much faster."

Another snap.

"You were sleeping, and I didn't want to bother you."

He growls.

I throw up my hands. "Fine. Next time I'll wake you up. I'd have loved to see you crawl through that tunnel."

"Talking to your warg again, princess?" Dain says as he appears. "You're always easy to find. Just follow the sound of your voice. How was your morning adventure?"

I fall in step with him. "I found a back door. Jacko was alarmed about it. Is everyone awake?"

"They are. Just waiting for you and . . ." He stops and looks behind me. "Where's Alianor?"

"Not with us." I see his expression. "Did she come after me? Oh no. That's just what we need—another delay." I sigh. "Would you come back to the tunnel with me? We'll go through from there and cut her off. Malric can walk back to camp."

"Wilmot won't like this. He was already grumbling about losing time yesterday."

"Which is why we're going to hurry." I pick up speed. "Now it's—"

"Your highness?" a voice calls. We glance to see Kaylein running toward us. "Rowan?"

"We're going to find Alianor," I call back. "She isn't with me."

Kaylein waves a piece of paper. "Because she's gone."

I pause one heartbeat, and then race over to her so fast Jacko, Malric and Dain all give a start.

My heart hammers so hard I can barely hold it without shaking. Alianor has left. She found something that said her clan kidnapped those travelers, and she's taken off on her own. We drove her away. We judged her, and I didn't talk to her about that.

I take the letter, read the first few lines, and my heart stops pounding. Seems to stop completely.

Alianor didn't leave because her clan took the travelers hostage.

It's worse than that.

So much worse.

CHAPTER THIRTEEN

I read the note again, to be sure I haven't misunderstood. I haven't. Two facts are very clear. Alianor has left, and Alianor is in danger. No, make that *three* facts: It's all my fault.

I shove the last one away. Mom says that when a leader makes a mistake, they have to pick up the guilt and set it on a shelf. Not a high shelf where they'll forget about it, but one just above eye level, where it's temporarily out of sight. Moving the guilt aside doesn't mean denying it exists. When I was little, anytime I made a mistake, I wanted to find someone or something else to blame. Dad taught me to take responsibility. Don't take all the blame, if it *isn't* all yours, though, because that's just as bad.

Dad said think of responsibility as a tart cherry pie. That's my favorite, so when I cut it, I can't help making my slice just a little bigger than my fair share. When taking responsibility for something that went wrong, cut yours just a little bigger than you deserve.

So I cut my share of blame here, and I put it on the shelf for later, when I can take it down and study it more and see where I went wrong.

The point now is to focus on those first two facts. Alianor is gone, and Alianor is in danger.

I was not wrong when I thought something in that pack had bothered her. Nor wrong that she'd taken that silver chain and hidden it from me. What I *was* wrong about? Her reasons.

I lift the note, written in a looping script on a page torn from her healer's journal.

> *Dearest Rowan,*
> *There is something I need to do, and I've come to realize I need to do it alone. The others are right—you need to push on to the mountains and find out what's happening with the monsters. You can't stop to help a few people when many times that number are in danger. Normally, I'd be the first to tell you that, and it IS the right thing to do. The right thing for YOU to do. And this is the right thing for me to do, because this problem is mine, and I cannot ask my friend to endanger her kingdom by helping.*
> *I found something in one of the packs. At first, I thought I was mistaken. I must be, because it made no sense. But then, when I was coming to catch up with you, I found something else that removed all doubt.*

I found a bracelet. A bracelet I gave to Sarika, my sister, who is studying in Roiva. Or she's supposed to be studying in Roiva, and there is no reason for her to come home before the winter holidays. Yet the pack contains clothing that looks like hers and books from the university, where she is taking classes in geological science. The books could be a coincidence. The bracelet is not. Sarika was coming home, and she has been kidnapped.

When I first found the bracelet, I hid it out of fear that you might see it as proof that my family was involved. That my sister was the kidnapper, not the kidnapped. Later, I realized that I'd acted in haste, and that I should speak to you about it. That's why I wanted us to explore the tunnels. But I could tell you were unsettled, and I think you saw me with the bracelet.

I thought more on the matter, and I decided that even if you didn't blame my family, the others would. Also, while you might be able to persuade them to search for her, you really do need to continue on your mission.

This is my mission. You don't need me right now. My sister does.

I will be fine. Please continue on, and I will meet up with you as soon as I can.

Your friend, always,

Alianor

Berinon—who has known Wilmot since they were children—jokes that the hunter's emotional range runs from mildly annoyed to mildly pleased. That's not entirely true. Mom says he has a temper, and Dain says he's seen it, though only directed at him when he's done something dangerous. I've never been sure how Wilmot felt about Alianor. Now I know, because he isn't furious that she's delayed our mission—he's furious that she's put herself in danger.

I'm a little annoyed about that, too, if I'm being honest. Does she really expect that we'll keep going and abandon her in the forest? I don't believe she'd ever force us to delay our mission to help hers. She can be reckless and occasionally thoughtless, but she isn't that manipulative. The truth is that she's convinced herself we'll carry on. She's also convinced herself that she'll be fine out there.

I still feel guilty. She wanted to talk to me, and I didn't want to talk to her. Worse, I realize this is what Jacko tried to tell me last night. Not that there was a back entrance to the cave, but that Alianor used it and never returned. She must have discovered that rear exit while exploring, and then realized she could stuff a fake shape under her sleeping blankets and slip away without alerting the guard. Or, at least, without alerting any guard who could speak, rather than just chatter or growl.

We're at the other entrance now, with our packs on, as Malric confirms that Alianor did indeed come through the cave tunnels.

"The kidnappers' trail went in the direction we were heading," I say as Wilmot stares out into the forest, his arms crossed. "May we follow it as far as we can and then make a decision?"

"I don't see that there's any decision to be made," he grumbles. "That fool girl put us in an impossible situation. What happens if she's hurt? Or worse? How would your mother explain that to Everard of Bellamy? *Yes, we were responsible for your daughter, but she made her own choices.*"

He grumbles some more. He feels as if he needs an excuse for going after Alianor, that he can't just say he's worried about her. Dain would do the same, and I guess this is where he gets it from. That isn't Wilmot's fault. I'm sure he never taught Dain to hide the fact that he worries about others. I always assumed that some of the less positive traits I "inherited" from my parents—my mother's temper, my father's recklessness—came from actual heredity. But I wonder if it's more about learning from people we admire, even if they'd be horrified to know *what* we were learning.

Wilmot was found as a baby, and it's always been presumed he was abandoned. Even if he'd been too young to feel abandoned, he grew up hearing people whisper that his family gave him away, and that might make it hard to admit he cares about people.

Dain's family did the same, and then he was raised by a man who obviously loves him, but I'll bet Wilmot never actually says that. So Dain struggles to admit his feelings for people. Even now, with Alianor gone, Dain's saying nothing, but the way he's fussing with his pack and casting anxious glances at me says everything he can't.

Wilmot sighs. "We need to go after her."

I exhale under my breath. There's no way I want to keep

going and leave her behind. I just appreciate not having to fight Wilmot on the matter.

Once we reach the path, Malric confirms that Alianor's trail continues on.

"And how does she expect to track the kidnappers without Malric?" Wilmot gripes. "I'm not sure whether I'm relieved she didn't steal him or annoyed."

"I think . . ." I begin carefully. "I think we should be careful about using the word *steal* with Alianor. She would never have taken Malric, but even if she did, it would be borrowing him, which I'd have allowed if he permitted it."

Wilmot gives me an awkward pat on the back. "Of course. I'm just being a cranky old man."

"You're younger than my parents, aren't you?"

Cedany laughs. "I think the princess is telling you, diplomatically, that you don't get to use the cranky old man excuse."

A few steps in silence, and then someone says, "Rowan's right, though, that we should be careful which words we use when we talk about Alianor."

To my surprise, this is Dain.

He shrugs. "If she steals, we can't pretend it isn't stealing. If she lies, we can't pretend it isn't lying. But it's easy to accidentally keep reminding people what they are and where they come from."

I slow and look at him.

He waves me off. "Stop looking at me like that, princess. I don't mean that *you* remind *me* where I come from. People do, though, and it's . . ." He rolls his shoulders in another shrug.

"It doesn't help. This is about Alianor, though. Obviously, we made her feel like we wouldn't believe her sister was a victim. The only one she thought she could talk to was Rowan, and that isn't right. That's how we got into this mess."

He glances around, realizes everyone's watching him and shoves his hands into his pockets, mumbling something un-intelligible as he waits—hopes—for us to look away.

We continue in silence until the trail forks. Wilmot looks from one branch to the other and curses under his breath.

"She went right, didn't she?" I say. "And to discover what's driving the monsters this way, we would need to continue left."

He nods.

"How did she know which way to turn?" I ask.

He points at the trail. In some places, it's hard-packed soil, but here it's soft earth, and the foot impressions are clear. One small set of prints—Alianor's boots—and two other sets.

"Only two people?" I say. "Or am I seeing wrong?"

"Only two. Running, from the looks of it."

"Running? Why?"

He doesn't answer, meaning he has no answer to give. No idea why there would only be two people, both running, when we estimated there must have been at least five travelers, plus a kidnapper.

"Maybe two of them escaped their kidnapper," Kaylein says.

"They'd be smarter getting off the trail, then," Wilmot says. "But yes, that makes sense."

When he sighs and turns right, Cedany raises a hand. "Allow me to go after Alianor. I know this forest, and I'm a decent enough hunter to follow her tracks." She slides a glance

Kaylein's way. "Kaylein could come with me. I know she's Rowan's bodyguard, but the warg does that admirably, and it would help to have her sword if we run into trouble."

Wilmot shakes his head. "We'll all go. The other path heads directly west, but this one goes northwest. It's not as if we have a precise goal in mind anyway."

"There's a settlement to the northwest," Cedany says. "That's likely where this trail leads, and they may know more about the monster migration." She pauses. "Unless they're the ones who took Alianor's sister." Another pause. "Let's just say there's a reason I kept moving east to ply my trade."

Wilmot sighs deeply, and then waves for us to take the right-hand branch.

We've barely gone a mile when we reach the dead harpy.

Malric's the one who finds it. We're walking along, and he stops short, growling for me to stop, too. Another growl to tell me to stay put, and he disappears into the forest.

"Couldn't he have done his business when we all stopped?" Dain mutters. "At this rate, we'll be lucky to get to the mountains before winter."

A moment later, Malric appears with something in his mouth. He throws down the bundle, and the harpy lands on its back, wings flopping open, tiny lips drawn back over needle-sharp teeth.

"They never get any less ugly, do they?" Cedany says with a shake of her head. She bends over and prods the harpy.

"Judging by the rigor, it's been dead since yesterday." She flips it over and examines a small spot of blood, parting the short fur to reveal a pinprick hole. "Dart, I think?"

She frowns and backs onto her haunches to study the beast. Then, with a grunt, she checks its neck.

"Broken," she says.

"Its neck broke after it died and fell?" I say.

Wilmot shakes his head. "No poison works quite that fast. That's why we avoid using poison arrows in hunting."

I glance at Wilmot. "A sedative dart, then—like Yvain uses. After which the harpy broke its neck in the fall. Or whoever shot the dart broke its neck after it fell."

While we use sedative mostly for relocating monsters, there are times when it's the easiest—and most humane—way to kill a rampaging beast that isn't suitable for relocation. Sedate it, and then kill it.

"I'd vote for the latter," Cedany says as she checks the beast's mouth and eyes. "The harpy attacked someone without a proper bow. They managed to sedate it with a dart and then snapped its neck before it woke."

No one asks why they couldn't just leave it unconscious until they made their getaway. That works for an accidental encounter—such as when you stumble upon a predator in its own territory and just need to get off that territory safely. However, these harpies are hunting as they migrate, and as we saw earlier, they aren't quick to give up and move on. Leave it sedated and when it wakes, it might follow you back to your camp. Or your village.

"Where's that settlement you mentioned?" I ask Cedany.

"Maybe a half mile? I'm only guessing. We passed it quickly when I first came this way. I was told they don't like outsiders. Our guide had tried to establish trade with them— it would be good to have a stopover on the way to Tamarel— but they ran him off."

Wilmot nods. "They aren't Clan Hadleigh or Clan Bellamy, and those are the only clans with proper settlements in the woods. There used to be a Hadleigh community nearby, but they moved on after the Michty River dried up. I wonder if that's where these new people are."

"Using the old Clan Hadleigh settlement," I say.

"Could they have Alianor's sister and the others?" Dain asks.

Wilmot glances at Cedany, who says, "I've never heard of them taking hostages for ransom, but I suppose it's possible. Either way, we need to be careful."

CHAPTER FOURTEEN

The village is ahead. We hear it before we see it. Jacko and I climb a tree for a better look. Dain follows, mostly—I'm convinced—to tell me *you're going too high, get back down here, princess, that branch won't support you, one of these days you're going to break your neck . . .*

"Haven't broken it yet," I say as I stretch out on a branch. Jacko hops onto my back and chatters at Dain.

"Are you sure that jackalope isn't part squirrel?" Dain mutters. "He climbs like one, and he scolds like one."

"So do you. Especially the scolding."

"It's *warning*, princess. Someone needs to do it. That jackalope only encourages you."

"He's my trusty squire, not my bodyguard." I peer through the branches at Dain. "Unless you'd like to be my trusty squire."

He snorts.

"You could have a uniform," I say. "It would be very color-ful. I like colors. Really bright ones."

"Are you surveying the village? Or chattering like a jay?"

I make a jay's chattering call, and he rolls his eyes, but his lips twitch in a near-smile. Then I peer down. The village is about two hundred feet ahead and, as expected, it's along the bank of the now-dry Michty River, a former Clan Hadleigh settlement. The area has been well cleared, which protects it from monsters—the forest being at least fifty feet from the nearest house. That also makes it easy to survey.

There are about twenty houses, which would have made it the biggest settlement in the forest. Yet when the river dried up, there was no reason for Clan Hadleigh to stay, so they packed their things and moved on. The newcomers moved in, like birds finding an abandoned nest. From what I can see, though, only about half of the houses are occupied. A few more have had the windows boarded up, which probably means they're being used for storage. The rest have been partly dismantled and then left to rot.

Ten occupied houses. Fifty people at most. I see a few milling about. They're all men until I spot a woman with a yoke and buckets, returning from wherever they've found a water source. That would be another reason Clan Hadleigh moved on. While the river flowed, they had easy access to fresh water. Now the people need to travel to find it.

I count only about a dozen people—nine men, two boys and the woman. Others must be off on a hunting trip or trad-ing expedition. Maybe that's where the women are, as it is

— 131 —

with Clan Hadleigh, whose women handle expeditions while the men work as river guides.

I'm scanning the forest when I spot movement. Someone in the trees. No, someone in *a* tree. A sentry, perched on a wooden platform.

I quickly tell Dain what I see.

"One sentry?" he whispers.

I nod.

"Man? Woman?" he asks.

"Does it matter?"

"I guess not."

"I can't tell from here. Man, I think?"

We climb down to warn the others, and Wilmot decides we'll split up. Dain and I will get closer to that sentry with Malric. Wilmot will circle downriver, and Cedany and Kaylein will circle up along the foothills. At first, I'm impressed that Wilmot's letting me go without an adult guardian. Then I realize it's because we've already spotted the sentry, so the safest job is sitting and watching him while the others approach the village.

In other words, we get the boring job. Like "patrolling" the dropbear cabin perimeter while the others dealt with the actual dropbears. Of course, that turned out to be far more exciting—and dangerous—than anyone expected. My luck— good or bad, depending on how you look at it—holds here, because as soon as we're close enough to see the sentry platform, we stop short.

"It's empty," Dain whispers.

We backpedal into the forest. Then we look around.

Malric and Jacko sniff the air. A grumble from the big warg tells us he's not picking up any scent.

The sentry spotted us. Or heard us, as much as we tried to be quiet. They've realized we're accompanied by a canine and moved downwind to approach us without being scented.

I bend at the knees, upright and still looking around, as I put Jacko on my shoulders. Then I pull my sword. Dain waits until I'm armed and then takes out his dagger.

Malric's gaze shoots east. He glances at me and then draws my attention in that direction. It takes a moment before I catch movement through the trees. I nod and show Dain. He grunts. I motion that we'll approach. I switch my sword for my dagger, which is less impressive but more useful in the dense forest.

Dain leads the way. He's quieter, and Malric wants to watch my back. We keep our eyes on a sliver of dark red among the green and brown trees. As I draw closer, I realize it's the back of a tunic. The person wearing it is looking in the opposite direction.

I touch Dain's shoulder, asking him to hold up. He does, and I consider the figure. The person is definitely looking in the opposite direction. Not searching for us. Watching something.

Watching some*one*. Silver glints in the morning sun. Silver metal and blue sapphires. My old hair clip. The one now worn by Alianor.

I ease three steps left, Malric following. Yes, the sentry is watching Alianor, who's seated on a log, bent over something.

I can see the sentry better, too. It's a boy, maybe a half-foot taller than me, with light hair and broad shoulders. He isn't just watching Alianor, either. He's sneaking up, and he has something in his hand.

A rock. He's holding a rock.

He's going to hit her over the head.

I race forward, ignoring Malric's warning snap and Dain's hiss. I move as fast as I can, sticking to green undergrowth that doesn't give away my footfalls. As I go, I take Jacko off my shoulders and set him on the ground.

The boy is so intent on his goal that he doesn't notice me until I press my dagger tip to the back of his neck.

"Drop the rock," I say.

He wheels, rock rising. I slam my left fist into his arm, and he drops the rock and lunges at me, but I dance out of the way. Dain rushes in, dagger raised. I snag the boy's calf with my foot, yank, and down he goes. That's when I switch my dagger back to my sword, because, like I said, it's a lot more impressive, especially when it's held at the throat of someone lying on his back with my boot on his chest.

I'm braced for the boy to try rising—I don't want to accidentally slit his throat—but he just lies there, staring so hard I almost reach up to be sure I don't still have a jackalope on my head.

I survey the boy. I don't see a weapon, which is my biggest concern. He's about my age, maybe a bit older, with wavy hair the color of sand and skin just a shade darker. He's wearing a dark-red tunic, a dark-red bandana and no shoes. That's what I really notice—no shoes and no weapon. I think he must have removed his boots to sneak up, but his feet are covered with dirt. Odd, especially as the weather grows colder, but I don't question foreign customs or personal preferences.

Alianor comes running over and stares down at the boy almost as hard as he's staring at me. Then she looks at us.

"Guess that letter didn't work," she says.

"Did you really think we'd stay away?" I turn to the boy. "Identify yourself."

He blinks, and I try again in two more languages, but when he answers, it's in the common language, which is what Tamarel and bordering countries use, with variations in dialect. His accent is one I can't place.

"I am Prince Trysten of Dorwynne," he says.

As Dain snorts, Alianor walks up beside the boy and says, "And that is Princess Rowan of Tamarel."

His hazel eyes narrow. "Do not mock me."

"Oh, believe me," Alianor says, circling him. "We *will* mock you. Our warg is more a prince than you. Bare feet. Ragged clothing. Dirty face."

It's the last that makes him scowl. "My face is clean."

"The point is that you are no prince of . . . where was it? Some made-up country? You really do take us for fools."

"Actually, there is a Dorwynne," I say. "A small country to the west of Roiva."

"Never heard of it." Alianor looks at the boy. "Have you heard of Tamarel?"

His face darkens. "Of course. I've heard of Princess Rowan, too. But she is not . . ." He trails off as he eyes me more closely. "*Her* face is dirty."

"It has one streak of dirt," Alianor says. "Which you only noticed because you can't stop staring at her."

Dain steps forward. "Enough of this. Who are you really?"

"Prince Trysten of Dorwynne." He looks at me. "That *is* an ebony sword in your hand."

"And a warg on her left side, a jackalope on her right," Alianor says. "She is very clearly—"

The boy scrambles up so fast I have to yank my sword back so I don't skewer him.

"Princess Rowan." He executes an impressive half bow. "Pleased to meet you."

"Pleased, huh?" I say. "We saw you with that rock. You were going to hit our friend over the head with it."

"What? No. I had the rock in case she attacked me. But you need to leave. Now. All of you. Before—"

"I'm not going anywhere without my sister." Alianor turns to me. "They have Sarika. I saw her. She's their captive."

The boy ignores her. "Leave. Quickly. Come back tonight, and we'll talk. But whatever you do, do not take your pets into the village."

I straighten. "They are my companions, not pets."

He waves off the distinction, looking genuinely agitated. "Whatever they are, you must not—"

Alianor's dagger flies to the boy's back. "Don't you dare try to stop me from saving my sister."

"I'm not. I'm just saying—"

"You're saying nothing. You're our captive now."

The boy lunges. Alianor's blade flashes, and Dain jumps in to stop her, and she turns the dagger on him. A yowl from the treetops, and something falls, hurtling toward Alianor. Before anyone can react, the creature is on her back, its teeth going straight for her throat.

"Dropbear!" I say, and I raise my sword, but Dain grabs the beast from Alianor and stumbles back, holding it out at arm's length.

The dropbear twists and leaps at Dain. I raise my sword again, but it has jumped into his arms. Then it turns and hisses at Alianor. That's when I see its—*her*—slightly ragged left ear.

"Huh," I say as I sheathe my sword. "Seems you found your dropbear, Dain. Or she found you."

"She tried to *kill* me," Alianor says.

"She was protecting Dain."

Alianor throws up her hands. "From what? Me? I was only telling him not to interfere . . ."

She stops and turns. We all do, looking around to realize the boy is gone.

Alianor waves at Malric. "You just let him leave?"

Malric sniffs and sits on his haunches.

"He wasn't a threat," I say. "He's unarmed and doesn't fight very well."

"He was a hostage," Alianor says. "We could have exchanged him for my sister."

"Well, Malric didn't know that." I lay my hand on the warg's shoulder. It isn't quite a pat—he's not the petting sort—but he grunts, as if appreciating my defense.

I look around. "The boy's gone, and you're here, which is the important part. Let me get the others, and we'll retreat to talk. I don't think the boy will raise the alarm, but I also don't think, judging by what he said, that we want to be found out here."

Alianor does not want to retreat to talk. She wants to take action. I don't blame her—I'd do the same if it were Rhydd in that village—but we need to know more before we act.

Once we're all gathered another hundred feet from town, Alianor tells her story. There isn't much to say, except that she knows where her sister is, beyond any doubt.

"In that village. Being held captive."

"Are you sure she's a prisoner?" Wilmot asks. "Did this boy confirm it?"

"He didn't deny it," she says. "But yes, I know she isn't there of her own free will. I saw her being led out of a building. Then she was taken back to the house where they're keeping her. It's one of the homes with boarded-up windows, and her hands were tied behind her back, so if you're going to tell me she's their honored guest . . . ?" She glowers at Wilmot.

Wilmot's expression stays neutral. "All right. She isn't there voluntarily. Do you know why she'd be captured?"

"For the same reason that boy told Rowan to stay away. She's valuable. Either for ransom or as a political prisoner. People usually know better than to try kidnapping one of my father's children, but these villagers either don't realize who they have, or they don't know what happened to the last people who kidnapped a Clan Bellamy warlord's daughter."

There's satisfaction and pride in her voice at the last part, but I can't suppress a shiver. I've heard the stories. At one time, the children—especially the daughters—of Clan Bellamy warlords were the most valuable targets in Tamarel. Take one of them, and you could negotiate with the warlord for safe passage. Alianor's grandfather got tired of this, set one of his daughters out as a trap, killed the entire crew who took the bait, and then refused that clan access to the woods for a decade.

I could point out that the boy never said *why* I should stay out of the village, but presumably Alianor is correct. I'm a target, and he was concerned about me being caught with my companion monsters for fear they'd be killed. I always worry about that myself, especially with Malric.

I shiver again at that thought. The others continue talking as they decide what to do about Alianor's sister. She has to be rescued, of course, but how—

Malric leaps in front of me so fast I yelp. The dropbear in Dain's arms hisses, and Jacko scrambles onto my feet, brandishing his antlers.

From inside the forest, a voice chuckles. Then, as we all go for our weapons, eight armed men step from the trees and surround us.

CHAPTER FIFTEEN

The moment the men step out, Kaylein moves in front of me and Malric moves behind me, both so fast that it's like doors slamming on either side. Jacko chitters and brandishes his antlers, and the men point and laugh. It isn't a mocking point-and-laugh, though. It's weirdly casual, as if they're fellow travelers, amused by my fierce jackalope companion.

"Stop right there," Kaylein barks when the oldest man—gray-haired but able-bodied—steps forward. "Move any closer, and you'd best be prepared for a fight."

The man inclines his head. "We have no wish of that, Princess Rowan." His gaze goes to me. "I do address you correctly, do I not?"

When I hesitate, he says, "Trysten told me who you are, though I'd have guessed from your entourage and your monster companions."

The boy—Trysten—warned them about us? After he'd told us to leave? A trick, then. Warn us off so we'd go, and then he could return to the village and tell everyone. I curse myself for not seeing the ruse.

"*Prince* Trysten, you mean?" Alianor says sharply.

The man shrugs. "The boy has an active imagination. He tells us that we have the sister of a girl in your party." His gaze crosses the group and rests on Alianor. "I presume he meant you?"

She straightens. "Alianor of Clan Bellamy. Daughter of Warlord Everard."

"That's what the young woman's companions claimed," he says, his voice mild. "I wasn't certain whether to believe them."

"You should. I presume you know what happens to those who interfere with my father's children."

He frowns. "No, I fear I do not, my lady. We aren't from your country."

"If you're in our forest, you ought to know," she says. "Otherwise, you might make the very serious mistake of kidnapping one of us."

"Kidnapping?" His brows rise.

"Are you going to pretend she's your guest?"

The man eases back, still unperturbed. "No, I would have called her a hostage."

Alianor snorts. "Same thing."

"Is it? I would have thought, being the bandit lord's daughter, you would understand the difference." Before she can answer, he turns to me. "May I address you directly, your highness? Or would you prefer I speak through your guardians?"

"Address me," I say. "And explain this situation."

"The problem is harpies. They nested near our village this spring, and it has caused no end of trouble for us."

"I don't see what harpies—" Alianor begins, but I shoot her a look, asking for silence.

"Sarika's group camped a few miles from here, and the harpies, always on the lookout for food, attacked. They made off with two of the travelers. Two of their companions—including Lady Sarika—gave chase. There were, I believe, a few more in the party, who seem to have struck out on their own rather than help the others."

He pauses, his gaze on mine, as if waiting for me to argue. I don't. This wasn't the story I'd envisioned, but the pieces fit. A quick attack by the harpies, grabbing two travelers. Two more follow, in hopes of rescuing their companions, which is why we only saw two sets of footprints on that path. The tent without any packs indicates that the remaining travelers grabbed their bags and ran before the harpies could return.

I don't say any of that, and I hope I don't give it away in my expression. I try to put on my "listening face," as Mom calls it, the one a ruler uses to show she's paying attention while not betraying her thoughts.

"Continue, please," I say.

"So Lady Sarika and her companion tried to follow the harpies, who were returning to their nest. This happened at twilight the night before last. Several of our villagers were in the forest, collecting from our traps, and they heard the commotion. They were only armed with daggers, so they used the darts we've come to carry at all times, for dealing with the harpies.

The darts contain sedative. They shot two of the harpies, and that was enough for the others to lose their ability to keep their prey aloft. One of the travelers broke his arm in the fall, but the woman tumbled into a small tree and escaped with only bruises."

He pauses again, and this time I think he's waiting for praise or gratitude. I only incline my chin, as regally as I can. "It is fortunate your people were nearby to help. However, I fail to understand why Lady Sarika is still in your village. I could understand giving all four a chance to recuperate after their adventure, but you've acknowledged that Lady Sarika is a hostage."

"We took a risk helping the travelers," the man says. "The harpies are monsters, and if what I know of your clan is correct, your highness, you understand their intelligence. Ravens and crows can recognize individual humans. Harpies are even better at that. Every time we act against them, they remember it and retaliate. The travelers can move on. We cannot. Therefore, we requested compensation for our aid."

"By taking four people hostage?" Alianor says.

"No, my lady. They gave us your sister."

"Wh-what?" Alianor says.

The man looks at me. "They told me who Lady Sarika is and that she could be traded for our payment. We objected, of course. We wanted to return with them to their packs to see what they might be able to trade. They tricked us and fled, leaving Lady Sarika. That was yesterday afternoon. We have been puzzling over what to do ever since."

"While keeping my sister tied up," Alianor says.

"She is understandably upset about what happened. She risked her life for her companions, and they left her behind as if she were a trinket. I'd much rather set her free and trust she'll stay until this is sorted, but she has a temper." He looks at Alianor. "It must run in the family."

"Before we begin any negotiations, I'll need to speak to her," I say.

The man hesitates.

"You can't expect me to take your word for this," I say. "Not when Lady Sarika is here to give her own account."

He nods. "You are correct. I hesitated because we've already been tricked once, by her companions."

"Then allow Alianor and another of our party to speak to Sarika and confirm your story—and that she has been treated reasonably. I will stay with you and my guard while that is done. Alianor isn't going to flee with her sister and leave me behind. If all is well, we will compensate you for your troubles. We travel with only the essentials, but we can manage a small payment and, beyond that, I trust you will accept a debt from the queen."

He shakes his head, and I stiffen. He's going to demand something I can't part with. My sword. Or Malric—I've noticed his men studying the warg with interest.

"There is only one thing I want, now that I have a Clan Dacre monster hunter here." He meets my gaze. "Get rid of these harpies."

Alianor selects Wilmot to accompany her. The village leader—Geraint—allows Cedany to go with them as far as the door and stand watch there. Meanwhile, I remain at the village entrance with the others. Geraint invited me to come in and have an early lunch, but Kaylein refused. As much as I'd love a meal that isn't dried meat, there's a danger in all of us entering the village proper. Entice us into a house for a meal, shut the doors and our entire party is locked up.

Would they do that? From what Cedany said, these villagers aren't known for hurting travelers. They just aren't throwing open their doors to outsiders. Yet they're obviously quick to take a hostage if they don't feel they've been compensated for their aid.

I could argue that you shouldn't jump in to help and *then* demand payment. That'd be like me saving someone under attack and then putting out my hand for a piece of silver. But admittedly, the villagers aren't really asking to be paid for a rescue—they want compensation for the trouble to come, when the harpies retaliate.

As for what they've asked me to do, well, it's my job, isn't it? I could argue that they don't pay our taxes, and so they aren't entitled to my monster hunting. Yet that makes me no better than them.

"What do you think of them, your—Rowan?" Kaylein asks as I survey the village.

"On a scale from cutthroats to saints, I'd say they rate about a four."

"I'd have gone for three myself," she says.

Dain shakes his head. "I'd have said five. Average. People are always looking to get something in return."

"Well, then, I have been blessed to know good people," Kaylein says. "And you have been cursed to know bad. Rowan's opinion is probably the most balanced. They are neither cutthroats nor saints. Just people living in difficult circumstances. Cedany says she has had to grow a tougher skin, living as she does. She—"

Kaylein stops, her gaze sharpening and then softening in a smile. "I do believe there's a rather attractive young man trying desperately to get your attention, Rowan."

I turn to see the boy—Trysten. He's on the edge of the forest, beckoning. Dain starts toward him, and Trysten gestures to say no, he wants to talk to me. Dain keeps stalking Trysten's way, calling back, "I'll handle this." When I glance at Kaylein, she's struggling against a laugh.

My brows knit, but she only shakes her head and says, "Is that the false prince you were speaking to earlier?"

"It is."

While I can't hear the conversation between them, it's obvious Dain tells him off for tricking us and setting his villagers on us. It's equally obvious that Trysten protests his innocence. He tries to say more, but Dain's already stomping back to me.

"I suppose he insists he didn't tell them about us," I say.

Dain grunts.

"What *did* he say?" I ask.

"That he'd alerted them to intruders before he spoke to us, and they must have overheard our earlier conversation. He obviously thinks we're all stupid. Telling us he's a prince. A barefoot, raggedy-clothed prince standing sentry in a backwater village."

Kaylein asks, "Did he say it *before* he realized Rowan was a princess? Perhaps when she had her sword at his throat?"

I nod. "You think he was scared and hoping, if he claimed to be a prince, I wouldn't kill him."

"Perhaps," she murmurs. "Or perhaps he was just trying to impress a pretty girl. Either way, once he realized who you were, he didn't dare admit he'd lied."

I'm considering this when Alianor, Wilmot and Cedany return.

"It's true," Alianor says. "Their version of events is accurate."

"You don't look happy about that," Kaylein says.

Alianor lifts one shoulder in a shrug.

Wilmot says, "It might have been easier if they'd been lying. Then we'd have an excuse to free Sarika by force. As it is, it looks as if Dain and I will be dealing with harpy nests."

I clear my throat. Wilmot looks at me, and I brace for a fight, but he only sighs and says, "And the royal monster hunter, of course."

Geraint says there are three nests of young harpies. At least seven juveniles. The young are fledglings, big enough to be left alone while the adults hunt but not big enough to pose a threat to us.

The plan is simple. The adult harpies lost their prey two nights ago, and Geraint says they didn't see them hunting last night, as they were probably still dealing with the deaths of their brethren. By now, the fledglings will be starving and the adults will be desperate. They'll leave the nests before dusk. We'll climb up then and deal with the fledglings.

"Kill them?" Geraint says.

"That's a last resort, and I don't see the need for it here. We'll use your sedative, knock them out and take them with us. Then we'll dismantle the nests so the adults cannot return. We'll relocate the fledglings. The adults will follow us, but we aren't in danger from them, given the size of our group. Once we put the fledglings deeper into the mountains, the adults will be occupied with them, and then we can move on."

Geraint exhales. "Good. As much as I want to hate those things, I'd rather not see all the young ones killed." He gives me a rueful smile. "Apparently, I'm getting soft in my old age."

"We can save the fledglings and relocate the adults," I say. "With the nests gone, they'll have no reason to return. No matter how angry they are, they'll have learned this is a poor area to raise their young."

Wilmot doesn't grumble about losing yet another day. It'd be hard to do that when the only choice is to abandon Alianor's sister. Also, we *are* monster hunters, and this *is* a monster problem.

Alianor spends the rest of the afternoon with Sarika. I long to meet her sister, but Geraint doesn't trust us. Keeping me and Sarika apart ensures we can't sneak off with her—or fight our way out with her. He wants those harpies gone, and I can't blame him for that.

By late afternoon, we're heading out, with Geraint and a few villagers along to assist us. Cedany and Alianor stay behind with Sarika. Geraint suggests Kaylein do the same, since she isn't a monster hunter. She won't leave my side, though. Alianor and Cedany are capable of looking after themselves. We leave the dropbear with them. She's very unhappy about that, but the villagers have small cages, which they use for relocating nuisance animals, and we lock her in one of those so she can't follow Dain.

It's only a mile to the nests. And we need to climb *down* to reach them, rather than up. The Michty was the biggest river in the land, and when it dried up, it left a canyon. The harpies built nests in the cliff walls. On the walk, I ask Geraint how long the beasts have been there. Since spring, he says. He'd never seen harpies this far east, but he's been seeing a lot more monsters recently. When I ask about them, his answers support the theory that the monsters are on the move in this particular region.

"They're on this side of the riverbed," he says. "For a stretch running maybe a mile south."

In the swath where we'd found the dropbears and colocolos, along with the other harpies. This flock must have diverted, discovered the canyon and seen no reason to keep migrating.

We approach the cliffside as the sun begins to drop. We discuss splitting up, but if the harpies come back, we need the advantage of numbers. Besides our group, we have Geraint and four of his men. Half their village is away on a hunting expedition—as I'd guessed earlier—so he's split his forces between guarding us and guarding the village.

When Geraint offers to take one man and peek over the cliff, I want to refuse. Wilmot accepts before I can.

"It's our job to clear the nests," Wilmot whispers after they go. "Do not take on more than necessary. If his men are attacked, we must be here to save them."

The two creep toward the cliff. Then Geraint's companion stretches out on the ground and peers over the edge. A moment later, they jog back to us.

"All clear," Geraint says.

I instruct the villagers to stay ten feet from the cliff's edge. Their job is to watch for the returning harpies.

Once they're in place, Wilmot, Dain, Kaylein and I start forward. Malric follows, but I position him at the edge, where he can keep watch. I ask Jacko to stay with the warg. To my surprise, he doesn't argue. He just keeps glancing toward the villagers, clearly unsure of what to make of this new arrangement. Malric seems to feel the same, as he keeps one eye on the sky and the other on the men.

"I don't think Malric trusts them," I whisper as we head out.

"Because he's smart," Dain mutters. "Smarter than some prin—" He cuts himself short. "Less trusting than some princesses."

"I wouldn't trust them with my valuables," I say. "But I don't see a problem with this. Do you, Wilmot?"

"If I did, we wouldn't be here." Wilmot glances at Malric and frowns. Then he shakes his head. "He's being cautious. As should we. Trust Malric to keep an eye on them. Jacko, too. We need to pay more attention to your jackalope."

"I already made the mistake of underestimating him," I say.

"You misinterpreted." Wilmot waves us on. "Now let's get this done. I'd rather not sleep in the village if we can be on our way tonight."

CHAPTER SIXTEEN

Three nests. Eight juveniles. They're younger than I expected, which worries me. With the harpies migrating, they must have laid their eggs late. I'd rather deal with older monsters, where I don't need to worry as much about hurting them. On the other hand, with these ones being too young to fly, the job should be easy enough.

The problem is positioning. The harpies have wisely built their nests under a sheltering overhang. That means we can't get a clear shot to sedate them with darts. I suppose that's a good thing, or the villagers might have tried this themselves. What we need to do is scale down the cliffside and inject the young monsters by hand.

I don't like it. I really don't. Each nest contains at least two juveniles, and I don't see how to inject them fast enough to avoid alerting the others. Once alerted, they could panic and fall to their deaths. Or their alarm cries could bring their parents.

When I glance over to tell Wilmot, he's watching me. He already sees the problems. He's waiting for me to see them, too.

"We can't sedate the fledglings fast enough," Dain says. "There are too many of them, too close together."

For one heartbeat, I'm annoyed that he "stole" my answer. But that isn't fair. He's a monster hunter in training, just like me. He needs to be able to figure these things out for himself, and he wasn't trying to show off.

"Thoughts?" Wilmot says.

"We need to find another way to sedate them." Dain glances down toward the nests. "Maybe get on a ledge and shoot darts?"

"Have you perfected your dart skills yet?"

"He hasn't had time," I say. "We could ask one of the villagers, but I don't want to endanger them that way." I consider. "Do you think the babies would accept food from someone other than the adults? We could dangle sedative-soaked food over the edge."

"That's a good idea," Wilmot says. "But I believe they're young enough to be even more trusting than that. Particularly if the food is given to them by . . ." He glances my way.

"A monster magnet?" Dain says.

Wilmot's blue eyes warm in a near-smile. "It does have its advantages. Kaylein, if you can help them prepare the meat, I'll figure out a safe way to get Rowan and Dain down there."

Fresh meat will be best for this, so we send one villager back for some while I ask Malric if he can catch anything. He brings me a rabbit long before the villager returns, and Jacko adds a mouse. We prepare strips of meat and dab them with sedative. As Dain, Kaylein and I do this, Wilmot and one of the villagers scout for the best spot. By the time we're ready, they are.

Wilmot has decided that the best way down is up. Get to the bottom of the canyon and climb. The walls are about fifty feet high, with the nests in the middle. It's also a matter of safety. Climbing down, I could tumble fifty feet. Climbing up, I'd fall no more than half of that. Of course, I have no intention of falling.

We use a path to get down. Malric and Jacko stay at the top with two of the villagers. The others join us.

Going up is easy. This is where, as I can't resist pointing out to Dain, my tree-climbing skills come in handy. He ignores me and settles for grumbling and cursing as he makes his way up to the nests.

Wilmot is below, arrow notched as he watches the skies. Kaylein is poised beside him. When I looked down from the cliff top earlier, some of the fledglings had been sleeping, but others peep as we climb, and I squint up to see a tiny simian face watching me as it leans from the nest.

I slow to study the small face. It's calm, eyes bright and intent. Curious, as with most baby predators. Prey animals will be more skittish, and older predators more aggressive. These little guys are the perfect age for this mission. As I draw close, two more heads pop up, bright eyes watching me ascend.

I slow to let Dain catch up. If anything goes wrong, we need to both be in position to defend one another. Once he's at my level, we cover the last few feet. Then I'm peering into a nest, and two little harpies are peering back.

"No, princess," Dain says.

"No what?"

"Don't say it."

"Say what?"

He glowers at me, but I only meet his gaze, wide-eyed.

"They're sooo cute," he says.

I know he's mocking me, but I only nod. "They are, and I'm glad you feel comfortable saying so, instead of pretending you fail to recognize the adorableness of baby monsters."

"I meant that's what *you* wanted to say."

"Because it's true." I hold out a strip of sedative-infused meat. "Apparently, even ugly monsters have cute babies."

"It's the eyes," he says. "Babies have oversized eyes, which humans think is cute. It makes us want to take care of them."

"Look at you with the science. Also, you're stealing all my lines. First calling them cute and then explaining why they are."

"I never called them—" He bites off the rest and scowls at a baby harpy watching him. "Fine, they're kind of cute. But you are not taking one home."

I watch one baby nibble at the meat as a second makes its way over. They're like little monkeys with wings, which I guess is what the adults are, too, except the babies don't have their skeletal heads and beady eyes and creepy long fingers and protruding fangs. They also don't have the look that says they want to gnaw your face off.

As Dain said, the babies have oversized eyes, which are so much cuter than beady ones. They also have tiny grasping fingers and toes, and little ears that flick as we talk. When they open their mouths to eat, even their miniature needle-teeth are adorable.

There are three fledglings in the nest on my side. One ate the meat and is already yawning. The second is nibbling at the strip, and the third, who was sleeping, is now blinking at me as it peeks from under a downy wing. Adorable.

"No," Dain says.

"They're really small. I'm sure one would fit in your—"

"No. There will be no more baby monsters, princess."

"Says the guy with the baby dropbear."

"It's a juvenile. And it isn't my fault she came back. I tried to get rid of her." He catches my look and grumbles. "Fine, I tried to set her free. I didn't actually want to get rid of her, and I'm glad she's back. Happy?"

"Yes, and even happier that she *came* back. She'd probably been following us the whole time. She only left because you told her to, which you had to do, but now that she's back, it's her choice."

As the second harpy curls up, tucking its tiny face under one wing, I reach to pet the third. It chomps onto my index finger and clings there, looking at me.

"Not so cute now, is it?" Dain says.

"Actually, yes, it is still terribly cute."

I lower my face in front of the harpy's. The little beast blinks and slowly releases me. It licks my finger and then rubs against my hand.

"I choose this one," I say. "The perfect combination of fierce and cuddly."

I let Dain sputter while I feed the little harpy. Then, as it drifts off to sleep, I ease over to the middle nest. Those two eat without complaint—they're hungry, having probably not eaten a proper meal in days. We see no sign of the adults, who are diligently hunting to fill these little bellies. I feel almost bad about that—thinking of them returning to empty nests and missing babies. But they're obviously attentive parents, who'll find their young.

As we finish up, one of the villagers lowers a basket over the edge of the cliff. We tuck in three fledglings. He hauls it up, puts them into a cage and we repeat the process twice more, until all eight are safely up.

Our next job is dismantling the nests. For that, we do something else that feels almost as cruel as kidnapping the babies. We push the nests off the ledge onto the rocks below. That's the most efficient way to destroy them. Then the villagers beat the remains with sticks as we climb down.

By the time we reach the bottom, they have finished and started up the path to the top of the cliff.

"Good work," Wilmot says.

Kaylein smiles. "You made that look easy."

"It *was* easy. They were so hungry they didn't need *me* feeding them. They took the meat from Dain's hand, too. We got lucky."

Wilmot shakes his head. "Never credit luck on a mission, Rowan. I know you're nearly as uncomfortable with compliments as this one"—he nods toward Dain—"but if you deflect praise and call it luck, others will echo that and you'll lose the recognition you deserve. You both came up with a good plan and executed it with care. *That's* why it was easy." He thumps Dain on the back. "Now let's get up top before the parents return."

I nod as we head for the path. "Malric, Dain, Kaylein and I will stay with the fledglings, safely away from the village, while you get Alianor, Cedany and Sarika. The faster we can—"

Jacko screams above us. It's a scream of fear and rage, and I'm already running when Malric roars. Another scream, this one human. I bear down, running as fast as I can, heart pounding so hard I can barely see.

I left Jacko behind. Left him where the harpies could get him.

Even as I think this, I know I didn't thoughtlessly forget him. I left him with Malric, knowing Jacko would be safer away from the nests. Yet I hadn't thought of this—what happens if the parents return when the villagers have the fledglings? Before we can get up the cliff?

That cliff seems endless. It'd been an easy descent, but this feels like scrambling straight up. My boots slip and slide and struggle for purchase, each stride forward costing me half a step back.

Still, I'm ahead of the others, and when Kaylein shouts for me to wait, I pretend not to hear her. I feel terrible for that, but I don't change my mind. I can't. I hear Jacko's shrieks and Malric's snarls and the cries of the villagers, and their panic fuels my own.

Finally, I'm on the cliff top and running toward the sounds. Ahead, Malric has his prey on the ground. He hulks over it, every hair on end, making him look the size of a pony. Jacko is beneath him, atop the prey, chattering in outrage.

Seeing them, I exhale. They are fine. They've countered the attack. I can't make out the harpy pinned under Malric—the long grass hides it—but there must be only one.

Then I take two more running strides, see past that grass and . . .

It's not a harpy. It's Geraint pinned beneath the snarling warg, Jacko on his chest chattering angrily. Chattering angrily at *Geraint*.

The other villagers cluster ten feet away, two brandishing daggers. The other two have bows, but they're holding the harpy-fledgling cages, arms wrapped tight around the boxes.

I slow, trying to interpret what I'm seeing. Did Geraint accidentally frighten Jacko? Step on him? Tease him? If Jacko was a nervous rabbit, I could see him overreacting. But he's a jackalope. Step on him, and he'd only chatter his outrage. Tease him, and he'd stalk away. Neither of those things would upset Malric either—he steps on Jacko all the time, and he's usually the subject of the young jackalope's teasing.

"Call off your warg, girl," Geraint says, his voice a low growl underscored with fear.

I bristle at the last word, but it's Kaylein who strides past, sword drawn, saying, "That is the princess of Tamarel. Show a little respect, *old man*."

"She isn't *my* princess, and I show respect where I receive it. I extended my hospitality, and the moment she's away, her monsters attack. If she wants to resolve this problem, she will call them off now."

"What did you do to them?" I ask.

Geraint sputters. "Do? Nothing. They attacked—"

Malric growls, shaggy head lowering over the man, lips curling to show off those impressive fangs.

"Give us the harpies," Wilmot says, and I jump a little,

startled by his voice at my side and by what he's saying, which seems the least of our concerns right now.

"Get this warg—" Geraint begins.

"Give us the harpies first. Pass over the boxes, and then Princess Rowan will ask her warg to retreat, and you will escort us to the village to retrieve our companions."

As Geraint sputters, cold dread slithers through me. He never intended to give us Sarika, and now he has Alianor and Cedany, too. At first, I didn't know why Wilmot was asking for the harpies, but he must just be insisting on the full terms of our agreement. Give us the harpies to safely remove, so we fulfill our contract.

"The harpies," Wilmot says, his voice low. "Now."

"Do you honestly expect me to trust you after this?" Geraint gestures at Malric above him. "You'll probably release them right outside our village and bring the full wrath of the flock down on our heads."

"We would not. However, if you do not take us at our word, you may send two villagers to accompany us and witness the release."

"I'll do no such thing. You can have your people. Then go."

"My people *and* the young dropbear."

Dain tenses. He's near the cliff top with his bow notched. Hearing Wilmot mention the dropbear, his head shoots up, and even from here, I see his eyes narrow.

"There's no place for a dropbear on your journey," Geraint says. "We'll tend to it."

"As you'll tend to the young harpies? As you planned to tend to the princess's jackalope?"

I stand there, confused. The harpies? The dropbear? Jacko? I don't understand.

And then I do. I remember the boy, Trysten, and what he'd said to us.

Whatever you do, do not take your pets into the village.

It hadn't made sense. Yet I'd missed a clue there. A very important one in his wording.

Not my companions. Not even my monsters or beasts.

My *pets*.

I'd corrected him automatically—it's a common mistake. Yet in this case, his choice of words was very telling.

While we were gone, Geraint had grabbed Jacko. That's what Wilmot is guessing, and it fits what I heard. Jacko's scream. Malric's rage. The warg attacking Geraint and pinning him until we returned. Jacko voluntarily taking refuge under Malric.

The harpy fledglings. The young dropbear. My juvenile jackalope companion.

What do these have in common? Things they don't share with Malric or the adult harpies?

They're small and young. Small enough to easily transport. Young enough to need humans to care for them. Young enough not to be particularly dangerous. Young enough to be trained.

Trained as pets.

CHAPTER SEVENTEEN

"Y ou—you—" I can barely get the words out. I've
heard of such things, of course, and I always
thought they were terrible tales of terrible epi-
sodes that happened once upon a time, like the stories of
people being sold into slavery. None of that is remotely legal
in Tamarel, so it must not be legal anywhere. That's what I'd
thought when I was little. Then I grew up and realized they
were not horror stories of times long past. Even in Tamarel,
where indentured servitude—being forced to work until a
debt is repaid—is illegal, it still happened to Dain. In other
countries—distant ones, thankfully—they do practice slavery. And in other countries, there is an active trade in monsters, both for menageries and as pets.

If you want monsters as pets, you're going to want them
young.

And where are you going to find those juveniles? Old enough to be weaned but still dependent on others?

Where the monsters feel safe to build their nests and dens. In the mountains. In the Dunnian Woods.

"You trade in monsters," I say. "You steal them from their parents and sell them as *pets*."

"And you hunt them, *Princess Rowan*. You kill them. Which do you think they'd prefer? You have pets of your own. Yet you object to us making a living allowing others to enjoy the same privilege. Is owning monster pets only for the wealthy in Tamarel? Only for the nobility?"

"No," Wilmot says. "Owning monsters is illegal for all. Rowan's *companions* are free to leave her at any time, as are her humans ones. They come to her by choice. Stay with her by choice. You are on Tamarelian land, breaking our laws. I would suggest you reconsider your choice of settlement. In the meantime, all I care about are those harpy fledglings and our companions. Give them to us and we'll be on our way."

"You don't get your companions unless you pay us our due for rescuing Everard of Bellamy's brat."

I stiffen, but Wilmot keeps his voice low, almost pleasant. "If you speak of his child that way, I would strongly suggest that you do not know Everard of Bellamy. Although that is evident by the fact that you hold her hostage. We have done as you asked by capturing the fledglings and destroying the nests."

"You never wanted that," I say. "You lied about the harpies harassing your village. You just wanted the fledglings, and you couldn't figure out how to get them yourself. Lucky, then, that I came along and solved your problem. If you'd just suggested

— 162 —

relocating the fledglings yourself, we might have fallen for it. But you had to try for Jacko, too."

"That was a mistake," Geraint says. "You may keep him. We'll take the harpies and the dropbear."

Kaylein walks up to Geraint, still flat on his back under Malric, and crouches beside him. "Please tell us again what you'll do? Since you have us in such an awkward position."

"Oh, but I do. My men are armed, as you see, and ready to defend our claim."

She snorts. "I'm not sure which is more amusing. The idea of defending a claim to which you have no right, or the idea that your men pose the least threat to us. You have four. So do we."

"Two are children."

"And I'd pit them against the best of those." She waves at the quartet. "These *children* train *daily* under the best fighters in the land. Your men barely know how to hold a weapon. And what weapons they've chosen. Two bows, with the arrows still in their quivers, and two daggers to fight against our swords. Our *child* over there"—she nods toward Dain—"could take down both your archers before they get an arrow notched."

Geraint says nothing. He seems to be thinking it over, probably wondering what bluff he can pull, but in the end, he realizes the futility of that option.

"Leave us the harpies, then," he says, as Malric lets him rise. "We will return the dropbear and your companions."

"You made a deal," I say. "We are not about to renegotiate—"

"You want these harpies?" says one of the men holding a box. "Take them."

He throws the wooden cage as hard as he can, dashing it into the rocks. I yelp and rush forward, only to realize my mistake. We are faced with armed attackers, and I cannot be distracted by anything. The box hits the ground before I could have stopped it, the wood shattering, sedated baby harpies tumbling out. I wrench my gaze away and hold my sword high.

"Go on, Rowan," Wilmot murmurs. "We have this."

I hesitate only long enough to glance down and see blood on the rock. Then I sheathe my sword and run to the harpies. Four of them were in that box. Two seem only dazed, raising their heads and blinking hard. One is mewling, a bloodied splinter caught in its wing. The fourth lies still, but when I lift it, its breathing is strong—it's just smaller than the others and more heavily sedated. I tuck the three into the remains of the box and lift the fourth as I tug out the splinter.

"So this is your royal monster hunter?" the man sneers. "A child cooing over hurt harpies?"

"Yes," I say, raising my head to look straight at him. "This is your royal monster hunter, for as long as you are on our lands. Someone who cares enough about her people to fall for a trap helping them with a monster problem. Someone who cares about monsters, too, because slaughtering them is not her job. Nor is shoving them into boxes to sell at market like chickens and cows. There is only one thing worse to me—caring so little about them that you'd rather kill them than give them to me."

The other villager with a harpy box lifts it over his head.

"Stop!" Dain shouts from his spot. "Move those hands, and I fire this arrow into your shoulder, and you will never lift anything heavier than a rag again."

The man's hands twitch.

"Are you deaf?" a voice says from the forest. "Or does that seem an idle threat?" Cedany walks from the forest, bow strung. "If you doubt he can make the shot, go ahead and test it. You'll lose the use of that shoulder and the other one, too."

Alianor appears, followed by a girl I don't recognize. Except, of course, I kind of do. She looks like an older, stouter version of Alianor, with darker hair. Both of them are loaded down with the packs we left at the village.

"We got tired of waiting," Cedany says. "Also, we overheard them talking about where they could sell the harpy chicks, which didn't seem like what you'd planned. Terribly odd. We decided to come and get this straightened out. We may have left two of your men sleeping in the cabin. I asked to see their sedative darts, marveling at how they work, and they showed me. So gracious."

Alianor walks up to the man with the harpy box and takes it from him with a "Thank you!" She leads her sister to me as Cedany moves toward us, arrow still aimed.

"You're going to let us leave now," Wilmot says. "We're going to take the harpies and, hopefully, get them relocated before their parents attack all of us. Remember that—the longer this takes, the more likely they'll return. Follow and interfere with us . . ."

"And you'll be dealing with seven angry people and a flock of angry harpies," Alianor says.

"Wait!" I say. "The dropbear."

"Oh no," Geraint says. "If you take those harpies, we're keeping the dropbear."

"That isn't—"

One of the men lunges at Sarika. She's walked too close to him, paying too little attention. His dagger plunges into her side. Alianor's scream matches her sister's, and in a flash, arrows and steel fly.

Geraint shouts for his men to stand down, but they're like guard dogs kept on short chains, those chains now snapped. They attack in a frenzy as Alianor drags her injured sister away. Then two more villagers rush from the woods. They'd realized the captives were gone and come after them.

Geraint goes straight for Wilmot, identifying him as the leader. Two men come after me, but they don't get within striking distance before Kaylein is on them, sword flashing as she fights both at once. Another villager, seeing her occupied, dashes toward me, grinning, cudgel raised as he sees himself taking down the princess of Tamarel.

Malric's on him before I can blink. There's another man, though, right behind, and Malric decides I can handle him . . . probably because he's armed with a wooden pike. My blade slices through that in one blow. Then he yanks a knife from its sheath, and at the same moment, two more villagers come at me from either side. Kaylein backs up to help me, but she's still fending off the first two men, both skilled fighters.

Wilmot orders retreat.

Take the harpy boxes. Take Sarika. Then retreat as fast as we can. We could still win this battle, but there's no need—we have what we demanded. Except for Dain's dropbear. I try saying so, but no one's listening, and when I catch Dain's eye, he only meets mine with a grim look and shakes his head.

We cannot stay for the dropbear.

I want to say he's wrong, that I will get that dropbear for him, just as he rescued Jacko from drowning for me. Yet that places the safety of my people below that of a single beast. I can only make a mental promise that I will get his dropbear back, even if it means a year's worth of allowances to buy her.

That makes me retreat faster. There's nothing more to be gained here. This is the difference between hunters and warriors. Warriors would need to stand firm and prove themselves. Our concern is the monsters, and we have—almost—all of them safe. I'm carrying both boxes of harpy fledglings while Alianor protects her sister.

We fight to injure, not kill. That, too, is the difference between hunters and warriors. We only need to escape, and most of these men seem like little more than farmers with bows and daggers. We hold them off and inflict just enough injury for them to stop pursuing us.

That's not the only thing that makes them decide we aren't worth the trouble. The distant scream of a harpy says the parents have returned. Returned and found their nests smashed, babies gone. Harpies might be far from my favorite monster—even less so after our encounter in the woods—but the guilt at hearing their anguish is so sharp I have to bite my tongue to keep from calling out and returning their young.

Thankfully, I don't do that. Even more thankfully, as we'd been retreating, I'd fed the waking juveniles more sedative-infused meat. They're asleep, and only twitch at their parents' distant cries.

We pause long enough to make sure Sarika can continue on. The stab wound is more than a mere scratch, and she's in pain, but with Cedany and Kaylein supporting her, she insists she's able to walk.

We've left the villagers behind. Which also means leaving Trysten behind. Now I realize he'd warned us with good reason. I'd have liked to talk to him more, to make sure he was all right with Geraint and the others. There's no way to do that now, though. Just something to discuss with my mother later.

We continue on for another couple of miles, moving along the top of the Michty riverbed. When we think we've gone far enough, the others find a safe spot on the cliffside while Kaylein and I gather moss and leaves, and make the broken box and the intact one into the best nests possible.

We place the boxes in the new spot and hurry to the forest. We've barely done that when a couple of the fledglings wake and begin screeching, and soon their parents' answering calls tell us they've been heard.

After the harpy fledglings are reunited with their parents, we get deeper into the forest and find a place to rest. Our first thought, of course, is for Sarika. Both Alianor and Cedany examine her more carefully. The wound will require stitching. The dagger didn't seem to have injured any internal organs, but it is clear she cannot continue on this trip with us.

"I'll take her back to my cottage," Cedany says. "If you don't need Kaylein, perhaps she could accompany me."

Kaylein brightens and then pulls back, shaking her head. "My place is with the princess."

A look passes between them, Kaylein turning away quickly, gaze lowered.

Cedany nods. "Understood. Alianor? You were willing to forgo the adventure to help your sister earlier. Perhaps you could assist us."

"Of—of course," Alianor says, though she stumbles on it, and shoots me a furtive glance before straightening. "My place is with my sister."

The corners of Sarika's mouth lift. "I do appreciate you coming to find me, Ali. In the past, you'd have sent someone else, while you continued on your adventure."

Alianor squawks. "I'd never—"

Sarika lifts a hand to cut her off. "All right. Perhaps I only *felt* as if you'd continue on, leaving your much less adventurous sister behind. I'd hardly have blamed you. I am not made for this sort of thing." She looks at her bleeding side. "Obviously."

"You went after your comrades when they were taken by harpies," I say. "While others fled into the forest."

Sarika makes a face, as if this reminds her she'd been abandoned by her comrades. Then she manages a soft smile. "That was more impetuousness than bravery. As furious as I am with those villagers, I'd never have managed to rescue anyone on my own. I didn't even have a weapon." She chuckles under her breath. "Perhaps I thought I could bring them down by shouting mathematical formulas."

"That'd be enough to scare me," Alianor says.

"My point, dear little sister, is that you have grown and matured since I last saw you, and I believe these adventures—and the companionship—are to thank for that. You ought to stay with your friends. I need to get home."

"Why are you coming home?" Alianor asks. "You should be in school."

"There was an . . . issue. The point is that I should continue on my way. I will be fine with Cedany, though I'm sorry you'll lose her help . . . and that she'll lose an adventure. We were talking earlier about how much fun she was having, being attacked by evil harpies, being held captive by evil villagers. So much fun."

Sarika's expression makes me laugh. However, I'm not happy letting Cedany and Sarika head off through the woods on their own. Not when Sarika is injured, and we left those "evil" villagers very annoyed with us.

I glance at Wilmot for help.

"I believe we can spare Kaylein," Wilmot says. "As much as Rowan will miss her, if the princess agrees, she should go with Cedany. The four of us—and Malric—will be a suitable party for the rest of this journey. We're all thankfully uninjured and well armed."

Kaylein protests, but it's obvious she'd like to spend more time with Cedany, and I'm happy I can give her that. Whatever is growing between them—friendship or more—Kaylein deserves it. She's worked so hard to get where she is, and Mom always says everyone needs more than work in their lives.

Cedany, Kaylein and Sarika will stay here for the night, resting and camping. We'll continue on. Wilmot's right that I'll miss Kaylein. Cedany, too, who'd been an interesting companion and a useful one, for both her bow and her healing skills. And then there's Sarika, whom I haven't even had a chance to speak to, but I'm fascinated by her studies and would love to learn more. That'll have to wait, though. They will be there when we finish our journey. Plenty of time to talk then.

We say our goodbyes and continue on. It's fully dark now, and we don't dare go too far, but we want to make a bit of time and none of us are tired.

We decide to stick to the top of the Michty riverbank. Tomorrow, we'll discuss following the riverbed. It's not the path we intended to take, but we're here now, and it's a clear and open area. Too clear and open at night, though, when we can't see well. Daylight will be different.

By the time we do stop, we're exhausted. Wilmot lights a fire and warns Dain, Alianor and I that we'll need to help with the guard duty, now that Kaylein and Cedany are gone. I offer to take first shift, but Malric is already in place by the fire and growls when I come near. It's very hard to argue with a giant wolf, especially when you're too tired to find words. So I go to bed.

Malric must stand guard most of the night, because when I wake in the morning, Wilmot has only been up for a couple of hours. He grumbles about the warg overworking himself, and I agree, yet I cannot help but appreciate the long rest. We all needed it. I'll just need to make sure Malric gets a chance to nap later.

We're getting ready to set out for the day, and Dain and I are looking around making sure we haven't left anything behind, when a voice from the forest says, "I think you forgot something, your highness."

I give a start, and Dain pulls his dagger. My hand is on my sword when a figure steps from the shadows.

It's the village boy—Trysten—holding a box. He thrusts it out to me, and through the bars, red eyes peer back. I let out a squeal of joy.

Trysten chuckles. "I thought you might want her." He steps up to Dain and extends the box to him. "I believe she's yours?"

Dain hesitates and glances at me, as if he's misunderstanding, and Trysten is returning the dropbear to me.

"She *is* yours, isn't she?" Trysten says.

Dain nods and takes the box. He sets it down and opens the door, and the dropbear flies out and attaches herself to Dain's shirtfront.

Trysten laughs. "Definitely yours."

It takes a moment. Then Dain says gruffly, "Thank you."

"He means that," I say. "I've been trying to figure out how to get her back. We had to leave her behind when . . ." I remember exactly who Trysten is, and my voice chills. "When your people drove us off." I pull my sword and take a step back. "If this is a trap—"

"It isn't. And they are not my people."

"Oh, right, because you're a prince. You really do think we aren't very smart."

"Uh," Alianor says. "He actually is a prince. Kind of. Sarika explained. It's a long story. A long and weird one."

"Which I'm happy to tell, once we're on the road," Trysten says.

"Do you see a road?" I say.

— 172 —

His lips twitch. "Once we're on the trail, then. I'm coming with you."

Wilmot returns from washing in the creek. "What's going on here?"

"He's a prince," Alianor says. "Also cute. Can we keep him?"

Dain sputters, and Trysten flushes. I stare at Alianor.

"What?" she says. "You get a cute jackalope. Dain gets a cute dropbear. I get a cute prince. Seems fair." When Trysten goes even pinker, she smacks his arm. "Oh, I'm kidding. You are cute, but I require more in a pet—or a boyfriend. Keep working at it." She winks at him. "If you can cook, we may have a deal."

Trysten goes beet red and looks to me, as if I'm going to save him.

"She's teasing you," I say. "Obviously." I turn to Alianor. "No, you may not keep him. He's staying here. With his people."

"They're not my people," he says again. "I was being held captive. Kind of. And I *am* a prince. Kind of. Like your friend said, it's a long story but"—he drops to one knee—"to the princess of Tamarel, I throw myself on your mercy and beg for a favor, royal to royal. Take me with you. I will explain everything, and you will not regret it."

Wilmot sighs the deepest, most put-upon sigh. Then he waves to Trysten. "Come along. We'll take you as far as the next settlement, provided your story is sound."

Trysten rises. "Thank you." He pauses and then glances down at his still-bare feet. "You wouldn't happen to have a spare pair of boots, would you?"

Wilmot sighs again and heads to the packs.

CHAPTER EIGHTEEN

Dain has extra boots. They're a bit small—but Trysten takes them with thanks and insists they're fine, and he's so appreciative that Dain can't even grumble. Also, he has his dropbear thanks to Trysten, so he can hardly begrudge him the use of his boots.

As for why Trysten is barefoot, that's the first thing I ask, once we set off. Trysten walks beside me, Malric to my rear, Wilmot in the lead, Alianor and Dain just ahead of me, Jacko hopping along beside us.

"They took my shoes," he says. "And my boots. In winter, I'm allowed socks, but nothing more. It's really hard to flee in bare feet."

I blink over at him. "They refused you boots so you wouldn't run away?"

Dain glances back. "Didn't look like you were a prisoner the first time we saw you, standing sentry duty."

"It's . . . complicated. I won't call myself a prisoner or even a hostage. More of a captive."

"Same thing," Dain says, though he doesn't roll his eyes or snort his derision.

"Mmm, maybe?" Trysten says. "To me, you take a hostage to demand something. Sarika was a hostage. A prisoner is someone who has committed a crime. A captive, on the other hand? I think of that as someone you're holding for a reason. We also call them political prisoners." He glances at me. "Do you have those in Tamarel?"

"People we put in prison because they don't like our political system? No. Not at all."

"I mean people you're holding for political reasons. Like two countries broker a peace deal and then exchange children to make sure both sides keep the peace."

I nod. "We have something called fostering, which is to strengthen ties between families and, yes, sometimes to make sure there's peace between the clans. We'd never consider them *prisoners*, though. My father fostered at the palace after his parents died. Alianor's fostering there now."

"Definitely captivity," she says. "I'm forced to take lessons under the best trainers in the land. Forced to eat the best food and sleep in the best beds. With servants hovering about so much I can barely brush my own hair without someone offering to do it for me. The things I do for my family, all because they want a spy in the royal palace."

Trysten looks at her.

She lifts a shoulder. "Joking and also not joking. My family is unusual."

"Well, my situation is a little different." He stuffs his hands into his pockets. "I said I'm a prince, and I said 'kind of,' which probably makes it seem as if I'm lying." He glances at me. "Do you know much about my country, Dorwynne? I suppose not, if you're the monster hunter. Your brother—it's a brother, right?—is the heir to the throne."

"Actually, I was. I'm the older twin. We switched roles this spring."

"Oh." He looks uncomfortable. "I'm sorry. I know how it can be, in a royal family. It seems like the scheming never stops. Can you still win it back? You're a *really* good fighter. You can challenge him to combat, right?"

Alianor bursts out laughing and glances back at us. "Please challenge Rhydd to combat, Rowan. I'd *pay* to see you two battle it out." She pauses. "No, actually, that'd be the most boring fight imaginable. The moment one of you got hurt, you'd stop. Or you'd just circle each other, not wanting to strike. Maybe a pillow fight. Can you pillow fight for the throne?"

"Rowan doesn't want to be queen," Dain says, irritated. "She gave it up."

"I'm better at monster hunting, and Rhydd is better at politics. The point is that I was raised to be the heir," I say. "So I do know a little about Dorwynne. I believe there's a king but no queen. Not a royal consort, either. Just . . . wives. Plural."

"Right. The king had three, all with children, all of them with a chance at the throne."

I nod. "I remember that. In Dorwynne, it doesn't go to the oldest. It's won by combat." I glance at him. "Didn't you have a royal ascension recently?"

"The last king stepped down two years ago. One of his sons took over. It's always a son. Always a king. That's the law. Anyway, that's also how I ended up out here. The new king only has one wife so far, and she doesn't have any sons. So he sent away all the brothers he felt were threats."

"Including you."

"Well, that's where it gets really complicated. I'm not the new king's brother. I'm his son."

Both Dain and Alianor stop and turn around. Ahead, even Wilmot slows, as if he's been listening in.

"Uh, what?" Alianor says.

"My father had me when he was really young. He was betrothed to my mother. But then stuff happened, and the marriage was called off, but my mom was already pregnant with me."

"How does that make you only 'kind of' a prince? You're the king's *son*."

"People have considered me a prince, at least since my father took the throne. But if I'm recognized as a prince, then I'd be his current heir. So he's decided I'm not."

"Does this make any sense? To anyone?" Alianor shakes her head. "The guy wants a son, right? So he doesn't have to worry about being overthrown?"

"He wants an heir, but he wants one that no one can question, and they can question me because he wasn't married to my mom. Also, he's not a very popular king, and no one really likes his wife, so there was talk about putting *me* on the throne, which is crazy, but . . ." He looks at me. "Politics, right? It's *all* crazy. Or at least it is in Dorwynne."

I say, "So your father—the king—sent away his brothers and you, until he has what he considers a proper heir."

"Exactly."

"I can understand that if you ended up in another country, with a royal family. But you were with traders. Black-market traders."

"Right?" He throws up his hands. "Politics. It's weird."

"Oh, I'm not sure it's the *politics*," Dain mutters.

"Hey, I brought back your dropbear. Anyway, I'm not supposed to be living with a bunch of illegal monster-pet traders in the forest. I'm supposed to be in Tamarel, being fostered—is that the word?—by Queen Mariela, alongside her two children."

"Uh . . ." I say. "No. Even if you never made it to Tamarel, I'd have heard of the arrangement. We have almost no trade—or contact—with Dorwynne."

"Which is why my father chose it. Or maybe it was his wife. Probably his wife. Anyway, they told my mom that I was going to Tamarel, and she's heard lovely things about your kingdom, once you get past the monsters. Me? I'd only heard about the monsters, which sounded awesome, so I was happy to go. Except there apparently was no arrangement with your mother. I was brought into the forest and handed over to those people, and I've been living with them for over a year."

"Without shoes."

"I ran away a few times. Which wasn't the best idea. There are a lot of monsters out there, and most of them can kill you. So I started behaving better and pulling my weight around the village, hoping they'd relax. Meanwhile, I was putting together a stash. Weapons, supplies and, yes, boots. But when I had the chance to run last night, I could either grab my pack or the dropbear."

Dain nods and mumbles a thank-you.

"That is the weirdest story I've ever heard," Alianor says. "So you really are a prince."

"Kind of. Depends on who you ask." He looks at me. "But you are definitely a princess. A princess who carries a huge sword, and hunts monsters, and has a pet—sorry, *companion*—jackalope and warg. That's way cooler than a kinda, sorta prince with no boots." He grins and then peers into the distance. "So, can I ask where we're going, and what we're doing out here?"

It's midday, and we're walking along the dry riverbed, between huge canyon walls. We can see Mount Gaetal ahead. That's where the Michty River started, according to Clan Hadleigh. To be honest, though, it's more legend than verified fact. We're at the edge of the mountains, heading in to the most dangerous part in our world. I've heard of people in other countries going on expeditions just to explore their mountain ranges, but people don't do that here. Or, if they do, they don't live to share their discoveries with the world.

People do pass through the mountains, obviously, but they take specific routes and they get through as quickly as they can. That's what allows someone like Geraint to take over a settlement, pay no taxes to Tamarel and poach monsters.

Even when we know outsiders live in the forest—like Cedany—we don't levy taxes. Paying taxes means you receive services, like schools and sheriffs and roads. Cedany doesn't need schools and roads. She also can't call the sheriff if her cottage is broken into—or filled with dropbears—because we cannot reasonably expect anyone to venture into the forest to help. And we cannot reasonably be expected to send patrols to hunt for bandits or illegal traders. It's just too dangerous.

The lack of exploration means that no one has ever confirmed the Michty River began at Mount Gaetal. People said it did, and that seemed reasonable, and there was no reason to risk lives answering an idle question.

When the Michty River dried up, it was no longer an idle question. Members of Clan Hadleigh investigated and yet . . . well, there is a limit to what anyone can be expected to do when the investigation takes you into a region infested with monsters. Also, there's a limit to what one hopes to accomplish beyond satisfying curiosity. The death of the Michty River was devastating to my father's clan, and it affected Tamarel overall. But it wasn't a small stream, where you could find a beaver dam blocking it and fix the problem. We didn't know why the river had dried up, and we couldn't foresee a way of "fixing" that even if we did know. So it remained a mystery.

As we walk along the riverbed, I think about this. Then I catch up to Wilmot and say, "Do you think the death of the river has anything to do with the migration?"

"I've considered that," he says. "It would have been catastrophic for the monsters who lived there. But . . ." He shrugs.

"It's been five years. Why would we start seeing problems now? And the monsters affected aren't all river-dwellers."

I nod. "I remember when it happened. Jannah did need to deal with new monster problems. She called them displaced populations—the river was gone, so the monsters that lived there moved elsewhere and that caused trouble. Like ceffyldwrs and encantados being seen in smaller rivers."

"Yes. There were also creatures who took advantage of this." He waves around the canyon walls. "Mountain goats and bighorn sheep and others moving from the mountains to live here, and bringing predators with them."

"Any environmental shift causes disruption in the monster populations. That's what Jannah taught us. This was a big one, but it wasn't catastrophic. And you're right that it doesn't seem like it would cause a sudden rush of harpies and drop-bears and colocolos five years later."

"A ripple effect is still possible."

I think about that before asking what he means. Then I nod. "What happened with the river caused other issues, and we're just seeing the effects now."

"Correct. We can't rule out—"

"Stop!" Dain shouts.

He runs in front of us. We follow his gaze. We're walking through a narrow part of the canyon. Like any river, the Michty widened and narrowed, depending on the surrounding environment. Here, the sides are solid rock, full of tight curves and narrow stretches. We're in one of those stretches. Each wall is about thirty feet away. On one of those walls, just above eye level, is a khrysomallos.

That's what caught Dain's attention. That's what has him pulling his bow slowly. A large, golden-haired winged ram. Several ewes and lambs dot the ledges above the ram.

"It's . . . a khrysomallos," Trysten says as he comes up beside us.

"I know."

"I mean, it's a sheep. A very pretty sheep, and Geraint's crew were always on the lookout for lambs, but it's still a sheep." He glances over, his brows knitting. "You aren't going to kill it for dinner, are you?"

"Of course not."

"Good. Eating monsters is unpleasant. Also, killing the flock's ram would be cruel. He's their protector."

"Mmm," I say. "Not exactly. He's mostly there to father babies, though he's also supposed to stand guard. The females can fight, too."

"Then keep an eye on all of them," Dain says. "Everyone move slowly. Don't draw their attention."

As the ram nibbles grass, Trysten glances at Dain. "Is this a joke you're playing on the newcomer? I might not be a monster expert, but I know khrysomallos. They're sheep. Very pretty winged sheep."

"We had an encounter," I say. "One had been wounded by a farmer. I think Dain still has the bruises. Even a regular ram is dangerous if it's angry."

"Ah, understood. Well, then, yes, let's proceed with caution. Everything seems fine—"

The ram lifts his head and looks straight at Dain. Then

he drops his head, brandishing his thick, curled horns, and paws the ground.

"That's very strange," Trysten says.

"Yes," Dain replies in a strained voice.

"We're not within twenty feet of his herd."

"Yes."

"And yet he seems very angry. With you."

"Yes."

Trysten cocks his head as he looks at the snorting monster. "Could it be the one you encountered earlier?"

"No."

"Perhaps it's just you, then. Your looks. Or your smell."

Dain glances over sharply.

"*Scent*," Trysten says quickly. "I meant scent."

I glance at Wilmot, only to see he's watching me. Waiting for me to issue instructions. He's relaxed, one hand on his dagger, clearly not alarmed and happy to use this as a training exercise.

"Dain?" I say. "Stay where you are."

"I'm not going anywhere."

"I think the ram is just warning Dain," Trysten says. "But I wouldn't mind a weapon, if you happen to have an extra. I hate to be a bother, but . . ."

I glance at Wilmot. He considers and then nods. No one should be unarmed out here. We'll just keep an eye on Trysten.

"Take my dagger," I say.

"No," Dain says. "Take mine." Gaze still locked on the snorting ram, he passes over his dagger. "Be careful. It's a special one."

"Thank you."

"Rowan?" Alianor says.

"Everyone stay where you are," I say. "Something's not right here."

"You think?" Dain mutters.

"Trysten may have a point," Alianor says. "It's possible that khrysomallos just doesn't like the looks of Dain. We had a dog that always growled at men with beards."

"I don't have a beard," Dain says.

She sighs. "My point—"

"I'm going to need to ask everyone to be quiet," I say. "Give me a moment to figure this out."

Is it possible the beast just doesn't like the looks of Dain? I suppose if the ram had a bad experience with someone who looked like him, that could happen, but it seems unlikely. And while this is the second khrysomallos we've had trouble with, the first had a valid reason. It's easy, then, to have it happen to us again and blame the wrong thing.

The first time there was a reason. This time, there must also be a reason. A different one.

Is it the bow? I consider telling Dain to put it away, but the ram was pawing the ground before he had it out.

Is it definitely Dain? I can see where the ram's looking, and Dain is the only one near . . .

Wait. Malric is to our rear, and while it's far from where the ram's looking, that is significant. Malric is staying where he is, and he isn't looking at the ram—he's staring at the opposite cliff.

The ram isn't snorting and pawing because of Dain. It sees something behind him. Malric has already figured that

— 184 —

out. The problem is that neither of us can see what it is. The warg is looking for it, gaze scanning the canyon wall. I do the same, and see nothing but earth and rock.

We're in a narrow and tight section of the canyon, with curves ahead and behind us. It seems possible that the ram senses something beyond one of those curves, but he isn't looking that way. He might also see something on top of the canyon wall or a hidden snake on the canyon floor. There's a moment when I remember the dropbear and think that's the problem. But she isn't still clinging to Dain's chest. She climbed down a while ago and has been playing with Jacko. The two are a few feet from me. The more I consider it, the clearer it seems: The ram is either looking at Dain or at something directly behind him, on the rocks.

I follow the ram's gaze and see only a rocky wall. There isn't a bush for a predator to hide in. Nor a cave where it might lurk in the shadows. There's nothing—

Movement. Just the barest flicker of it.

Something's there.

CHAPTER NINETEEN

"**P**rincess . . ." Dain says.

"Shhh. There's something behind you. Don't look. You can't see it anyway. I can't either."

"Uh . . ."

I hush him and peer at the canyon wall. I definitely saw movement. So why can't I—

There. The tip of a tail. I'd seen it flick. It's a furry tail, the same brown as the canyon walls. Once my eyes lock on it, my gaze sweeps along to see . . .

Another tail?

Two creatures?

I almost laugh aloud as I realize what I'm seeing. A laugh of pure delight at figuring out the puzzle and the delight of spotting a monster I've never seen in the wild.

A nekomata. A spirit cat. Legend says that they're the ghosts of wildcats who lived so long that their tails split in two. Yes, legends don't always make a lot of sense. The "ghost" part is because they seem invisible in their natural environment—the mountains. Plenty of monsters and animals have camouflage to keep them hidden from prey and predators. Among mammals, though, nothing wins the camouflage game like a nekomata.

Once my eyes adjust, I understand why the nekomata seemed invisible. It has mottled fur the color of the rock, with an irregular pattern that tricks an eye expecting stripes or spots or patches. Its skin helps. It can change color. Not like a chameleon—it can't turn bright blue. But its skin shifts between light and dark, and that extends to its nose, its lips and the inside of its ears. So those, too, blend with its surroundings. It also has very short, fine fur, so the skin-color change subtly tweaks the appearance of its fur from beneath. Though I can't see its eyes from here, I know they will be a muddy gray, blending with the dirt and rock.

And all of that, while fascinating, doesn't change the fact that it's a wildcat—one twice the size of the cath palug—and it is *very* dangerous. The nekomata is one of the leading killers of travelers through the mountain passes. It waits on a ledge, blending in with its surroundings, and then leaps, grabbing the last person in the party and disappearing before anyone realizes what's happened.

If we'd been walking closer to that side . . . I shiver and focus on the current problem.

"Nekomata," I say. "On the cliff behind you."

"No one move," Alianor says, her voice tight. Then her gaze cuts my way. "Sorry, it's just . . . nekomata."

I nod. There are many monsters Alianor has never encountered and many she's never even heard of. For Clan Bellamy—who lead travelers through those mountain passes—the nekomata is one they would know well, and rightly fear.

"I don't think it's going to attack us," I say. "It wants the khrysomallos. We're just in the way. Wilmot, can you see it?"

"I do now," he says grimly.

"You're fine, Dain," I say. "We see it, and it's thirty feet away. Malric?"

I glance over to see his gaze now fixed on the cat monster as it crouches on a narrow ledge. Both of its feline tails flick now. It knows it's been spotted, and it isn't trying to hide anymore. It watches us, and I watch it, over a hundred pounds of pure muscle, a beautiful and deadly feline.

"Let's move," I say. "Alianor and Trysten? Keep your eyes on the flock, please. We're watching the nekomata."

Wilmot leads the way, his bow out, arrow aimed at the nekomata as we move. Everyone else eases sideways. I glance at Malric. He's sitting, meaning he plans to stay in place until we're safely gone.

I'm the last of the main group. Jacko and the dropbear stay close to my feet. I take two more steps . . . and the cat monster spots the small predators. It rises up, tails swishing. Its tongue flicks over its teeth, as if it's imagining how the jackalope and dropbear might taste.

"No," I say firmly. "Please. We don't want to hurt you."

The nekomata's gaze swings my way. Murky gray eyes lock on mine.

"We're passing through," I say. "We're armed." I lift my weapon, showing it without waving my sword in threat. "You wanted lunch. I understand that. But we aren't it. Not me. Not my companions."

I hold my sword in one hand—not easy, given the weight of it—and hoist Jacko. He settles into his spot on my shoulders and then chatters at the cat. The dropbear creeps up to my leg, latches on and hisses at the nekomata. Then she climbs onto my hip, and while I have both hands on my sword again, I'm really hoping I don't need to use it, what with the jackalope and dropbear clinging to me.

The nekomata stands and swishes its tails. It eyes us, head tilted, as if to say, "Well, you don't see that every day." Then it crouches.

"Hold!" I say.

Wilmot murmurs, "She's right. Aim but hold."

The nekomata isn't crouching to spring my way. I can see that from my angle, though the others might not. When it leaps, it only springs to a higher perch. Then it sits, lifts one paw and begins to clean it.

I exhale. "All right. We're clear. Just—"

"Rowan!"

It's Alianor, and my gaze flies back to the nekomata, but the monster is still on its perch. A bowstring twangs, and the ground shakes, and I spin as two ewes charge.

"Jacko, down!" I shout.

He jumps from my shoulders, but the dropbear stays on my hip, holding fast and pulling me off balance as I swing at the first ewe. I land a glancing blow, and the other hits me in the opposite hip. I stagger. Another ewe is charging, the ram right behind her. Arrows fly, and two hit. One ewe goes down. Another lets out an enraged cry of pain.

Footsteps thud as Alianor and Trysten run for me. The ground continues to vibrate. I pull back to swing at another ewe. Then Trysten shouts, "Ceffyl-dwr!"

At first, I think I've heard wrong. Maybe it's some kind of Dorwynne battle cry that just happens to sound like a monster name. After all, we're nowhere near water. Then Trysten charges and I spin to see a ceffyl-dwr galloping toward me, ground pounding beneath its hooves. There's one heartbeat where I start to raise my sword. Then I see the blaze on its nose. A familiar blaze on a familiar nose.

"No!"

I shout at the same time as Alianor. She runs to stop Trysten as Doscach veers toward the ram. The ceffyl-dwr rears up and comes down on the ram's broad back. The beast bellows, and Doscach spins and kicks, hitting the ram and knocking him back. Before the khrysomallos can recover, Doscach is beside me, lowering his head. I grab his long green mane in one hand and the dropbear in the other, and I swing onto Doscach's back as I shout for Jacko.

I don't need to bother with that last part—the jackalope is already in flight. He lands perfectly in front of me and hunkers down, holding on. Doscach lunges, but the ram is barreling straight for him.

A whinny from above, and then a shadow passes overhead. Sunniva dives straight at the ram, who lets out a bellow of terror. A khrysomallos ram might be able to defeat a small pegasus filly, but apparently he's never had one dive at him from the sky.

The ram falls back. A ewe leaps at Doscach's flank, but I kick her off. Then both the ewe and the ram fall behind as the ceffyl-dwr gallops away.

"Go!" I shout to the others. They don't need me to say it twice. I'm safe, and they're the ones on the ground with the angry herd.

Doscach zooms past them, and when I twist, Sunniva is diving at the ewes, who are already scattering. And the nekomata? It stands on the ledge, watching as if this day is turning into one its kittens will tell their kittens about: the family legend of the time a human, dropbear and jackalope escaped a crazed flock of khrysomallos, aided by a dive-bombing pegasus.

When we're finally safely away, the monster sheep having given up the chase, Trysten stares at me with a look not unlike the nekomata's.

"It's my ceffyl-dwr," I say as I hand the dropbear down to Dain. "My companion. The pegasus, too."

Trysten chuckles. "I presumed that, though at this point, I wouldn't be surprised if a ceffyl-dwr and a pegasus randomly joined forces to save the royal monster hunter."

"They didn't 'save' her," Dain says. "They just helped. Rowan would have been fine."

"I appreciated *everyone's* help," I say, as I swing off Doscach's back. "So you guys got tired of waiting for us back home, did you?" I say as I rub his nose. "It helps to have a pegasus to scout, I bet." I glance at the others. "They must have spotted us when we entered the canyon."

I give the ceffyl-dwr a strip of dried meat from my pocket, and he slurps it up. Sunniva lands, as graceful as a feather, and two-steps, shaking her roan-red mane ever so prettily.

"I haven't had apples in three days," I say. "Nor carrots or anything you like. Just this." I hold up another strip of meat, and she sniffs and trots away.

"Last time she's helping you, ingrate," Alianor says. "Hey, Sunniva, you have apples at home, you know. As many apples as you can eat. Why not just admit you actually came for your princess?"

Sunniva just keeps trotting, tail high, wings rippling.

"Or maybe she came for Doscach," Alianor says. "He wanted to see his princess, and she couldn't bear to be without her handsome water stallion."

Sunniva stops and glances at us, and it's coincidental, but even Wilmot smiles as he claps a hand on Doscach's back.

"Well, there's not much water here," Wilmot says. "Not anymore. But since you've decided to come along, I suppose we'd best stick to the riverbed for easy walking. Everyone stay in the middle, please. Out of a nekomata's range."

"Actually," I say, "the nekomata's hind legs allow it to leap an astonishing—"

I catch Alianor's narrow-eyed glare and stop.

"Sorry," I say. "Not the time. Just stick to the middle."

Trysten falls into step beside me. "*I'd* like to hear more about the nekomata. Maybe not whether they can reach me here, but I'm definitely interested in learning about them."

Dain makes a noise that sounds like a snort, but when I glance over, he's busying himself feeding the dropbear.

"Oh, I can tell you all about how far nekomata can jump," Alianor says. "I have stories you don't want to hear."

"And if we do?" I say, smiling at her.

"Well, then." She waves a circle. "Those who want the horrible tales, gather close. Everyone else, keep your distance . . . and watch the cliffsides."

CHAPTER TWENTY

We've stopped for the night. We walked as long as we could before finding a place to sleep. We don't leave the riverbed for that. We're at an astonishingly wide part of it, with the mountains beginning to rise on both sides, and the empty ground is actually safer than venturing into the dark hills. Or it is as long as we post two guards, able to watch the expanse of open land. There's a small river here, too, one that might even be the remains of the Michty.

While the others eat, I sit by the stream and watch Doscach play. It's not quite deep enough to submerge him, and he reminds me of myself and Rhydd, playing in the shallow stream behind the castle. We'd lie flat on our stomachs in a weird half swim, half slither as we pretended we were exploring a deep lake. That's a whole lot harder to do for a long-legged horse, but he finds the deepest part and throws water like a baby in a bath.

He's making Sunniva jealous, too. She doesn't understand the appeal of water beyond drinking. That's made me wonder whether pegasi avoid it or whether she's just never learned to swim. Clearly, though, Doscach is having fun—alone—and she is not happy. She trots along the bank, occasionally dipping a dainty red hoof in, only to yank it back and shiver.

"Such a princess," I say to her.

She snorts and tosses her head.

"Well, this princess is going to take a bath. Jacko? I know you hate water, so please keep an eye on me from the shore."

The jackalope stands tall, whiskers twitching. Malric grunts and stretches out. I strip from my tunic, leaving on my autumn-wear undershirt. Under my leggings I have another pair that go only to my knees, soft cotton for insulation. As chilly as the water is, I'd be tempted to strip out of everything for a good wash, but it's best not to give anyone the shock of stumbling on a stark-naked swimming princess.

I hop in and yelp as the cold water envelopes me. It's refreshing, though. These long days of walking means dirt and sweat, and the water feels glorious.

As I paddle about, Doscach shakes his head over me, splattering me with water. Sunniva's mane is lovely—silken dark-red strands—but Doscach's is a wondrous thing, long and dotted in barnacles that click when he tosses it. It's sticky, too, like some seaweed.

We swim and goof off, and even Malric wades in, though he acts as if we're children playing in a pond—so terribly annoying, when he only wants to get his feet wet. Jacko patrols on the bank. Sunniva works herself into a pretty snit, alternating between testing the water and trotting off, as if she doesn't care that we're having fun without her.

I dive under and run my hands through my curls. When something tugs my hair, I surface to glower at Doscach, but he's twenty feet away. And behind me is Malric, intently eyeing a fish.

"Someone tugged my hair," I say, looking at Malric.

If wargs had eyebrows, he'd be lifting his, giving me a look that says he'd never do anything so silly. I flip my wet curls over my shoulder and turn around, and *someone* grabs them, giving a sharp pull that sends me splashing down on my back. I surface again to see Malric watching his fish. With a sniff, I turn around, facing the other direction as I float on my back and—

A fish flops onto my stomach.

I jump up with a yelp and the fish's tail gets caught down the neckline of my undershirt. As I pull it out, Malric looks over as if to say, "Huh, how'd that get there?" When he reaches for it, I smack it against his snout. Then I toss it onto the bank, and both Jacko and Doscach run to grab it before Malric does.

"Did you just smack your warg with a fish?" a voice says.

I look to see Dain walking over, with the dropbear trundling along beside him.

"He started it," I say, glaring at Malric, who's growling at Jacko, the victor in the fish race. I raise my voice. "That's what you get for throwing your fish on me. It's Jacko's dinner now."

Dain snorts a laugh as Jacko drags the fish, nearly as big as him, away to begin his feast. I start rising out of the water, and Dain's eyes widen and he quickly turns away.

"I'm dressed," I say.

"Not very well."

I look down. "I wear less when we go swimming."

"That's different. A swim outfit is meant to be seen. Those aren't."

I sigh and let myself sink into the water, to float on my back. "Is this better? My hair streaming out, a maiden floating downstream, past the gallant hunter—isn't that a ballad?"

"Yes, and she was dead."

I frown. "I thought it was a romantic ballad."

"It is. She drowned on the back of one of those." He points at Doscach, fishing upstream. "The villagers saw the ceffyl-dwr take her into the water, and they called for the monster hunter, who gallantly rode to her rescue, only to see the fair maiden floating downstream."

"Dead?"

"Yes."

"And that's romantic?"

"Apparently."

"Weird." I flutter on my back. "Well, I'll be a living maiden, floating down the river." I tug my hair to fan around me. "Do I need flowers in my hair?"

A frog lands on my hair. Dain snickers as I scramble up to dislodge it.

"So much for my moment of floating beauty," I grumble.

"If you want someone to tell you you're pretty, ask Trysten. He'd probably make up a ballad, too."

I wrinkle my nose.

"Haven't you noticed?" Dain says. "He stares at you the way Doscach stares at Sunniva." He waves upriver, where the ceffyl-dwr tosses a fish at Sunniva's hooves, only to have her dance away.

"Does he?" I say.

"Yes."

"Weird."

I paddle on my back again. Sunniva comes down to lower her head and sniff at me, but when I lift a wet hand to pet her, she trots away.

"You know, you could use a bath," I call to her. "You've got a spot of dirt right there. And over there. But if you don't want to look nice . . ."

She snorts and keeps prancing along the bank.

I glance at the dropbear, snuffling along the water's edge. On the far side, Jacko lifts the fish's tail and chirrups, as if inviting her to join the feast. She paces along the edge and then peers up at us.

"There isn't a tree bridge," I say. "But I can help you across, if you trust me."

I put out my hands. She considers and glances at Dain, who waves for her to go on. She jumps into my arms, and I carry her over to Jacko. Then I return to Dain.

"It was nice of Trysten to bring her," I say.

He nods.

"I wouldn't have left her there," I say. "I didn't know how to go back for her right away without endangering anyone, but I wouldn't have let them sell her."

He nods again. "Thank you."

"You're uncomfortable having Trysten along," I say. "Is it because you don't trust him? Or because you just don't like new people? You seemed fine with Cedany, but she's an archer, and she helped save you from the harpies. Also, she's a grown-up, so she doesn't hang out with us as much."

"I don't *not* trust Trysten. If that makes sense."

"You don't think he's going to hurt us or trick us, but you don't know him well enough to say you trust him. Same here." I sit on a submerged rock and wring out my hair. "Thank you for giving him your dagger."

"I didn't want him having yours." He pauses. "And he should have a weapon." He pulls the dagger from his side. "Wilmot gave him a spare, so I got mine back."

He runs a finger along the blade. Is it conceited to say it's a beautiful weapon if I'm the one who gave it to him? I didn't make it, so I think that's okay. It's Berinon's handiwork—he kept up his blacksmithing as a hobby and makes the best weapons in the castle. The design was mine, though, with a jackalope on the side, to thank Dain for saving Jacko. It's also to remind him that if he wants monsters to like him, he needs to admit he likes *them*. I glance at the dropbear and smile. It seems Dain might have been listening.

"She needs a name," I say.

He sighs. "I know."

"Droppy? Droppo? Bearo?"

He chuckles and shakes his head.

"Remember when we first met?" I say. "I was trying to convince you that Jacko was my companion, and you said if he was, then I should tell you his name. Only I hadn't actually given him one."

Dain's brows arch.

I pull my knees up on the submerged rock. "Like you and the dropbear, I was uncomfortable admitting he was mine for good. Worried that as soon as I said I liked him and wanted him to stay, he'd leave and I'd feel bad. So I hadn't given him a name. I just called him 'jackalope.' When you challenged me, I said his name was 'jacka . . .' Then I stopped myself, and you heard 'Jacko,' so that became his name."

He sputters a laugh. "Seriously?"

"I would have changed it, except you said it was a dumb name, so I had to keep it. Just to be contrary." I glance at the dropbear. "You have to the count of ten to name her, or she's going to be 'Droppy' forever."

Genuine panic lights his face.

"I'm kidding," I say. "Take all the time you want. Just do give her a name, Dain. Admit you want her to stay."

"I . . . I don't know. I mean, yes, I want her to stay, but names? I don't know how to do that."

"How did you name toys? Or pets? Did you have . . . ?" I trail off and my cheeks heat as I see his expression. "I'm sorry. I didn't think—I never do, do I? I'm always . . ." I flail my arms, water splashing. "Saying insensitive things that I don't mean to be insensitive. I forget that your . . . your experiences might not have been the same as mine. I'm sorry."

His lips quirk. "I did name my stick once. It was a very special stick that I found and carved myself. I called it 'My Special Rat Stick.'"

"MSRS? Em-ess-ar-ess?"

"Like Doscach? Nope, I'm not even that creative. It was just My Special Rat Stick. I may have mocked you for Jacko, but that's exactly what I would have called him."

"How about names from stories? Some maiden you admire in a bard song."

He snickers. "Name my dropbear after a girl I liked in a song? That's just weird. You're way better at names. You pick one."

"I shouldn't—"

"Pick one, or she's going to be Droppo forever."

"Being female, it should probably be Droppa. Or Droppy."

"Nope, Droppo it is." He rises. "Come on, Droppo. Time to go. Remember, if you hate your name, it's the princess's fault. She refused to—"

"Fine, just hold on. How about . . . Desdee?"

He hesitates. "That means something, doesn't it?" He sounds it out. "DSD." A mock-glare my way. "Dain's Special Dropbear?"

"You asked for a name. That's what you get."

He looks at the dropbear, eating fish. "Dez, then. I'll call her Dez."

"You can, but we'll both know her real name. It'll be our secret." I glance at her. "Right, Dain's Special Dropbear?"

He shakes his head and sits back down, and we keep talking, enjoying this rare time together, with our monster companions.

Mount Gaetal looms above us.

We are near the foot of the great mountain, and we've barely seen a monster. All right, that's not entirely accurate. Since the khrysomallos and the nekomata, we've seen more monsters than we would hiking through Tamarel proper, but they've all been the harmless sort. A couple of mountain-dwelling jackalopes, not much bigger than Jacko, yet fully grown, and gray-black to his brown coloring. Some colocolos in the river valley. A few more khrysomallos, who barely lifted their heads as we passed.

It would be immature of me to admit disappointment, wouldn't it? *I'd really hoped for a chance to study new monsters as they dragged my companions away for dinner.*

It's good that we don't encounter any serious threats. Yes, I did hope for more non-dangerous monster encounters, but at least we aren't being slowed down by mini-adventures. Yet what truly bothers me is the fact that we aren't seeing anything except small predators and prey, and very few of those. We shouldn't even have dared get so close to the great mountain. It should be far too dangerous. Yet it is not, and that is troubling.

If the monsters aren't here, where are they?

"What has it been like since the Michty dried up?" I ask as we walk along what remains of the river, now nearly twenty feet wide.

Wilmot shrugs. I glance at Dain, who gives the exact same response, though he adds, "I've never been here."

"Neither have I," Wilmot says. "Not since the river disappeared. The last time I was anywhere close, I was still living inside the castle walls. Jannah was preparing for her trials, and we concocted a mad scheme to sneak up here together. I decided we'd reach the mouth of the Michty and stand at the foot of Mount Gaetal, and after that, her trials would be easy."

He shakes his head. "We stopped about a half-day back. By then we were both injured. We escaped two pairs of wyverns to find our packs being torn apart by wargs. We snuck away, only to be attacked by a herd of ceffyl-dwrs."

Wilmot's eyes warm in a fond smile. "Jannah always joked that after that, her trials did indeed seem easy."

"So it wasn't like this fifteen years ago," I say. "But we don't know whether it's been like this since the river went dry."

"There was no reason to investigate. It's certainly not what we encountered that summer."

"Can we get closer to the mountain?" I say. "Is that safe?"

Wilmot just keeps walking, and I think maybe that is my answer, but after a half mile he speaks again.

"I believe we can press on a little," he says. "It isn't even midday yet. At worst, we could retreat here before dark and consider a new and safer path."

Trysten clears his throat. "At the risk of asking a very foolish question, a new path *where*? I know you're here to investigate the monster migrations, but where exactly are you heading?"

Silence. Wilmot seems to be considering again, in his slow and careful way, so I decide to begin.

"We aren't heading any specific place except closer to the mountains," I say. "To see if we can figure out what's happening. Maybe a forest fire or other natural disaster sent the monsters fleeing. It could be connected to the river drying up, or it might have nothing to do with that. If we can get this close, yes, I'd like to continue on and see what we find at the mouth of the river."

I look at Wilmot, who nods. Then I glance at Trysten.

"Is that all right?" I ask. "You joined us to get to safety, not to head deeper into the mountains."

He assures me it's fine, and we quicken our pace to see how close we can get to the mountain before nightfall.

CHAPTER TWENTY-ONE

I've never been this close to mountains. Even when we took Tiera to live with the other gryphons, their aerie had been at the edge of the mountain range, in the foothills. From there, Mount Gaetal had been only a shadowy peak against the horizon. It's bigger than anything I could have imagined, and it just keeps growing as we walk.

When Wilmot said we'd see how close we could get before sunset, I thought he was . . . well, being Wilmot. Clearly, we'd reach the base by early afternoon, with plenty of time to retreat before the sun dropped.

Yet after an entire afternoon walking along the Michty River corridor, we still don't reach it. The mountain just gets bigger and bigger, until I cannot help being just a little bit frightened by the sheer size of it. Frightened and awestruck.

By late afternoon, Wilmot figures we're still a quarter day's walk away. He decides we'll camp here, in the emptiness of the former riverbed, along the banks of the new river.

Doscach doesn't want to stop. He even tries to get me to ride on his back, as if I'm just too tired to continue.

As the young stallion paces, I watch him while the others prepare for our evening meal.

"Something's wrong with him," I say to Wilmot, keeping my voice low so I don't alarm the others.

"I don't think *wrong* is the word. It's good that you're learning to pay attention to your monsters. Especially him and Sunniva. She's a prey animal, and he may be a predator, but he'll be mistaken for prey. Big prey that could feed anything in the forest for days. They'll both be on guard even more than Malric."

Wilmot nods at Sunniva, who's trying to entice Doscach into a game of chase. "She's comfortable here."

"But he's not."

"Is that because he senses a problem with our campsite?" Wilmot asks. "Or because he wants to keep going? That's the question you need to answer."

"How?" I look around at the others already setting up camp. "You think it's safe, obviously, or you wouldn't let us stay."

He nods at Sunniva. Then he nods at Jacko and Dez, both darting around her hooves, saying they're ready to play if Doscach isn't. Finally, he hooks his thumb at Malric, dozing in a patch of late-day sun while occasionally opening one eye to glare at the younger monsters, as if their commotion is keeping him awake.

"They can all tell Doscach is out of sorts," Wilmot says. "But none of them are concerned. They seem to have decided he just wanted to stop someplace else, maybe with a better pool for bathing."

I study Doscach and the others.

"Do you sense anything wrong here?" Wilmot asks.

I shake my head. "I think he just wants to press on. I don't know why, but I don't see any problem with where we are."

"If that changes, let me know. Otherwise, let's try fishing for our dinner. I'm very tired of dry meat."

I dream of shadows come to life. Shadows that creep through the camp and snuff out the fire, and no one notices, because whoever was supposed to stand guard is asleep. Everyone's deeply asleep, because of the darkness and a fog that wends through the camp, a fog that seeps into the lungs and sends us to dreamland.

Sends everyone *else* to dreamland, that is. I am awake. At least, I am in the dream. Something's woken me, and I stare up at a sky covered with shadow. That shadow seems to hover right above me. Tendrils of fog still float about, whispering that I should sleep. Yet something deep inside whispers that this is too important to sleep through.

The fire is out, but I'm not cold. My blood scorches through my veins. My clan blood, whispering that this is so important. Then Jannah's voice at my ear, telling me to get up. Just as I begin to rise, a cold nose presses against the back of my neck.

I give a stifled yelp, and Doscach appears, his damp mane tickling my forehead. The gills on his neck move, as if he's breathing through them, which he never does outside the water. But this is a dream, and in a dream, nothing needs to make sense.

Doscach lowers onto his front legs, telling me to climb on his back. Because it is a dream, I do. I don't need to think in a dream, to make decisions, to worry whether I'm doing the right thing. I don't need to take my sword or put on my clothing or tell anyone what I'm doing. It's only a dream, and the shadow is gone, stars shining bright overhead. That fog still slithers through the camp, making me sleepy and content, moving as if in a trance.

Only a dream.

When I look around, everyone is asleep. The fire is indeed out, burned down to ashes. Wilmot sleeps beside it, as if he's collapsed there. Malric snores next to my sleeping blankets. Only Jacko stirs, and I smile at that. Even in a dream, he's the one I can't leave behind. He notices I'm on Doscach's back and jumps up, only to stagger and blink.

I reach down, but he can't quite make it. He's dopey and sleep-dazed. I ask Doscach to lower himself again, and he does, and I scoop Jacko into his place. Then we're off.

Doscach is a creature of the water, happiest there. Yet, unlike many aquatic mammals, he moves just as fast on land, and he stays on the water's edge, running at full canter toward the mountains. As Jacko chitters on my lap, I pet and soothe him, and I smile up at Mount Gaetal, majestic and beautiful against the night sky.

I almost wish I *were* awake, to count this among the perfect moments in my life: racing on a ceffyl-dwr's back, holding my jackalope, hearing the burble of water and the wind sighing in the trees, inhaling the faint smell of campfire. Yet were I awake, it would not be so glorious. I'd be in a panic, seeing that terrible mountain drawing near, my companions left behind, me on Doscach's back, clad only in my nightclothes with nothing but my dagger, sheathed on my hip. No, this is better as a mere dream.

And then it is not.

I don't know exactly how I realize I'm awake. I don't pick up a new smell or see a new sight or hear a new sound. It is as if I'm swaddled in soft hides, blissfully warm and sleepy, and then, slowly, those hides fall away, my mind clearing and the cold night wind slapping me into wakefulness.

I'm not dreaming.

I'm awake.

I am on Doscach's back.

Running full-tilt toward Mount Gaetal.

Wearing only my thin nightclothes, with my feet bare and nothing but a dagger at my side.

"No!" I say as I jerk upright.

Jacko startles and blinks up at me, as if still half-asleep himself.

I yank on Doscach's mane. "No! Stop!"

He only runs faster, and this waking dream turns to a nightmare. I am on Doscach's back, and he is running to Mount Gaetal, and I am trapped, like in the legends where a ceffyl-dwr's mane binds its victims to its back.

Maybe this is what the legends actually mean—that once you climb on, you cannot get off, because it's galloping at such a speed that throwing yourself from the monster's back means certain death.

I've been tricked. Like a maiden in a bard's song, who comes across a beast in the woods and befriends it, only to realize it is an evil creature. Doscach never wanted to be my companion. He only pretended to be until I lowered my guard, and now he's snatching me away to devour me . . .

Yet, even in my panic and groggy state, I realize that's ridiculous. I have never heard any true story of a monster befriending a human as a trick. Why would they? Their needs are simple. If Doscach wanted dinner, there were far easier ways to get it than hanging out with a princess for weeks on end.

I have joked about Malric devouring me in my sleep, but that's more about me than him—my lack of confidence in his true feelings about me. I have heard of animals turning on their masters and killing them. Never monsters, though; not unless it is a situation like the one those terrible villagers trade in—taking monsters from the wild and selling them as pets. In that case, yes, a monster can be even more dangerous than an animal. It has been enslaved and will kill for its freedom.

That is not what this is. So what is it?

The answer comes as soon as that sleep-fog clears from my brain. Last night, Doscach very clearly wanted us to keep walking. I'd worried he didn't like the spot we'd chosen, but that hadn't seemed to be the problem. What I never considered was the other end of the spectrum. He wasn't warning us against staying in that spot—he wanted us to continue on because there was something farther upriver he wanted us to see.

We'd been so close to his goal, and then we stopped, and his reaction was frustration and annoyance. And now, sleepy and mistaking the moment for a dream, I'd climbed onto his back and he was taking advantage of it.

Fully awake, no matter how much I might have wanted to see what the ceffyl-dwr thought was so important, duty and responsibility would have won out. I have a duty to my guardian—Wilmot—not to go tearing off into the most dangerous part of our world, no matter how curious I might be. I have a duty to my people not to risk my life satisfying that curiosity. Yet even while I think that, I struggle to *feel* it. I can blame sleepiness, but I think the true blame lies with my blood. My Clan Dacre blood.

Earlier, in that dreamlike state, I'd sworn my blood was catching fire, urging me up, urging me toward *something*. An unknown something. The urge still beats there, like a second heartbeat, pushing me onward. Prodding me to just see. Just take a look.

This is important, it whispers.

I do try to stop Doscach. I must. I could never face Wilmot otherwise. But we're moving so fast that I must feel like no more than a gnat on his back. I yank on his mane, and I knock my heels into his sides, and I shout at him to stop. He does not.

And then, just as I am wondering whether I could throw myself free—whether that truly does risk death—Doscach veers . . . and leaps from a rock. I scream, one arm holding tight around Jacko, the other grabbing as much of Doscach's sticky mane as I can hold.

We drop through air for what feels like forever. Then we hit water, and I scream again, my mouth filling as I clutch Jacko with all my might, his little heart beating like it's about to burst from fear.

We are underwater. Doscach has plunged into . . . I don't even know what he plunged into—the river wasn't even deep enough to submerge him, yet he's all the way under the water and swimming, and we are trapped on his back.

Trapped and being taken into the darkest depths of this pool, where we will drown, just like in the stories.

Except I'm not trapped, I realize. I'm voluntarily on his back now. I push to free myself, but my hand stays tangled in that sticky mane. I can't use my other hand—it's holding Jacko.

One arm holding my jackalope. The other caught in Doscach's mane. I cannot swim to the surface. I am going to drown. *We* are going to drown. Jacko and I—

Our heads burst from the water. It's another heartbeat before I dare open my mouth and gulp air. I'm still gulping it when the young stallion leaps onto land, hooves clacking on rock, the sound echoing all around us.

I scramble off him, one arm still tightly wrapped around Jacko. I don't care if I can't see anything except black. I stagger away from Doscach, feeling my way around until I can sit on what feels like rock. Then I blindly examine Jacko. As my fingers find his chest and feel it rising and falling with quick breaths, my eyes adjust enough to make out his form on my lap. He's shivering so hard his whole body seems to convulse, and I hug him against me, both for warmth and comfort. He snuggles in, his purr still ragged with fear.

Hooves clop, and the dark form of Doscach moves toward me. I clutch Jacko and snap, "No!"

Doscach stops. I can make out enough now to see his head lowered, emerald-green eyes glowing. He makes a noise deep in his throat.

"I understand that you wanted to show me something," I say. "I understand that I wasn't listening to you. I understand that you brought me here for something you think is important. But the way you did it was wrong. *Wrong*. You frightened us. You could have *drowned* us."

He inches closer, head lowered, looking up at me through inky lashes.

He didn't mean to scare us—for him, water isn't frightening. He wouldn't have let us drown—he saved me from that once before. He's young and, in his frustration, he made a mistake, which I've done myself. Yet whatever his intentions, we *were* frightened, and he needs to know that.

Wilmot has told me many times to remember that Sunniva and Jacko are not grown monsters. Neither is Doscach. I'm still a child myself, even if I rarely feel like one, but to them, I'm an adult. Their guardian. It's my job to teach them, as Wilmot teaches me.

"It was wrong," I say. "Wrong."

I hold out Jacko, still shaking and chattering. When Doscach nudges him, the jackalope hisses, and Doscach pulls back. He whinnies softly and paws at the rock.

"I should go back," I say.

My voice doesn't echo now. It isn't loud enough, lacks the conviction I ought to feel.

I *should* go back.

But how? Lifting Jacko, I pick my way over the rocky ground until a shimmer in the darkness tells me I've reached the pool.

I squint around. I can't make out any light, though there must be a little somewhere for me to see anything. Then I look up and spot a hole in a ceiling above me with moonlight seeping through.

I realize I'm in a cavern, and the only obvious exit is through a pool of deep, ink-black water. If I could dive and swim, I might head the wrong way and drown. And what about Jacko? Even if we survive, another scare like that could stop his heart.

I should leave, but I see no way to do that.

Once daylight comes, light will shine through that hole and help me figure this out.

But even then, I'll be at the foot of Mount Gaetal, dressed in a wet shift, armed only with my dagger, needing to walk a mile to my companions, who may have already left the camp as they search for me. If I'm not killed by a monster, I'll die of hypothermia or exposure.

I sink back onto a rock and rub my eyes. When Doscach's wet nose nudges me, I start to snap at him. Then I stop.

Doscach knew the way in. That means he can get us out. I'll be safer out there with him. He is both a mount and a predator, able to help protect me. Jacko will be frightened, but he'll realize Doscach is getting us to land.

How do I get Doscach to help me? Let him show me whatever he brought me here to show me.

That feels like rewarding bad behavior, but I don't see a choice.

I hug Jacko and set him on my shoulders. Then I rise.

"All right, Doscach. What do you need me to see?"

CHAPTER TWENTY-TWO

It should be easy, right? The ceffyl-dwr brought me to this cave to show me something. Instead, he trots about as if the answer is obvious.

I start to explore as best I can. We're walking on slick stone. There's stuff growing on it. As a scientist I should be more specific, but I can barely see my hand in front of my face. I know only that there is "stuff" on the rock.

I find fish, too, or the long-dead remains of them. When my fingers touch a particularly long bone, Doscach gets very excited, pushing it toward me. It's from an animal, and he clearly expects another reaction, snorting and dancing when I fail to leap up in astonishment.

"I can't *see*, Doscach," I say. "It's too dark."

Still grumbling, I carry the bone into the light. It takes time to figure out what I'm holding. It's a large leg bone, neither particularly sturdy nor slender. I frown at it. Doscach nudges me and prances away, and I turn to glower at him. Then I see his own legs.

"It's a ceffyl-dwr bone," I say. "Is that what you wanted me to see? A ceffyl-dwr died here? One you knew?"

I'm not sure what to make of that. If it was part of his birth herd, then that would be a tragedy for him but, at the risk of sounding terribly callous, I'm not sure what I'm supposed to do about it.

Does he think I *can* do something? Heal his dead pack mate? No, he's a monster—he's smarter than that.

I squint up at the source of light. While the hole seems big enough to climb through, I hadn't considered doing so because it's at least twenty feet off the ground. Now, with my eyes better adjusted, I'd estimate it's more like fifty feet.

No. I must be seeing wrong. The ceiling can't be that high, or this cavern would need to be inside a mountain as big as . . .

As big as Mount Gaetal.

I'm *inside* Mount Gaetal.

If the ceiling is that high, how big is this cavern?

I begin to explore. Doscach keeps close and Jacko stays on my shoulders, alert now and audibly sniffing. As I walk, I look for another source of light and soon spot a second hole. Through it, the moon shines bright. I continue walking, only to pick up yet another, even brighter source of light. By then, I've walked at least a hundred feet. This cavern is *immense*.

I reach the brighter source of light, and I have no idea what it is. The ceiling stretches impossibly high here, and it seems as if the walls themselves glow. Some kind of phosphorescent vegetation? None of it is reachable from here, but I could get closer. To my left, there's a slope. If it *is* phosphorescent vegetation, I can gather some to get a better look around the cavern.

The ascent begins easily enough, then it gets tough, and I need to set Jacko down. He begins climbing alongside me. When he disappears into a crevice, I have to laugh. Apparently, he's recovered. Soon, though, he begins chittering.

As I peer into the crevice, he backs out, tugging a fish skeleton as long as my arm. He dives back in and returns, dragging another, the bones rattling over rock.

"Isn't that strange," I say. "Something must have dragged them up here. A cath palug, maybe?"

I continue climbing as Jacko hops about nimbly from ledge to ledge. As the glowing light illuminates this passage, I begin to see shells. Dozens, even hundreds of shells, apparently left by birds. Odd that there's so many of them.

I climb another foot and give a start as I find myself staring into the eye holes of a fish head. Another skeleton, this one wedged between two rocks. In a cavern this big, with so many nooks and crannies, why would a predator drag prey so high? I hoist myself onto the next ledge and let out a yelp.

It's another skeleton. A fish with teeth. An encantado—a monstrous river dolphin. The skeleton alone is at least six feet long. How could anything nimble enough to climb this high drag it up here?

I look up to see what appears to be another dolphin-like skull on the ledge above. I climb and suck in a breath that echoes through the cavern.

Nothing dragged them up here. Nothing could.

How would fish and aquatic mammals *get* up here? If the water was here, too. If they were living their lives, tucked away in their holes or swimming along and then, suddenly, the water was not there, and they were stranded.

I stare down at the lower encantado skeleton, and I shiver as I imagine its fate. The water is gone, and it flops and wriggles over the edge of its home cave . . . only to land on more dry rock. It dies away from its family.

I touch dried vegetation. Water plants left without water, shriveling and disintegrating.

My gaze sweeps the cavern. A cavern so big that in the dim light, I cannot even make out the whole of it.

Water. All this had been filled with water. And now all that remains is that pool below.

The pool. Doscach had swum up the small river that remained of the Michty. That's what the pool is—the source of what is now a river a tenth the size of the original.

This cavern is the mouth of the Michty River.

So where did the water come from? Where's the original spring—or springs—that fed it? I look up, but I'm not sure that's the answer. It's more likely down. Underground springs that began under the mountain. There must still be one or two flowing, but they're minuscule compared to what had been here.

I remember the ceffyl-dwr bone. Below, Doscach paces, hooves clacking on stone above which other ceffyl-dwrs once swam.

Ceffyl-dwrs don't live underwater, but they may have lived just outside the river and hunted in this cavern. Those bones may have come from a ceffyl-dwr who'd been injured and trapped when the water stopped flowing.

Is it possible Doscach was born to a herd that lived here? The river dried up about five years ago. If Doscach was a horse, he'd be a full adult by now, ready to fight for his own herd, but monsters mature more slowly.

He brought me here to show me something, and I may be wildly theorizing, but I think this is where he lived once, as a foal. As we drew close to the mountain, he became more agitated. Not upset or excited, but somewhere between the two.

Going home. Back to a place where he would have been happy. A place that disappeared, perhaps even fracturing his herd, as they were forced to hunt for new territory.

This certainly doesn't solve the mystery of the river, but it gives new information that I can take home to scholars. And I think it was important to Doscach to see this place again. If it was important for him to show it to me, then I am honored, and I forgive him for the way he went about it.

I peer up at the glowing walls. As long as I'm here, I might as well try to gather some specimens and have a closer look at the bones Doscach brought me to see. I map out a safe path and ask Jacko to stay where he is, on the deep ledge, inspecting the encantado skeletons.

I climb with care, until something slices my hand. Luckily, I'm prepared for that. Now that I know where I am—in a former water basin—I'm more aware of the possibility of sharp barnacles and broken shells. So when I do cut myself, it's only a shallow slice, my caution stopping me from grabbing too forcefully at things I cannot see.

Whatever cut me is wedged into a crevice I used as a hand-hold. I tug myself up and squint. At first, I see nothing. Then I gasp. It's a scale as big as my palm. It seems jet-black, but when I move, it catches the light as if the covering is iridescent.

I carefully wiggle it free. It is indeed the size of my palm. A massive fish scale. My mind races with possibilities, all the aquatic monsters in my bestiary books.

Sea serpents? Those are ocean beasts.

Is it possible I've discovered a new monster? A freshwater version? One so big it lived and died in this cavern?

I don't have an easy place to carry the scale, so I tuck it back where I found it. Then I go higher, hunting for more scales or—better yet—part of a skeleton. I see plenty of the latter, but only from smaller fish and animals. When I reach the glow, it turns out to be a moss. I touch it and look for any irritation on my fingertips, in case it's toxic, but they seem fine. I tuck two handfuls of the moss under my sleep tunic. Then I retreat, retrieving the scale as I go.

Once on the ground, I set the scale down where I can find it again. Then I return to the ceffyl-dwr bones. With the glowing moss in hand, I examine them. It's one skeleton, fallen to pieces. Several ribs are broken, and there's a sharp rock the length of my leg beside the ribcage. Did it fall on the ceffyl-dwr before it could escape? Did whatever happened to stop the water cause this rock to tumble down and mortally wound the beast?

"Thank you for showing me this." I put my arms around Doscach and hug him tight. "You are forgiven for scaring me half to death. I know this was important, and I wasn't listening."

I give him another pat and then step away. "Let me get the scale and then we'll—"

Doscach takes off, hooves clattering on the rock as his dark form disappears.

I sigh and hoist Jacko onto my shoulders. "Seems we aren't quite done here yet."

I lift the moss, and when I can make out Doscach, I walk over. He's against a wall, his head stuck into a wide crevice. He pulls back and I peer inside to see it's actually a tunnel. More moss glows deep within it.

"Ah," I say. "So there's a back door. One that doesn't mean plunging into freezing cold water and terrifying a non-swimming jackalope. You could have mentioned this before, you know."

I head inside, and Doscach follows. It isn't long before I see why we didn't come in this way. He only fits for about the first twenty feet. Then the ceiling slopes until it brushes Jacko's antlers. Doscach's being thoughtful and giving us another exit, one he can't take.

"All right," I say, patting his nose. "We'll meet you on the other side, then?"

He nudges me forward, and I laugh.

"Yes, yes, Jacko and I will happily take the dry route. Believe me, this will make us both much happier."

I wave a farewell and bend to crawl along the blessedly dry tunnel.

CHAPTER TWENTY-THREE

I don't get far before the ceiling shoots up again and I can walk. The tunnel walls are smooth as glass. The ones in the cavern had been worn by water, but these are even smoother. Worn by running water? There aren't any barnacles here. No dead vegetation either. Could this have been a waterway into the main pool?

The geological sciences aren't my speciality. I remember the books in Sarika's pack. This cavern and its waterways could answer so many questions about the Michty River. If something stopped or diverted the flow, is it possible to restart it? Is it even wise to try? Nature has already moved on, the riverbed filling with fresh life.

I'm musing on this when Jacko chatters a quiet warning. I slow and then come to a stop.

As I peer down the tunnel—dimly lit by the phosphorescent moss—a sound echoes through the chambers. A rumble.

Almost like a groan, but so loud it's more like distant rolling thunder.

"Is that what you heard?" I ask.

Jacko has gone still on my shoulders. I can hear him sniffing, then he scrambles to dismount. Another sound comes. A . . . cry? I hesitate to call it that, even as a chill runs through me. It did sound like a cry. Like some animal I don't recognize.

No, a monster. My gut says monster. Which one, though? It's an almost birdlike noise. An image of wings flits through my head.

Birdlike. Wings. Monster.

A gryphon is the obvious answer, but after my time with Tiera, I will always recognize gryphon noises.

Harpy? Manticore? No, these have wings, but they aren't otherwise "birdlike" in the sense that they make sounds anything like those of a bird. Their heads are mammalian.

Wyvern.

While the flying reptiles have fox-like heads, the noise they make is an avian screech.

There are wyverns ahead, and I'm armed with a jackalope and a dagger.

The rumble comes again, and I frown as I tilt my head. That isn't wyverns. It must be the mountain. An earthquake? I almost laugh at the thought—that would be the worst luck possible. More likely it's the sound of the mountain itself, shifting.

Those who've guessed at why the Michty River dried up blame the mountain's structure, speculating that something inside shifted, sending the water back into the earth and other smaller tributaries. That might be an ongoing process, like a volcano rumbling for years before or after an eruption. That means that while the rumbling sounds bad, it isn't any reason for me to turn back. Especially when turning back means going *deeper* into the mountain.

Jacko looks behind us and then in front. I offer to pick him up again, but he wants to stay on the ground, and he wants to continue. We do so, with extreme care. I have my dagger out now, the moss stuffed into my clothing with the scale to leave my hands free. And then, as the tunnel curves, there is true light—dawn's light, somewhere in the distance.

"Look," I whisper, pointing for Jacko. "Light! Sunlight! We're almost there."

His quiet chitter nicely warns me that my "whispers" aren't as quiet as they should be.

"Sorry," I murmur and motion buttoning my lips.

The rumbling has stopped, but we still catch the occasional wyvern cry. At one point, it sounds as if two are bickering over something, maybe leftovers from the night's hunting. Then that stops, and all I hear is a distant scratching, like talons on rock.

Another ten paces and Jacko zips ahead to point out a crevice in the side wall. Until now, the walls have been smooth and unbroken. Here, though, there's a crack wide enough to slip through.

Should we slip through it? That is the question. While the sunlight comes from somewhere up ahead, so do the scrapes of talon on rock.

I crawl quietly into the crevice to take a better look. It's maybe ten feet long, and beyond it there seems to be another cavern. A dark cavern.

All right. This isn't an obvious alternate route, but if those wyverns are right at the end of the main tunnel—and we can't get out without passing them—I'll reconsider this one.

I'm about to withdraw when Jacko hops inside and nudges a rock on the floor. Before I can bend to look more closely, he picks it up and carries it to the main passage. Once I'm out, he drops it at my feet.

I crouch and touch it.

"Not a rock," I mumble. "A tooth."

It's a wyvern tooth. I recognize it because we had to kill one of the wyverns that attacked us this summer, and Wilmot returned to the body to remove the teeth for me.

I don't like the reminder that I had to kill a beast, but as Jannah said, these "trophies" can remind us of a failure—if we believe the violence could have been avoided—or of a harsh necessity, as with the wyvern.

This tooth is bigger than the ones I have. While I brought that wyvern down, Malric dealt the killing blow. I don't have my sword or my hardened leather tunic. With only my dagger and my nightclothes, I'm not fighting *anything* unless I have absolutely no choice.

The tooth also seems a little different from the ones I have. There's an extra ridge along the side. That could indicate age. I consider taking it with me, but I'd need to swap it for the black scale, and that's more scientifically interesting. The scale would also make a better weapon.

With reluctance, I set the tooth down. Then we continue along. The clicking of talons sounds to our right now, but muffled enough for me to know it's behind rock. All the more reason not to take that side passage.

I'm picking up my pace when Jacko chatters and bumps my leg. I stop and follow his gaze. It's aimed back at that crevice. Something moves, dark against the dim light of my phosphorescent moss. I plaster myself to the right-hand wall. Jacko does the same, and we both look toward that movement. It's gone now, leaving the tunnel quiet and still.

Did I imagine it?

One look at Jacko tells me I didn't. He's staring wide-eyed in that direction, fur on end. Another movement. I blink hard to see better, but the sunlight is coming from the opposite end.

And then a snout appears, followed by a head, peeking around the corner. It's a long snout, dark, and the shape confirms it's a wyvern even if I can't see the fox-like ears.

The beast sniffs, the sound carrying to us. From the size of its head, I see that it could be the wyvern whose tooth we found—it's definitely bigger than the ones we encountered before.

It seems darker than the others, too, and its head is smoother. While a wyvern has the head of a fox, it's probably better to think of it as part bat and part reptile. There are bats with that fox-like head and fur. A wyvern's wings are definitely bat-like—membranes stretched between the torso and the forelegs, which are part of the wings. Those forelegs end in talons, and the beast is awkward on the ground, like a bat, waddling on its wing tips and hind legs. I listen for that distinctive sound—more a dragging than a scratching—but I hear nothing. Even when the beast pulls back out of sight, it's silent. Then it peeks again, and this time, it stretches its neck out and . . .

There are no fox-like ears. No ears at all.

I shake my head sharply. Does that matter right now? Its ears are probably flattened against its head.

I stay perfectly still, barely daring to breathe, in the hope it will retreat. After a few moments, it does, with the click of nails on rock. I still don't hear the telltale scrape of a wyvern's front claws, but that doesn't mean anything. It's retreating. That's all I need to know.

Jacko and I set out again as quietly as we can. The jackalope keeps looking back, and I watch him for signs he hears or sees anything. He doesn't, and soon we are coming up on the end of the tunnel and see, fifty feet ahead of us, the sun rising through a cave opening.

I pause a moment to marvel at the dawn.

When the tunnel broadens, I peer around. Jacko does the same. We've reached another cavern. Water burbles nearby, as if from a stream. I can't see the whole thing at a glance, but the water seems to come from around a corner. Otherwise, it's silent, and I don't see signs of a nest or den. No bones or debris anywhere. It's as clean as if the cavern has been swept.

As I ease out, nails click on rock and I freeze. Silence. I strain to hear while trying to judge where the noise came from.

I detect a very soft noise, like distant movement in the same direction as the burbling water. Around the corner, out of sight. So I just need to make it to that exit without being heard.

I creep forward, thankful I'm barefoot. My steps make no sound. Neither do Jacko's. As we move, I keep glancing toward that water noise. At any moment, I could go from being "hidden around a corner" to fully visible.

Two more steps, and I see a pool of rippling water. Off to one side are some oddly shaped rocks. Ink-black ovals, as smooth as glass. I'd love to take a closer look, but this really isn't the time for geological curiosity.

I'm less than a dozen feet from the exit. Beyond it, there's a huge ledge and the tops of trees. We're maybe thirty feet off the ground. Certainly too high to jump, but I can climb down from this height. First, I just need to get out . . . quietly.

I creep three more steps, then four. A fifth step, and I stop short and squint toward the cavern with the water and odd rocks, not even sure what I'm seeing. A tail? That's certainly what it looks like. It can't be, though. It's at least two feet thick. No creature has a tail that big.

Maybe it's a wyvern's back leg. I nod. That makes sense. It does seem to be reptilian. It must be part of a leg, held at a weird angle. Still, I do not want to meet whatever creature is attached to that big leg.

Another step and then another, and when I look back, I'm certain it's a leg I'm seeing. It's just the curve of it, the rest hidden behind the wall of rock. Well hidden, it seems. That's a relief.

I keep going. Five steps left. Four. Three. Two—

Nails on rock. I turn, and on the other side of the cavern, away from the pool, something moves in the shadows. I can still see that partial leg, so it isn't that creature. It's definite movement, though.

Jacko presses against me. I want to scoop him up and run, but a sudden movement might alert these creatures. Also, Jacko can move just as fast as I can on his own. Better to keep my hands free and step backward.

I do, and sunlight hits me. The nails-on-rock sound continues, as a dark shape moves in the shadows twenty feet away.

Just keep backing up. Slowly retreat. Don't run. With predators, you should never run.

The shape begins to take form, and I almost exhale in relief. It's definitely a wyvern. While it might still be a semi-formless shadow, I can see the general shape of the head—the skull and snout—and the thick, reptilian rear legs. Most importantly, I see wings. I definitely see wings.

The wyvern has spotted me, and it's advancing slowly. I sense caution and curiosity in that approach. It's wondering why there is a human in its lair.

Don't mind me! Just passing through. Be gone in a heartbeat!

A laugh burbles up inside me, a nervous, frightened laugh that I manage to swallow. I just need to keep backing away.

Still in shadow, it begins emerging into dim light. Something about the way it moves is strange. It's not the wyvern's awkward bat-on-land teetering shuffle, but a steady forward gait. I still don't see any ears.

Enough with the ears! That is the absolute least of your concerns.

I can't help it. As frightened as I am, part of my brain is still a monster scientist. Is this a different subtype of wyvern? One only found in the mountains?

Would you like to stop and examine it?

I stifle another nervous chuckle. No, thank you.

As soon as I think that, the beast shifts, and I see ears. They're just farther back than I expected. There, see? Wyvern.

I'm on the ledge now, the full dawn sun beating against my back. I glance left and right, looking for the best way down.

Neither. From here, it looks like an actual ledge, without a path to the ground.

That's all right. I can scramble down the hillside. I edge left, which seems the more promising route. Jacko is still by my feet, close enough for his fur to brush my skin. He's staring at that emerging shape. His body starts to shake, nose silently twitching. I can't see his eyes, but I know they're wide. Wide with fear, which is understandable—a wyvern can carry off a fully grown jackalope.

One more step sideways, with Jacko almost *on* my feet, and then the beast's head emerges from the shadows and—

It is not a wyvern.

I . . . I don't know what it is. The head is reptilian and jet-black. What I'd thought were ears are short horns. The neck is long, and the beast has front legs, with claws. I still think I see folded wings, but they're in the shadows. Along its neck is a ridge, which I presume extends down its back.

What is this?

A little voice whispers that I know, but another one says I'm wrong. I must be wrong.

What does it look like?

A dragon.

CHAPTER TWENTY-FOUR

I've seen dragon art. There are even a few pieces that are said to come from real life, back when dragons existed, before Tamarèl united under Clan Dacre. They didn't look like this, though. They were bigger, for one thing. The size of gryphons, some said. Even bigger, others said. And they were red or green, sometimes both.

Maybe this is an unknown dragon-like monster. Or an evolved form of dragons, which has been hidden away in the mountains for generations. Legend says that humans killed the dragons. With their size and ferocity, they were a threat to human habitation and livestock. They bred and matured so slowly that extinction came easily.

Maybe there were survivors, and they evolved into this, a wyvern-sized creature that wouldn't attract the same attention, wouldn't pose the same threat and become the same target of human fear.

All these thoughts pass in a blur, because as excited as my inner scientist might be, my inner hunter knows I need to get out of here—*now*. Leave, and get someplace safe. Tell the others, and then decide whether this is a secret we keep. To protect these dragon monsters. That comes later. For now, I must protect my—

Something strikes down behind me, the air vibrating with a rush of wind. I turn slowly, and my heart stops.

A second dragon—as big as the first—has landed on the ledge. There's one moment when I stand in utter awe, seeing the beast in the dawning light. It is . . . incredible. As big as Malric, with a reptile's body, lean and graceful. Its horns curve backward, and it has a ridge all the way down its spine and tail. The wings are more bat than bird, thick and leathery. Four legs, unattached to the wings, each foot with gleaming talons. This beast is jet-black, like the other, but when the sun hits its scales, they gleam iridescent, and my free hand drops to the scale under my waistband, knowing now what I found.

Then the beast rears up, rising on its hind legs, wings extending. It opens its mouth, the inside black with sharp, strong teeth. And it screams. It lets out a cry like the ones I heard earlier—the birdlike ones. Those were simple communication. This one is alarm. A shriek to tell the one inside the cavern that they are under attack.

I race to the edge, ready to run down and . . .

And it's a straight drop. Sheer rock. Nothing I can hold onto to help me scramble down. I glance past the other monster blocking my way, but even from here, I can see the entire ledge is the same. There's no way to climb down.

The draconic creature inside the cavern begins coming my way. The other still rears on its hind legs, shrieking at me. I reach the other edge and . . . the same. A straight drop.

Back through the cave. That's my best choice. Run past the second draconic creature and into that tunnel and run, just run. The only question is whether I carry Jacko or if I should let him run with me, and as much as I want to do the former, I know it's better to let him run. He'll stay close, and I have my dagger, and I will not let them take him.

I grip my knife, turn and run, letting out a scream of my own, a battle cry that I hope will startle the first beast enough so I can pass. Out of the corner of my eye, I see it fall back, and I keep running toward—

Toward the tunnel. I don't see the tunnel ahead. There's a wall instead. A huge black rock—

A scream, a deafening scream of rage and the wall—the *wall*—is moving. That's all I register at first. That there was solid black in front of me, and now it's moving and . . .

I am not looking at a wall. I'm looking at a body. A massive torso sheathed in black scales blocks my path, and my gaze lifts just as a head appears.

My scream echoes the beast's. Its is rage. Mine is terror and shock, as I see a head bigger than my entire body, mouth opening to reveal teeth as long as my arm.

I grab Jacko. I don't think. I scoop him up under one arm, and I scramble backward with my dagger thrust out. My dagger . . . which is half the size of one of those teeth.

The dragon screams, and it *is* a dragon, there is absolutely no doubt of that. The other two are babies—juveniles, and this is their mother, and she is so immense that my brain cannot comprehend what I am seeing.

Those jaws open in another scream, and I am looking into the maw of a dragon that could swallow me whole. One chomp of those jaws, and I am dead.

I cannot get past her. There is no "past her" that I can see. She takes up all the space.

This is what I saw lying around that corner. What seemed to be part of a coiled tail, but I told myself it had to be a leg, because no beast had a tail that size.

She does.

I cannot get past her, and behind me is a ledge with a straight drop, a young dragon still on it.

Too bad. I have no choice here. I have to run for that ledge and try to slide or scramble down the mountain. My brain screams that this is not an option, but I don't see another one.

I cannot get past this dragon. She is never going to *let* me get past her. She's furious, and the only reason she hasn't killed me yet, I think, is her absolute shock at finding a human in her den. A human invading the home where she's raising her young. I don't even consider whether I can calm her down and convince her I'll leave quickly. No amount of monster-hunter talent or Clan Dacre blood is going to fix this. Her gold eyes hold only rage. Deadly rage.

With Jacko clutched under one arm, I begin my retreat. Behind me, the juvenile on the ledge hisses and screeches, but when it makes a move, its mother screams at it. Telling it to stay back. Telling it to stay safe. Telling it she will handle this. She will kill the intruder.

I am going to die.

I am seeing a dragon. An actual dragon, and it is beautiful enough to bring tears to my eyes, but this is the last thing I will see. Like my father, who dreamed of seeing a gryphon, and the first one he encountered killed him.

I have never dared dream of seeing a dragon, but I am doing it. I might be the first person in generations. Princess Rowan of Clan Dacre, royal monster hunter. The girl with the gift for monsters.

The girl with the curse of stumbling over them at every turn.

The girl who saw a dragon—an *actual dragon*—and died with that sight imprinted on her mind.

I keep backing up. Then the dragon's head snaps out. Her massive body doesn't move. It doesn't need to. Her long neck extends, lips curling, malevolence in her golden eyes . . .

She stops. Those eyes fix on mine, and joy leaps in me. She sees me. Really sees me. Her nostrils flare, and she inhales my scent, and she is going to realize I'm not a threat. I'm just a human girl in nightclothes, barefoot and clutching a young jackalope.

Then her jaws open, and she roars, and the very sound nearly knocks me off my feet. I wheel to flee and something hits me—*she* hits me, her cold snout slamming into me. I fall and instinctively pull all four limbs in around Jacko. I will save him. Whatever happens, he doesn't need to die here. He can escape.

I'm huddled over him, shaking in fear, so certain I am going to die, part of me just wanting it to be over with. But another part silences that impulse. My blood runs hot, like in that dream, and I swear I hear it singing through my veins. I clutch Jacko in one arm and press the other hand flat against the rock, dagger beneath it. I flex my dagger hand, and let myself shake, let the fear seep from me.

I am small, and I am frightened, and I am no threat. No threat at all.

I feel her breath on me. Strangely cold breath. Breath that smells . . .

I know that smell.

I shake off the thought. It doesn't matter. Just focus on being small and scared and then—

I flip over. I clutch Jacko tight and lift the dagger. Her head is right there. I could hurt her. I could hurt her badly. But I don't. I just hold the dagger and meet her gaze.

Her jaws crack open. Not opening wide. They barely part, and she hisses, and breath rolls out.

That exhalation washes over me, cold droplets spattering my face. I hold my breath. I don't know why—maybe just because those droplets gross me out. It's the right move, though. I've already inhaled enough, and it does something to my brain. Makes everything seem strange and light and weightless. Makes me feel . . .

I feel like I did last night, during that waking dream.

I blink fast and creep backward. The dragon roars, and her jaws snap inches from my face. I scramble up, and she swings her head, knocking me flying.

Then there's another scream. A very different one. A clatter on rock and an equine shriek, and one of the juveniles screeches. A blur of white over my shoulder. Before I can move, that blur gallops onto the ledge, hooves clattering.

It's Sunniva. I blink in shock, certain I'm seeing things.

The pegasus filly charges straight at the dragon, her wings out and raised, making the filly seem twice her size. At the last second, she rears, red hooves flashing. She screams again, and the dragon's head jerks back in surprise.

Sunniva sidesteps to me and bends onto one front knee, like Doscach does when he wants me to climb onto his back.

I blink against the fog in my brain. "I—I can't. I'm too heavy."

She whinnies and rears, hooves flying, warning the dragon to stay back. I lift Jacko, thinking she means for me to put him on her back, but she drops to both front knees and looks over.

If she can't carry me, then I'll roll off and leave her with Jacko. I swing my leg over her shoulders, and as Jacko clings on, I take hold of her mane and shimmy up, my knees close to her neck, sitting ahead of her wings.

The dragon snaps from her surprise. She roars, and her neck shoots out, like a snake striking, but Sunniva is already galloping from the ledge. The one young dragon rears on its hind legs. Sunniva veers at the last second and then launches over the side, her wings extending behind me. We drop, and my heart drops, too.

I've made a mistake, been selfish, she can't carry me and we're going to—

Sunniva adjusts her wings and stretches out her neck, and we begin to glide.

"Yes!" I whisper. "Just glide. Get me close enough to the ground, and I'll slide off and—"

A roar behind us. I look back to see the dragon charging across the ledge. Those massive black wings extend. Then she is in flight.

"Down, Sunniva!" I say. "Just get me down, and I'll roll off."

Sunniva flaps her wings, but we don't rise. We're barely moving, and the dragon is torpedoing across the sky.

I look down. We're still twenty feet in the air, above a rocky clearing without even trees to hide in. Sunniva's labored flaps keep us hovering when I want to go lower. I *need* to go lower.

I lean against her neck. "Just let me down, Sunniva. You can take Jacko."

I push downward with my hands, hoping she'll understand, but she's focused on staying up, struggling to flap her wings, unaware that the dragon is getting closer with each breath. Then a black cloud blocks the sun. I look up to see the underside of the dragon overhead.

Sunniva lets out a frightened whinny and flaps harder, going nowhere.

"Down, Sunniva! *Please*. Just—"

The dragon drops, her talons out. Sunniva's entire body jerks. Her wings give a tremendous flap, and we're flying across the sky, zooming easily out of the dragon's reach. Sunniva keeps going with strong flaps of her wings that tell me she'd been faking the weak ones. Doing what I'd done in the cave—pretending to be small and weak and helpless. Now she's sailing straight for the trees. The dragon roars behind us, but we're already between tall trees, through paths too narrow for the dragon to follow.

Once we're safely in the denser forest, Sunniva glides down. Her hooves hit harder than usual, the only sign that she's carrying extra weight. I slide off. Jacko leaps onto my shoulders and starts chattering happily.

"Good girl," I say as I stroke Sunniva's nose. "Good, strong girl. I don't know how you found me, but you deserve *all* the apples."

She's trembling. Exertion? Excitement? Or actual fear? With Sunniva, it's easy to say it must be the first two. Yet I know too well the difference between being fearless and acting like it, and when I put my arm tentatively over her neck, offering a hug, she buries her nose against my shoulder, and I embrace her.

"You did so well," I whisper. "I'm so proud of you. Standing up to a dragon!" I shake my head. Then I take the scale from my waistband and hold it up. "You deserve this. I'll make a hair clip from it for you."

She sniffs the scale and then takes two steps and tosses her pretty mane as if to say, "I did very well, didn't I?"

"You did."

I hug her again, and Jacko rubs against her leg. She lowers her head to nuzzle him, and I'm about to speak when a voice shouts.

"Rowan!" It's Wilmot. "Sunniva!" Then, "I saw the filly go down somewhere nearby."

"Over here!" I shout.

We run toward his voice, coming out beside a river, where Doscach is swimming alongside the group, leading them as they walk. The ceffyl-dwr must have brought Sunniva to the mountain to fetch me when I came out of the tunnel. Instead, she'd heard me scream and come to my rescue.

"You're all right?" Wilmot asks as he strides to meet us.

"I'm fine, but did you see . . . ?" I point at the sky, unable to finish. "You did see it, right?"

"The huge black dragon?" Alianor says. "Nope. Clearly a figment of your imagination." She hugs me. "Yes, we saw. We saw you on a pegasus, flying away from a dragon big enough to devour Sunniva in one bite." She glances at the filly. "Well, maybe two."

Doscach leaps from the water to nuzzle Sunniva, and for once, she actually lets him. Then he comes over to me and drops his head.

I smile and scratch behind his ears. "You didn't mean to send me into a dragon's den. I know that."

"Dragons?" Alianor says. "Multiple?"

"She has young. Two of them."

"Do you think they're responsible for the migration?" Dain walks over, Dez on his chest.

"I . . . I'm not sure. We need to talk about that. Preferably farther away from her den."

CHAPTER TWENTY-FIVE

We get into the woods, in a spot as dense as it can be while still fitting Doscach and Sunniva. The others begin dragging over logs as I feed Jacko and nibble meat strips myself.

"So I guess Geraint was right," Trysten says. "There *is* a dragon in Mount Gaetal."

I look over sharply. "What?" My cheeks heat. I'd been pleased, thinking I was the one who'd discovered the dragons. But people do pass nearby. They couldn't miss the sight of a dragon flying overhead. "How long have people been seeing it?" I ask.

"Hard to say. Geraint says travelers have reported spotting one since they moved into the settlement. Maybe five years?"

"Five *years*? And we hadn't heard anything?"

Wilmot and Dain join us, Alianor bringing up the rear as she eats a handful of fall berries.

"Dad heard a report," Alianor says. "Just one, though. He said they happen all the time, and it's always wyverns."

Wilmot nodded. "There have always been reports of dragons and, as Alianor says, they always turn out to be wyverns. Or gryphons. Or manticores. Even pegasi."

"It wasn't many reports," Trysten says. "Geraint was the one who thought there was something to them. Then, about a year ago, reports stopped, only to start again six months afterwards."

"When the monsters started migrating," Dain says. "That proves it's the dragon."

I don't answer, lost in thought.

"Why don't you tell us what happened, Rowan," Trysten says. "From the beginning."

When I finish, everyone is staring at me. Everyone except Dain, who's glowering at Doscach, where he sits nibbling on a fish.

"It's not his fault," I say.

"For what?" Dain says. "Taking you away in the night? Scaring you half to death by diving into a deep pool of water? Or prodding you into a *dragon's den*?"

"He wanted to show me the cavern," I say. "I think those bones belonged to someone in his herd, maybe even a parent. I think he lived here when he was young, and he wanted me to see what happened."

"What did happen?" Alianor asks.

"I'd like to talk to your sister about that. It was obvious that the cavern was once a huge reservoir of water that fed into the Michty River. It emptied relatively quickly, I think, which is why fish were trapped and died. I think the pool is what's left of the river. It must be fed by other springs. Then there's the tunnel I walked down, where the walls were worn smooth, as if by running water."

Alianor nods. "So something stoppers the water. Maybe an earthquake or a rockslide or something that blocked the flow and sent it other places. Whatever it was, it would need to be huge . . ." She trails off and grins. "Oh! I see what you're thinking."

"It's pure speculation," I say quickly. "Trysten says the rumors began around the time the Michty went dry. I don't know what the dragon could have done . . ."

"Home renovation," Alianor says with another grin. "You know what it's like. You move into a new place, and you make some changes. Well, unless you're a princess who lives in a castle."

Wilmot nods slowly. "At her size, the dragon could have been responsible, particularly if she was planning to lay eggs. The old books say the incubation period for dragons could be years. If she was pregnant when she came to Mount Gaetal— flying in from over the sea to lay her eggs—she could have stopped the springs in making her den. She lays the eggs and is spotted every now and then for several years. She would have been incubating them and storing food. Then they hatch, and she disappears as she tends to them."

"Reappearing six months ago," Dain says, "when she's hungry and looking for food for her family. That drives off the monsters."

The others nod. I say nothing, and Dain looks at me.

"You disagree," he says.

"Your theory makes sense," I say slowly.

"But . . . ?"

I glance at Trysten.

Dain sighs. "You don't need to worry about embarrassing me in front of others, princess. My ego isn't that delicate. You have another theory. Spit it out."

"I actually don't have another theory. I just . . ." I take a deep breath. "Why are predators fleeing? There's much easier prey out here than dropbears and harpies. And colocolos wouldn't even satisfy one of the babies—they're bigger than wyverns."

"Predators aren't fleeing because she's eating them," Dain says. "They're relocating because she's eating their prey. Only the colocolos seemed panicked. The others are just getting out of her way, leaving this area to her."

"That makes sense," I say. "And it makes sense that we'd see it more now, with the babies growing up and Momma hunting. I just feel . . ." I shrug. "I feel like this is a partial answer. A dragon family would definitely disturb the natural order of things. Some predators would move on. They probably did as soon as she arrived. Like Doscach's herd, wherever they ended up. Some prey would move on, too, especially animals large enough to satisfy her."

"But it's too much," Dain says. "What we've seen suggests there's more to it."

"It has to partly be the dragons, though, right?" Alianor says. "The timing can't be a coincidence."

Wilmot nods. "Yes, it's unlikely to be coincidental. Something is spooking the monsters who decided to stay, something that convinced the dropbears and harpies to move on, and panics the smaller beasts, like colocolos. So how could the appearance of baby dragons be linked to that?"

"Baby dragons . . ." I say slowly, and then I turn to Trysten, who nods grimly.

"I think I might be your link," he says. "Or, not me personally, but where I just spent more than a year of my life. With people who trade in baby monsters."

"Wait," Dain says, moving Dez to his feet as he twists toward Trysten. "You knew your village was hunting baby dragons . . . and you didn't tell us."

"First, they aren't my village, and I'd appreciate it if you remembered that. Maybe you can't believe anyone would stay with people like that unless they were locked in a cage, but I am not you. While my father might not recognize me as his heir, I was raised as a lord in his house where I was as much a prisoner as I was in Geraint's village. My father even forbade me from learning to fight and tried to limit proper exercise."

I frown. "Why?"

"So he wouldn't grow up to be a threat," Alianor murmurs. "He wouldn't be able to challenge his father." She glances over at him. "You look fine now."

"Entirely from nearly two years living in the forest. My mother did what she could to keep me healthy, but walking over the mountains nearly killed me. I was a very bookish boy. I will be again, when I get some actual books. My father tried to limit that, too—intellect is another way to defeat a ruler. My mother had to choose where to thwart him. I got more secret lessons in history than secret lessons in sword fighting. The point is that I was ill-equipped for life out here." He glances at Dain. "I don't expect someone like you to understand that."

Dain bristles. "Someone like me?"

"Competent. Confident. You know your way around the wilderness and around monsters. You would have found a way to escape, like Alianor did."

"That was mostly Cedany," Alianor says. "But I don't think anyone here is questioning your story, Trysten." She looks at Dain. "Right?"

"I wasn't questioning that. My concern is the plot to kidnap dragon babies, which he didn't share."

"Because I didn't know about it," Trysten says.

Dain sputters and waves at me. "You just told Rowan—"

"I told Rowan I *might* know what *might* be happening. What *might* be upsetting Momma Dragon so much. As a hostage, I wasn't part of Geraint's troop, and I wasn't allowed in on their secrets. It was a temporary situation. My mother isn't going to spend the rest of her life trusting that I'm safely in the care of Queen Mariela. The only thing keeping her from visiting me so far is . . ." He waves at the mountains.

"She can't easily come visit you," I say. "Nor can she expect you to easily come visit her."

He nods. "By now, though, she'll be insisting on a visit, and the more my father denies her, the more suspicious she'll become. Geraint wasn't telling me anything he wouldn't want me taking out of the settlement. For six months, I believed them when they said the baby monsters were orphans, and they were taking them to Tamarel for the monster hunters to help."

He looks warily at us, as if waiting for a snicker or an eye roll.

"I believed them when they said they wanted us to relocate the harpy fledglings," I point out.

Wilmot nods. "I'm always ready for an ulterior motive, and I didn't see that one coming."

"Well, I eventually overheard enough to figure it out," Trysten says. "But I still pretended to believe their stories. I was afraid of what they might do otherwise. When it came to the dragons . . ." He shakes his head. "Maybe I'm not as smart as I like to think I am, but I honestly didn't piece it together until Rowan mentioned the babies."

"Is this just a hunch, then?" I ask. "Or did you hear something that makes you think Geraint is involved?"

"They've been working on something," he says. "A big project. That's where the rest of the settlement is. This has been going on for months. Small groups leave and return, and then others leave and return. Lots of whispered conferences and secret meetings. Not everyone in the settlement is in on those. I knew they were stalking a big monster—a very, very lucrative one. I guessed gryphons. We've seen young ones flying overhead this year, but they're already too big to sell."

My heart clenches. "Young gryphons? Coming down from the north?"

"Yes, from the foothills there. When we started seeing them, Geraint said we should find the lair. Those ones are too big, but if it's a nursery, they'll keep raising litters there. I thought they'd been searching for that."

Tiera's nursery. Where I left her. That's a secondary concern, though, because I very strongly suspect that isn't their target. Not this year.

I glance at Wilmot. "But wouldn't the juvenile dragons be too big to sell as pets? They're already hunting. Already bigger than wyverns."

"While I'm sure there are fools who think a dragon would make a lovely pet, Geraint would aim higher," Wilmot says. "*Much* higher. These would be sold to royalty, as symbols of their powers. Or to countries, as machines of war."

"*Machines?* But—but they're . . . dragons are living creatures."

"So are soldiers," he says. "So is every person that a country sends into war."

For a moment, I'm too dazed to answer. My mother taught me this. While our unique geographic location means Tamarel has never been at war—not since it united—she has explained that war means sending men and women to fight, and we must always remember they are actual people, not pieces on a game board.

That seemed so obvious to me as a child. But now Wilmot suggests countries could use dragons in war, and I'm horrified. Yet how is that *worse* than using humans? I suppose one could argue that the humans have a choice in the matter, but I'm sure in some countries, they don't.

Wilmot continues. "A dragon would be worth more than ten gryphons. More than twenty unicorns or wargs. Sell a single young dragon, and Geraint and most of his troop could retire. Sell two, and they'd be rich."

I'm still struggling to process this when he says, "You only saw two?"

"Y-yes. I mean, there could have been more. I remember reading the old books that said dragon eggs take years to incubate. They speculated that the brood aren't all born close together, like chickens. Well, they are, relatively speaking—if chicken eggs take twenty days to incubate, and they can hatch days apart, then it makes sense that dragons could hatch months . . ." I remember those odd rocks I'd seen in the cave. "I think I saw more eggs."

Wilmot nods. "I'll wager Geraint has figured that out. If there are only two—or even three—juveniles, there may be unhatched eggs. While he wouldn't turn down a juvenile, a newly hatched baby would be even better. And if he can get both? Or eliminate the mother?"

"Kill her," I say.

"Yes," Trysten says. "If they want a baby monster badly enough—or the parents are particularly dangerous—they kill them to get the young."

"But a dragon? How would they even . . . ? You haven't seen her up close. It's just . . . not possible."

"Isn't it?" Dain says. "If dragons lived here once and are gone, what happened to them? Legend says they were killed off."

"And driven off," Alianor murmurs. "Then one returns. Takes a chance on having her babies here, as far from people as she can get. Her babies are still in danger, and they aren't old enough for her to take across the oceans. She's stuck here, and she's mad. She's really, really mad. And I don't blame her."

"I don't either," I say.

"So how do we put this right?" Trysten says.

"Calm her down," I say. "Stop the threat, and hope she calms down. Before she drives all the monsters to Tamarel." I pause. "Before she loses her babies and goes looking for the humans who took them."

"Serves them right," Alianor mutters.

I shake my head. "I saw the look in her eyes. How angry she was. With me. With *all* humans. I'm afraid if she goes looking for someone to punish, it won't be Geraint's troop. They'll be long gone. She'll fly to the nearest towns, and those aren't across the mountains, where Geraint will have taken her babies."

"Tamarel," Dain says. "She'll be furious and looking for humans to punish, and she'll come to Tamarel."

Dain, Wilmot and I spend the rest of the morning hunting while Alianor and Trysten gather nuts and berries. That may seem incredibly irresponsible of us. Didn't we just come up with a possible theory for the monster migrations? Shouldn't we be trying to stop Geraint's men?

Yes, but that isn't going to be a simple matter of walking to their camp and telling them to stop. We need a plan. We also need food. So Wilmot and I hunt as we plan, with the beasts doing their own hunting alongside Dain.

There's a very good chance that we're actually gathering food for the walk home. In fact, by the time the sun is high in the sky, Wilmot has decided that's exactly what we're doing.

I want to protest. Go home? But we just found the problem! And Geraint's men are upsetting the dragon more each day. We must act now!

That's how it feels, but it's not the truth. Geraint's troop has been trying to get a juvenile or an egg for months now. Yes, the mother dragon's angry. Yes, she's getting angrier. But this isn't a volcano ready to erupt. It's an ongoing situation.

This isn't a fight or even a negotiation. We can't get Geraint to agree to stop hunting dragons and walk away. The moment we were gone, he'd continue.

He must realize that enraging the dragon may be causing the migration. He doesn't care. The migration means more frightened monsters for him to catch, and when he gets a dragon, he'll be rich. That's what matters to people like him— what he'll get out of it.

We need to return home as fast as we can, and then get my mother to send a troop of law enforcers. Arrest Geraint and his troop, imprison them until the dragon calms down, and then exile them back to their own land.

"It feels like dumping the hard work on someone else," I grumble as we head back to camp, a brace of game birds over our shoulders.

"Yes," Dain says. "You sat in your comfy castle room and ordered other people to solve this problem. You didn't walk to Mount Gaetal yourself—nearly getting killed several times—and then stumble on dragons and narrowly escape with your life. Nothing like that."

I glare at him.

"Is the problem that you don't like telling others to take over?" Wilmot asks. "Or that you don't like not seeing this through yourself?"

"Both, I guess."

As we walk a little farther, Jacko and Dez zoom back from wherever they've been hunting. Jacko climbs up onto my head, and Dez settles in, clinging to Dain's chest.

"We need to make you a sling," I say. "While a jackalope on my head and shoulders might look ridiculous, it doesn't hamper me much. You need a support sling for her. Like parents use for babies."

Now I'm the one getting a glare.

"What?" I say, throwing up my hands. "You—"

A crashing through the bush has Malric grabbing the hem of my tunic. He lets go when Alianor bursts through.

"Have you seen Trysten?" she says.

We shake our heads. "Isn't he with you?"

"He was, but we were working separate berry patches, and then I spotted a new one, and I called to him, and he didn't answer. I went to where I'd left him, and he wasn't there. I ran back to camp, searching for him. He's gone."

"He must be nearby," I say. "I hope he didn't wander too far, but we'll find him."

"No, you don't understand," she says. "His things aren't in the camp. He took them—and all of our remaining food. He's *gone*."

CHAPTER TWENTY-SIX

I want an alternate explanation. While I don't know Trysten well, he's been nothing but helpful from the start, when he tried to warn us away from his camp. He brought Dez back to Dain. He's tramped along for two days without complaint. He's the first person to offer to fetch water or firewood.

"We should have known he was setting us up," Dain says as he stalks through our camp, checking to see what else is missing. "He's no prince. How did we fall for that? His story was ridiculous."

"It would be in Tamarel," Alianor says. "But it makes perfect sense for other countries."

"But a prince? He's too nice to be a prince."

"Uh . . ." I say.

Alianor squeezes my shoulder. "Don't mind him. The only prince he knows is your brother, who *is* kind. Dain's grumbling because he wanted a reason not to like him, and he couldn't find one."

"Shouldn't this make him happy, then?" I say.

"He is happy. Dain is never more joyful than when he's grumbling and scowling and stalking around."

"Is it . . ." I begin carefully. "Is it possible there's another explanation?"

"You too?" Dain says.

Wilmot cuts in. "The princess is asking a fair question, Dain. We cannot abandon the boy if there's a chance he didn't walk away." He looks at me. "What are your thoughts, Rowan?"

I walk around the camp. "What's missing? Food? Anything else?"

"Wilmot's dagger," Dain says. "And my shoes."

"Which he had on him. Did he take anything except food?"

Everyone shakes their heads.

"There's not much else to take," I admit. "Besides dirty clothing. Is it possible he overheard us talking about heading home?" I say. "That's in the opposite direction of *his* home. Maybe he decided to set out on his own. We haven't encountered many monsters, so he'll think it's safe enough."

"Not many monsters *here*," Dain says. "That'll change once he gets away from the dragon den."

"True, but would he realize that? We're two days closer to his home here. As for the food, he knew we were already hunting for more. Our priority is getting home. But should we devote some time to looking for him? At least have Malric search for a trail? He can't have gone far."

Wilmot squints up at the noonday sun. "Take Malric and Alianor, Rowan. Dain and I will get these game birds ready to go. We'll set out by midafternoon. That's as long as we can afford to search for Trysten."

This is not what I expected. Definitely not what I wanted.

Finding Trysten proved harder than we'd hoped. Malric located the trail, but it was obvious that Trysten had expected that and tried to thwart the warg's tracking abilities, wading in a stream to hide his scent. It took a long time to find his trail after that . . . and then he did it again, in another creek. By the time we've caught up, it's already midafternoon. Wilmot will not be pleased. If we'd hit another body of water, we'd have stopped there. Instead . . .

Alianor, Jacko and I are in a tree, with Malric standing guard below. We're looking out on a camp. Not our camp. Geraint's.

Geraint himself is there. He'd apparently been following us, staying just out of sight, while he waited for Trysten to return. We've been betrayed. There's no other way to interpret what I'm seeing. Trysten is in that camp, and he isn't a prisoner. He's sitting on a log, talking to one of the men, laughing and shaking his head as he eats a drumstick.

"So is he not a prince?" Alianor whispers. "Not even a captive? Sarika said he was."

"They told her that?"

"No, she overheard it." She pauses. "Unless she was supposed to hear it."

"Why?"

"To scare her. To prove they weren't kidding around by holding her hostage. They already had a *prince*. And then we come along, and he tells us the same story."

"Why?"

She shrugs, her gaze fixed on Trysten laughing below. "In case Sarika mentioned it, I guess. When we escaped with the harpies, Geraint sent Trysten after us with the dropbear. What better way to prove Trysten was sincere? Give us back the dropbear and then throw himself on your mercy. You're a princess, after all."

I stare down at Trysten, who's joking with a man about Kaylein's age. I want to say we've misinterpreted, but I don't see how that's possible, and I fear the impulse is purely selfish. I don't want to admit we could be fooled this badly.

"I'm sorry," I say. "I know you liked him."

She glances up, her brows rising as she shakes her head and smiles. "My heart isn't broken, Rowan."

"I know. I just mean . . ."

"That I said he was cute, and a prince, so that means I liked him. I did like him—as a companion. Otherwise?" She wrinkles her nose in thought. "I wasn't thinking of him that way. I'm sorry he turned out to be evil. Let this be a lesson to us. Never trust a cute boy."

"Cute but evil."

She sighs. "A tragedy."

"Agreed. Now let's go tell Wilmot the bad news."

By the time we get back to Wilmot, he is really, really not happy. He'd wanted to be on the road by now. Our news doesn't improve his mood.

"So what do we do now?" I ask.

"Is there any question?" Dain says. "Leave him, obviously."

"I don't mean about Trysten. I mean that he's passed on my conjectures about the dragons. We have to presume some of what I told him is new information. I confirmed the location of the den and the existence of eggs, and I said there was a back door in, through the river."

It's not until I put this into words that I truly understand what I've done. What I've given them. A way to sneak into the den while the mother dragon is gone, steal eggs and escape through the tunnels, where she can't follow.

I've learned so much since Jannah died. I've developed skills that will make me a better monster hunter. But I've learned things about myself, too, and those are just as important as archery or swordsmanship. Here, I make another leap, even if no one else will notice it.

When I realize I gave Geraint a secret way into the dragon's den, I want to blame myself. Take responsibility for a mistake while berating myself for my recklessness. Yet before I do, I stop, and I think, and I don't do that. I don't do it out loud, and I barely say it inside my head.

No one foresaw Trysten's betrayal. Not even Wilmot. When I told my story, we hadn't yet realized there could be a link to Geraint and his poachers. If I blame myself aloud, then everyone needs to leap in and reassure me it's not my fault. A leader doesn't need that reassurance. She knows when it's her fault . . . and she knows when it isn't. This isn't.

When I glance up, Dain's gaze is resting on me, his mouth tight. He's waiting for me to start that cycle of self-blame and necessary reassurances. Instead, I say, "So we need to figure out our next move," and he nods in satisfaction.

"The question—" I begin, and I'm cut short by a distant roar that has us all jumping.

It's the dragon. I will never forget that sound. Yet this roar is different. When she chased me, she'd been outraged at the trespass. I was in her den, and I have no doubt she'd have killed me for that mistake, but once Sunniva and I were in the forest, she didn't try to pursue, didn't circle and roar. I wasn't a threat. I was just a small human who should not have been so close to her babies, and once I was gone, she trusted I'd learned my lesson.

This roar is boiling fury. This roar is the dragon screaming at the entire forest.

"Something's happened," I say. "Something bad."

Wilmot nods gravely. No one says what that "something" might be. This is a mother who has lost her child, and I want to block my ears until it stops. I don't, because this is important. Important for us, and possibly for all of Tamarel.

Wilmot peers up into the afternoon sky. "We need to get deeper into the woods, where she can't see us."

No one points out that we didn't do whatever just happened. It won't matter.

I run to the nearby stream, where Doscach was fishing while Sunniva grazed along the sun-dappled banks. Now they're both poised, heads up; water streams from Doscach's mane as he tracks the dragon's progress through the sky.

I open my mouth when the sun disappears and thunder rolls through the forest. I look up. There's no storm coming. The sky is bright blue, dotted with white clouds. The sun has disappeared because there's an ink-black dragon blocking it, the beat of her huge wings like thunder.

Sunniva races over to me, a blur of white, and the searching dragon turns. I grab Sunniva's mane and half drag her toward the forest, shouting apologies as I do. She understands and doesn't even snap at Doscach as he prods her from behind.

I get Sunniva into the thickest stand of trees I can find, just barely enough room between trunks for her slender body. Jacko hops along at my heels, and Malric circles, his gaze on the sky.

I order the others to stay away until I'm certain the dragon hasn't spotted Sunniva's white coat. Once she moves on, we gather and listen to the dragon's screams. When I lean against Sunniva to comfort her as she shakes, Alianor nods and says, "Good idea," and stands beside me, our bodies blocking her white form. Dain does the same while Wilmot slips into a more open area to watch the sky.

The dragon's circles grow wider as we stand there. They don't come our way again, though. Then the roars stop, and those thunderous wingbeats cease.

"She's done," I whisper, exhaling.

From a nearby clearing, Wilmot glances over and shakes his head, motioning for us to listen. Then it comes. A babble of voices. Panic and running footsteps and a scream. A very human scream, and the ground vibrates beneath our feet.

The scream continues, along with cries for help. Then silence. Sudden and sickening silence.

"She's found them," Alianor whispers with a shudder. "She's found the poachers."

More shouts. Anger and panic mingled. Another scream, cut short, and I try so hard not to imagine what's happening.

The shouts taper off, and the dragon roars in frustrated rage.

"They've escaped," Alianor says. "She got two of them, but the rest made it into the forest."

Dain grumbles that we don't need the commentary, but it's a very quiet grumble, acknowledging that Alianor is as spooked as us, and this is how she deals with it.

Wilmot's head jerks up. His gaze swings in the direction from which we'd heard the dragon. She's still roaring, and it takes a moment to realize she's getting louder. Malric's gaze is fixed on the forest. He listens for another moment, and then he twists, lunging my way, striking my legs and telling me to move.

"They're coming," I say. "Geraint's men must be running this way."

"Split up," Wilmot says as he strides toward us. "Dain, take your dropbear. Alianor, take Doscach. I'll take Sunniva. If any of the beasts try to flee on their own, let them. Do not follow."

I open my mouth to argue. Split up? But there's a dragon coming. We need to stick together . . .

No. Sticking together increases our chances of being seen or heard. If by some chance the dragon manages to get into the forest, then it doesn't matter how many of us there are— we cannot fight her.

Wilmot didn't specify who would go with me, because that is obvious: Jacko and Malric. While I'm confident Dez will cling to Dain—literally—I'm less certain about the equine monsters, and I ask them to go with their respective humans, but it's quickly apparent that Doscach isn't letting Sunniva out of his sight while a dragon is circling. Sunniva doesn't want to leave my side either, but I can convince her to stay with Doscach, leaving Wilmot with Alianor. Then each group goes its own way.

CHAPTER TWENTY-SEVEN

I creep through the forest with Malric at my rear and Jacko at my feet. The sound of the others fades behind me. The dragon has stopped roaring her thwarted fury and settled for silent circling. Twice she passes close enough for me to hear the whoosh of her wings, though I don't see her.

Another twenty paces, and I stop. I shouldn't get too far from the others, and this seems a good place to lie low. Any sound of the fleeing poachers has disappeared, suggesting they've found their own hiding spots.

As soon as I think that, the bushes rustle, feet pounding the earth. I dive to the ground and flatten myself in the thick undergrowth. Malric hunkers down beside me, Jacko between us. I reach for my sword, reconsider, and take out my dagger instead.

Just let the poachers run past. I'll fight if I have to, but with any luck, they'll keep going. Even if they spot us, there's no reason to stop.

The footfalls and the crackling undergrowth grow louder and louder. I close my eyes and track their trajectory. They're heading just to the right of us, on course to miss us entirely. Stay still. Stay perfectly—

A squeal. A snort. The footfalls veer and head straight for us.

I leap up, expecting to see running poachers. Instead, it's two four-legged brown forms.

I quickly sheathe my dagger and pull my sword. The creatures smell Malric. One rears back, squealing, rising enough above the undergrowth for me to see it.

At first, I don't know what I'm seeing. It's a rabbit head, twice the size of Jacko's, with shell-shaped ears. The beast rears, hissing, showing a long body. The front quarters look like a badger's, the rear like a bear's—if both animals hadn't eaten in weeks.

It's a rompo.

With their skeletal frames and humanoid ears and tiny teeth, rompos are very creepy. They are not, however, dangerous. Unless you're already dead.

Rompos are scavengers. There's another name for them that adds to the creep factor. Corpse-eaters. It's said that they have a taste for humans and dig up graves. I shiver with revulsion as they hiss at me. But they aren't going to hurt me. I'm surprised they haven't already run away. The dragon has them spooked, making them braver than usual. Still, it's only two of them. Even Jacko isn't concerned as he hisses and waves his antlers.

"Malric?" I say.

He's beside me, growling, clearly watching them. As soon as I charge—

A noise sounds to my left. It's almost a humming sound, strangely musical. A bird, I presume . . . until I remember that rompos are said to sing. Yet the sound comes from my left. Then it comes from my right, too, and the two in front of me join in.

All right, so there are four of them.

At least four.

I'll charge the two in front, and Malric can handle any others—

A bellow from the forest. My head snaps up, imagining the dragon swooping. It's a human cry, though.

The two rompos in front swing their gazes that way, and the others stop singing. Someone is crashing through the forest, making as much noise as they can. It doesn't sound like either Dain or Wilmot—I can't imagine either making that much racket. Alianor, then? But the whoops sound male and—

A light-haired figure appears, waving his arms and shouting as he leaps into the path of the two rompos.

Trysten?

"Get!" he bellows. "Scat! Scram!" He looks at me. "Just make a lot of noise. They're only rompos. They'll—"

The one nearest leaps . . . straight at him. The other yowls and charges. Both hit him at the same time, and I rush in, switching my sword for my dagger, lest I slice open Trysten instead. Well, considering his betrayal, maybe I shouldn't be too worried about that. However, I need him to live so I can tell him exactly what I think of him.

The two rompos are on top of Trysten, snarling and snapping. He's fighting but it's punching and kicking, as if he's forgotten he's holding a dagger.

I sink my blade into the shoulder of one rompo and throw it aside. Then I slash at the other. That should be enough. The first has already fled, yipping in pain. This one, though, doesn't even seem to notice its injury. It's going for Trysten's throat, and when its jaws sink in, I have no choice. One sure slice across its own throat. Then I shove the beast off Trysten and whirl around to make sure the other beasts are gone. They are, and Malric is behind me, snarling at the empty forest as Jacko yodels his victory cry.

"They—they don't—" Trysten says as he pushes up. "They're just rompos. They're easy to scare off."

"Not when they're fleeing from a dragon." I spin on him. "And what are *you* doing here?"

He flushes. "Uh, helping you? Which didn't quite turn out the way I expected. See, knowing rompos, I figured I could run in, make a lot of noise and save the princess." He rubs at the bloody gouges on his neck. "Instead, I was nearly killed by a rompo. That would have been really embarrassing."

His lips curve in a wry smile, eyes meeting mine.

"She means why are you *here*," Dain says as he tromps from the forest, Alianor and Wilmot following. "After you betrayed us."

"What?" Trysten straightens, blinking. "When?"

Dain turns to me. "Did he get hit on the head when he fell?"

"Nah," Alianor says as she walks up to Trysten. "It's that twin brother you forgot to mention, right?"

"Twin . . . ?"

"The identical twin brother, who is also a hostage with Geraint. He's the one we saw this afternoon with them."

"I don't have a twin—" Trysten pauses. "That's sarcasm, isn't it?"

"We saw you with Geraint's men," I say. "Laughing and talking."

"Because I went back willingly."

"Exactly."

He waves his hands. "Not like that. I was tricking *them* into thinking I went back willingly. While we were gathering berries, I spotted one of the men. They'd been watching you. So I ran over and pretended I'd made a horrible mistake and wanted to come back. Really, I just wanted to see what they were doing."

"So you gave them the information about the dragons," Alianor says. "You told them what Rowan found—the back entrance and the eggs and the babies. They used that and stole a baby—"

"An egg," he says. "That's what I came to tell you. They stole an egg and . . ." He swallows. "They broke one. They snuck in and grabbed two eggs while she was hunting, and they broke one to slow her down."

"To slow her down?" Alianor says, horror on her face.

When I speak, my voice is eerily calm, my own horror pushed deep. "So she'd try to save the other baby. The one whose shell was cracked. They killed a dragon baby to give themselves time to get away."

Alianor wheels on Trysten. "You did this. You told them—"

"Nothing!" He raises his hands. "I told them nothing. Well, nothing that helped them find the dragons. They were already tracking you. Someone got close enough to overhear us talking about how you found the tunnel and about the eggs. I pretended I'd been standing guard at the time, so I couldn't confirm it. I said you guys didn't trust me. Which apparently wasn't a lie—"

Malric's growl cuts him short. The warg and the jackalope had been standing guard with Doscach. Sunniva had been grazing, but she's on alert now, her gaze fixed in the same direction as the others'.

As Malric lopes to me, Wilmot gets to his feet, bow out. We all draw our weapons.

"Come out," Wilmot calls. "We know you're there."

"Because we *want* you to know," Geraint's voice calls back.

Malric growls as Geraint steps out. The man laughs, and there's challenge in that laugh, as if almost hoping the warg will attack. Geraint holds a dagger, as do the two men flanking him, and I have no doubt that if Malric feinted in their direction, they'd fall on him.

I hate them for what they've done to monsters, and what they did to the dragon, but most of all, I hate them for this— that they're hoping for an excuse to hurt or even kill a warg who has done nothing to them.

Malric only growls and settles in at my side.

"They warned us about you, boy," he says to Trysten. "When your people brought you to us, they warned us not to be fooled by fancy words or airs. You might be book smart, but you're as gullible as any noble who wants to buy a harpy chick. You don't know your way around the world. We *let* you sneak off with the dropbear, so you'd lead us to the princess. Don't ever take up spycraft, my lord. You're as crafty as a toddler stealing a sweet from a market cart."

Trysten's eyes blaze with anger and humiliation. "I won't go back with you. I won't."

"Good. We don't want you. Your father was supposed to send for you this summer. Apparently, he doesn't want you either."

"All right, then," Wilmot says slowly. "We'll take the boy off your hands—"

"Oh no. He's a prince. He doesn't come free. We want a trade." He turns to Dain. "We'll take you."

"W-what?" Dain straightens. "Me?"

"We've seen you fight. We've seen you shoot. We've seen you hunt. We've seen you climb that cliff and sedate those harpies. You're as good as the girl." Geraint nods to me. "Without that pesky royal title."

He laughs at his own joke and then continues. "We can't ask for a princess. We can ask for an orphaned boy who only gets his place at the princess's side through charity."

"What?" I squawk. "Dain is not an orphan, and it's certainly not charity—"

"Just because one's parents are alive doesn't mean one isn't an orphan. Perhaps not legally, but inside . . ." He meets Dain's eyes. "I know that look. The look of a boy without family. We can give you that. A family who will welcome you and value your skills, far more than any princess or queen. You don't come from their world, boy. You know that."

"He has a family," Wilmot says through clenched teeth. "He has—"

He stops short, and I look over sharply, waiting for him to set this horrible man straight. To tell him that Dain is his son, and we are his family. But Dain's looking at Wilmot, and I can't see what passes between them, but Wilmot stops mid-sentence.

Before I can speak, Dain says, "I'll go."

"What?" I say. "No."

Alianor takes my arm, squeezing it. "He's right, Rowan. Dain isn't one of us and never will be. Better he goes with people who'll value him, and we take the prince."

I blink at her. Her eyes widen in a look I know well. She's up to something. They all are. Only in a nightmare would Dain agree to join poachers. Only in a nightmare would Wilmot let him go and Alianor trade him for a prince. We could get out of this. It would take a fight, but we'd do that before we'd ever leave Trysten or Dain.

Trysten is the only one who hasn't figured it out, and he's protesting loudly, but Dain insists he wants this. I realize I need to protest, too, or it'll seem strange if we're all happy to let our companion leave.

"We can't let him go," I say.

"I don't like it," Wilmot grumbles, but it's a fake grumble. "Are you sure you aren't doing this because you're upset about something, Dain?"

"No, I'm doing it because he's right. I don't belong here."

Wilmot insists on a moment with Dain, to be sure of his intentions. Geraint's men don't allow the two to go off and speak privately, but they give them some space. When they finish, Wilmot stalks back to Geraint.

"Spring," Wilmot says. "You may have him through the winter, and in spring, I want to check up on him."

— 269 —

"Of course. You know where to find us."

Wilmot snorts. "You're no fool. You've already abandoned that settlement. You stole a dragon egg. You aren't going back there."

"Dragon egg?" Geraint rolls his eyes. "You really believe this boy's mad tales?"

I open my mouth, but a look from Wilmot warns me to silence. If we press them to admit they have an egg, they might attack to keep us from following them.

They negotiate. Then we escort Dain to our camp, where he grabs his pack and walks away, Dez trundling along at his heels.

CHAPTER TWENTY-EIGHT

The plan is for Dain to sneak back tonight and tell us where to find the camp, so we can retrieve the egg. I don't like it. I don't like it at all. Wilmot insists we give Dain a chance, though. Trust him. Trust, too, that Wilmot would never expose Dain to danger. They want Dain, and they didn't mistreat Trysten. Dain will be fine. If he can't escape, we'll find and free him.

We don't move our camp, and Wilmot has told Geraint that. We are staying here "in case" Dain changes his mind and we need to renegotiate. It'd be more suspicious if we just moved on.

I'm supposed to take the next shift for guard duty, but I'm not sleeping. I'll drift off and then start awake feeling like I'm missing something.

Dain. We're missing Dain, and I cannot stop worrying about him.

Does anything that Geraint said resonate with Dain? Not that he would ever join poachers, but could this make him reconsider his place with the monster hunters? Question whether he belongs?

Does he feel orphaned? Abandoned by his family?

Does he feel as if he doesn't fit in? I'm a princess; Rhydd is a prince; Alianor is a warlord's daughter. Even Trysten is the son of a king and was raised in a noble family.

There's more that's keeping me awake, though. I trust that if Dain is questioning, we'll have a chance to discuss it. What's also bothering me is that every time I fall asleep, I drift into last night. Not the part where Doscach took me into the mountain, but before that. Back to my waking dream.

I keep seeing the moon and stars snuffed out by a black shadow that glides over the camp. I keep seeing that fog, smelling it, feeling my mind floating back toward sleep. I keep hearing everyone around me deeply slumbering.

You forgot this, a voice seems to whisper.

Forgot what?

It doesn't answer, just keeps replaying the dream that was not a dream.

I blink awake.

The dream that was not a dream.

But it *did* start as a dream, didn't it? I dreamed of the darkened sky and the gliding shadows and the mind-numbing fog and the others so soundly asleep.

Except they *had* been deeply asleep. Wilmot and I haven't discussed how I'd gotten past his guard, because I suspect he was embarrassed to admit he'd fallen asleep. That wasn't like him. At all. He is constantly telling us that if we get sleepy on guard duty, we must wake him rather than risk drifting off.

As I sit there in the dark, the fire flickering behind me, I see the dragon. I see her head coming down to mine, her breath washing over me, that smell familiar . . .

The smell of the fog in my dream.

The dream that was not a dream.

Narcoleptic breath.

The phrase comes from deep in my memory. I know *narcoleptic* has something to do with sleep. So "narcoleptic breath" would put you to sleep.

Is that possible?

When it comes to dragons, the most misunderstood lore relates to their breath. Some legends say dragons breathe fire. Others say they breathe ice. Or poison. Of the three, only the last is plausible from a scientific standpoint. Basilisks are said to be able to turn people to stone. The reality is that they spit a neurotoxin, which acts as a paralytic. The key isn't the actual breath, but the droplets expelled, like when a human coughs or sneezes. With monsters—and with some reptiles and insects—those droplets can contain poison.

Did I read the phrase "narcoleptic breath" in some scientific paper on dragons—a passing reference that I didn't quite understand, but which didn't seem important because I never expected to encounter actual dragons?

Is that what happened when the dragon breathed on me in her cave . . . I inhaled the droplets and it felt like cotton encasing my brain, making me fuzzy and sleepy?

Is that what happened last night? My dream that wasn't a dream?

An inky shadow passing over us, big enough to blot out the sky.

A black dragon drifting past.

The fog settled over us, making my brain fuzzy and dopey. Putting Wilmot to sleep. Keeping Malric from hearing me when I wandered off. And I wandered off because I was just dazed enough to think I was only dreaming, with Doscach apparently not being affected, either because of his amphibious nature or because he hadn't been close by at the time.

But does that make sense? The dragon is furious at humans. Would she just drift lazily over our camp?

Unless she wasn't "drifting lazily." She was spying on us. Checking us out. Investigating. And putting us to sleep so she could do it.

I remember Geraint saying that harpies recognized human faces, like ravens. They knew who'd harmed them and would retaliate against those specific people.

If harpies were that smart, then surely one could expect the same of dragons.

So the dragon sees us camped near the base of Mount Gaetal. She could knock us out and kill us, but she only investigates. When she realizes we're not the humans who've been threatening her offspring, she leaves.

I remember that moment in her den, when I thought I was about to die. When she'd seemed to be assessing me.

Recognizing me as one of those humans camped below her mountain.

And then?

Had she held back, considering what my presence in her den meant? Considering whether I was a threat?

I don't think she planned to let me walk out alive. But she did pause. She did try to sedate me rather than kill me outright. Sedate me while she thought it through? While she checked on the rest of my people to see whether they were also invading her home?

Idle speculation. What's important is that she did not kill us in our sleep. That she did not decide we should die "just in case." Humans don't always wait to see whether a nearby wolf pack threatens their livestock before they hunt and kill it. If their livestock *is* attacked, they don't always make sure that the wolves they've hunted down are the ones responsible before killing them. The dragon doesn't see all humans as dangerous, which is good. She acknowledged the possibility that we were not a threat.

And then I invaded her home.

I can't fret about that. I should talk to Wilmot and see what he thinks of my theories. As soon as I rise, though, I remember Wilmot doesn't have first guard shift. Alianor does. No matter—I can discuss it with her first.

I pull on my clothing and walk over. She turns, rubbing bleary eyes.

"Please tell me it's the end of my shift," she says.

I hesitate. She looks exhausted, certainly not alert enough to discuss the science of dragons.

"I can't sleep," I say. "I was going to offer to take over early."

I'm hoping she'll say no, that she's fine, and then I can talk to her.

Instead, she exhales loudly. "Thank you. I owe you one."

We talk a bit after that, as she prepares for sleep and I settle in with Malric at my side and Jacko on my lap. Then she's in her sleeping blankets, and it's just me and my beast companions.

"Anyone want to talk dragon theories?" I murmur to them.

Malric yawns. Jacko curls up, purring, clearly ready to go back to sleep. And so I sit there, wide awake and on guard, until something crashes deep in the forest. I leap up, listening. It's the crash of someone running. Or some*thing*. At first I think of Dain, but he isn't supposed to meet us until midnight. Then I remember the rompos and pull out my sword.

A second sound cuts through the first. A thunderous flap of wings.

My gaze shoots up. The moon shines bright, covering the forest in waves of light. Waves with one dark spot.

When the dark spot moves, stars appear behind it and disappear in front of it. A massive black shape gliding through the sky. The dragon is hunting.

I glance at the fire. Should I put it out? For now, she seems intent on her quarry. I can see her shape more clearly, great wings flapping as she tracks something on the ground.

If she catches her prey, we'll be safe. She'll take it and fly back to her den. The problem comes if she misses it and *then* spots our fire. I should probably extinguish it.

A thud in the forest. A thud and then a curse. A human curse.

I freeze. The dragon is chasing a person. Chasing one of the poachers.

Should I interfere? My gut says yes, but that risks my companions. I grip my sword tighter and strain to listen as the voice continues muttering, the person having obviously tripped and recovered.

It is not the voice of a panicked human. It's the voice of someone who doesn't know he's being stalked by a dragon. Someone running through the forest . . .

When he mutters again, my head shoots up.

Dain.

But Dain wasn't supposed to return until after midnight. That's why Wilmot was taking third watch—so he could wait for Dain.

There's no doubt now who I heard. Something has gone wrong. Dain had to leave early, and he's running back to camp, and he doesn't realize the dragon is stalking him.

I wheel toward the others.

They're fast asleep, and I'd waste precious time explaining. Malric is already up and coming to my side. Jacko is right there. Doscach and Sunniva are asleep in a clearing, too far away for me to summon, and I can't risk the dragon deciding they'd make a fine substitute for Dain.

I run as fast as I can. I don't worry about making noise. Better if I do. It might distract the dragon or even wake Wilmot and Alianor. I crash through the undergrowth, and Malric does the same, as if understanding my logic.

"Dain!" I shout. "Dragon!"

Only the crashing answers. Dain's racing through the forest, and when I dash out from a stand of trees, I can see him. We'd camped in the woods, but he's running through an open area that he needs to cross to get to us. That's why the dragon can see him.

"Dain!" I shout, waving my arms. "Dragon!"

He hears me then, his head shooting up.

"What?" he says, slowing.

"No! Run! Drag—!"

A roar cuts me short, and Dain spins and stumbles. As he does, I see something clutched in his arms. A black sphere as big as Jacko.

Dain has the dragon egg. That's why he's early—he had a chance to snatch it.

That's also why the dragon is chasing him.

"Put it down!" I shout. "Put the egg down and run!"

He's off and running, but with the egg still in his arms. He's seen the dragon, and now he's bending to lower the egg to the ground, and I'm running at him as fast as I can, Malric ahead of me, Jacko trumpeting his alert cry. And the dragon is swooping. Swooping so fast she's a black blur, talons outstretched.

"Dain!"

I don't even get his name out before she strikes. There is blackness. Nothing but blackness, a shadow that seems to swallow Dain whole and then she's winging up again, taking to the sky . . . and the meadow is empty.

A cry. A cry of panic and shock, and I follow it up to see Dain clutched in the dragon's talons. I run after them, my sword out, shouting for her to bring him back, that she can have the egg, we don't want the egg. The night swallows Dain's cries as the dragon keeps rising into the sky.

And then she is gone.

CHAPTER TWENTY-NINE

I run. I don't have time to return to the others. I try to send Malric back, but he ignores me. I'm running for Mount Gaetal, and I will not stop.

I find the river easily—I can hear the running water—and follow it to the mountain's base, where I locate the pool. Before I jump in, I check to be sure my sword is secured. A rustling in the bushes has me jumping, even as Malric only glances in that direction.

Alianor steps through, breathing hard from running.

I exhale. "Good. Can you tell Wilmot that Dain's been taken? I'm going after him."

"I'm coming with you."

I shake my head. "I need you to—"

"I'm not one of your hunters, Rowan. I don't need to obey your commands. Wilmot will figure it out or he won't. Better for you to have me at your side."

"Take Jacko. He can't swim. Keep him here—"

She folds her arms over her chest. "I am not babysitting your jackalope. I'm coming with you. He'll come or he'll stay."

There's no time to argue. Every heartbeat is another moment when Dain might die.

"Follow me, then. It's dark, but try—"

She hands me something from her pack. It's a hair clip I gave her—not the jeweled one, but one woven with a firebird feather. It picks up the moonlight and glows like a flame.

"Wear that," she says. "I'll be able to follow you. Now get in there and swim."

I try to leave Jacko on the shore. He won't hear of it. He climbs onto my back and clings there. When Malric tries to pull him off, the jackalope hisses, but Malric only bends his forequarters, telling Jacko to ride on his back. Then we're off.

I don't think about how I'll find the other side. If I do, I'll panic. I just keep going until I judge I've swum as far as Doscach did. Then I rise and surface in the cavern.

We all climb out, soaking wet and shivering. Alianor and I left our boots on the shore—they'd only weigh us down—so we're walking barefoot. As I move, I wring out my hair and clothing, but I keep moving, straight for that tunnel.

Jacko runs on ahead, leading the way. Alianor follows me, with Malric at the rear. We don't speak. We just move as fast as we can.

I'm trying not to think of what we'll find at the end of

this tunnel. If only Dain had dropped the egg. But maybe if he had, the dragon would have killed him for stealing it. My hope—my fervent, deepest hope—is that his panic subsided enough for him to strategize, and as soon as the dragon released her hold, he made a run for it.

I want to round a corner and see him racing toward me. He knows the tunnel exists. He knows not to run out to the ledge, which is a sheer and deadly drop.

I hope we'll barrel into him as he flees, and then we can escape together.

With every step, that hope fades. I don't hear his running footfalls, and soon I do hear other sounds—those of the dragon and her young.

I force myself to stop and whisper to Alianor. We're coming up on that side tunnel where the juvenile had heard me and peeked out. We'll use that same small passage to peek in. Or I will, while she stands guard with Malric.

We reach the side tunnel and I slow, straining to listen. Then I ask the others to wait, including Jacko. The jackalope chitters softly, and I nod and motion for him to stay at my feet. That satisfies him, and we move into the side passage.

From beyond the passage come the sounds I'd heard earlier. The rumble that I'd mistaken for thunder or shifting ground. The birdlike noises I'd mistaken for wyvern cries. The former comes from the dragon mother as she communicates with her young, who respond with those high-pitched bird noises. The sounds are calm, though. She has her egg back, and things have returned to normal. And Dain?

I swallow and take another step before I can peek out. We're on the opposite side from where the mother dragon rests, near the eggs and burbling pool. Moonlight fills the cavern, letting me see. This is a smaller room, scattered with bones and debris and what looks like sleeping areas. The juveniles' bedroom and play area, the space too small for their mother. I don't see either young dragon here, though. They're with her in the nursery.

I take one more step, and moonlight brightens the room as it flows through the cavern opening. I see more debris and—

My breath catches.

I see Dain.

He lies off to the side, curled up on the floor. I see him, and my heart stops.

He isn't moving.

He's lying there, clutching Dez against his stomach, and neither of them is moving. The dragon killed them. She got her egg back—

Dain's chest rises. I stare at one spot on his chest, completely focused on it to be certain of what I'm seeing.

He's asleep. They both are, the dropbear's chest also rising and falling as she breathes.

The dragon didn't give them time to escape. She put them down and breathed on them, putting them to sleep so they didn't distract from her main goal: recovering her egg.

Now she's got that, she's tending to it, making sure it's still viable, the baby inside still alive. Once she's certain, she'll deal with the supposed thief. She'll deal with Dain.

I just need to wake him. Slip in there, while she's busy on the other side, and—

Claws scrape rock. A shadow moves through the moonlight, and I shrink back. Then I peek again. One of the juveniles is making its way toward Dain.

I pull out my sword. As much as I don't want to hurt the young dragon, Dain is unconscious and defenseless.

I adjust my grip and watch the juvenile's slow approach. It's curious. Maybe it'll wake Dain. That would be perfect. Dain wakes up, and I can call to him. It would be safe. The mother dragon can't get into this tunnel. Call him here, and we can flee.

The young dragon stops near Dain, reaches out its long neck and sniffs him. Then it opens and closes its mouth, and I tense, seeing those serrated teeth, but the beast doesn't seem to be preparing to bite him. I can't tell what it's doing, and then I figure it out, and I almost laugh.

It's trying to sedate him. To use its narcoleptic breath to be completely certain he's unconscious. Of course, it's far too young for that, and instead, it just makes small coughing noises. Then, satisfied Dain is soundly sleeping, the beast reaches out one talon and pokes at his shoulder.

"Rowan."

Alianor's voice at my ear makes me jump. She motions me to silence, and I give her a hard look for that. I wouldn't need to be warned if someone didn't sneak up on me.

"Someone's coming," she whispers.

I nod. "Wilmot."

She looks doubtful. "It's more than one person."

"Wilmot and Trysten, then?"

"I . . ." She steps back and waves for me to follow. "Just come and check it out with me."

I glance back at Dain. "I can't." I motion for her to peek out as I whisper in her ear. "I'm hoping the juvenile will wake him, and he can run. I need to be here to call to him. Or to intercede if it attacks."

She nods. "I'll go check out who's coming."

"Take Malric."

Another nod, and she's gone. I bend down to Jacko and give him a pat as we watch the juvenile dragon. It's being careful. *Too* careful. I want it to prod at Dain, roughly. Wake him up before whoever's coming—

Footsteps thump in the tunnel, and I jerk my head up at the same time the juvenile does, its golden eyes turning my way. I back up until I can peer into the tunnel and see Alianor returning at a run, her bare feet slapping the rock. I motion wildly for her to slow down, but even as I do, I hear the pad of multiple feet, moving quietly but steadily.

Alianor swings into the side passage with me. "It's Geraint and his men."

"Did they see you?"

"I don't think so."

I hesitate. I'm not sure what to do here. I want to stop them from getting into the den. From stealing more eggs or hurting the juveniles. But a part of me also whispers that I could use the distraction of their arrival to rescue Dain.

What is my responsibility here? To my hunter? Or to the dragon?

My hunter *and* my friend. I must get Dain out, yet I must also try to avoid betraying the dragon.

Betray her? She would have killed you. Killed Dain.

It would be safer for Tamarel if she left. But if all her offspring were stolen, she might attack Tamarel.

While my priority is Dain, I cannot flee and let Geraint destroy her family.

"We're getting Dain," I whisper. "As soon as the dragon hears them, we're getting him out. Then you're taking him."

"While you do what?"

"I-I'm not sure. Just get Dain out."

"They'll kill you. Or she will. We need to—"

Something lunges behind me. I see it just as Alianor yanks me away—it's the young dragon who'd been checking out Dain. It opens its mouth and coughs.

Alianor's brows shoot up.

"It's trying to spray us," I say. "With narcoleptic breath it doesn't have yet."

"Nothing in that sentence made sense."

"It's fine. Just let it keep coughing at us."

I step back and motion for her to do the same. Malric leaps between us, but the dragon just hisses and then tries spraying again. Even the warg looks confused. He doesn't attack, though, just nudges us into reverse, which is what we're already doing, Jacko at our feet.

Then there's a cry behind us. A human cry of surprise that turns to anger, and I glance over my shoulder to see one of Geraint's men.

CHAPTER THIRTY

I wheel on him, my sword raised. "Go. This den is under the protection of Queen Mariela of Clan Dacre. Withdraw now and vacate her lands, and you will be spared any legal prosecution arising from your trespass."

The man stares at me, as does the other appearing at his shoulder. Then they both laugh.

"I thought it sounded good," Alianor grumbles. "But apparently, they want to do this the hard way."

She brandishes her dagger. They laugh harder.

"Step down, princess," Geraint says as he appears behind them. "This is a task for men, not little girls."

"Stealing from a dragon?" I say. "That's not a task. It's theft."

"Also *really* stupid," Alianor says. "Haven't you already lost a couple of men?"

"It's a risk we're willing to take," one of the others says. "To win the prize of a lifetime."

"Now step away from that baby dragon," Geraint says. "We'll toss you a copper for working your clan magic on it and keeping it calm." His smile grows. "We'll even make it a silver if you lead him right down this tunnel for us."

"A princess doesn't need . . ." Alianor begins.

She trails off as she realizes they know I don't need money. They're mocking us. As for the juvenile, I'd forgotten all about him when I turned my back, which is an unforgivable error. Fortunately, Malric's watching the young dragon. It is indeed calm, though that has nothing to do with us and everything to do with the fact that it hasn't learned fear yet. It's curious, its neck extended as it sniffs at Malric, who allows it.

And that's when we realize we've all forgotten the biggest threat of all. We're here, talking away, and Momma Dragon has been silent. Sneaking up . . . as much as a creature the size of two houses can sneak. I don't hear her. I don't see her. But I smell her breath, wafting down the main tunnel.

The men do, too. The ones at the end of the group turn and give a start, as they see what I cannot. The dragon, I presume, her head shoved into the tunnel as she breathes.

"Back!" Geraint calls, as several more men appear down the tunnel. "Hold your breath and get back. Let it subside."

"Then keep going," I say. "Clear this tunnel. Now."

"Actually, I think we will," Geraint says. "You've convinced us. Now just come and stand right over here." He points to the mouth of the tunnel. "Stand there, and watch us go. Don't worry about the dragon. She can't fit in here."

"Nice try," I say. "Her breath puts people to sleep."

Alianor's eyes round, and then she nods in understanding before waving her dagger at Geraint. "Yes, nice try indeed. Back out, as the princess said, and we will not be forced to feed you to this tiny dragon."

She points at the juvenile, now sniffing noses with Jacko. The men laugh.

"You think we're joking?" Alianor says. "This is the royal monster hunter. Friend to monsters everywhere. What greater way to prove that Tamarel welcomes the dragon than for Princess Rowan to teach her babies how to hunt and kill?"

"Hunt and kill humans?" one says.

Alianor shrugs. "Only the bad ones. It's an excellent national security plan."

Geraint sneers. "I have heard your father is a poor warlord. That he has forgotten the 'war' part of his title and prefers negotiation, wielding his silver tongue in place of a sword. You'll need to improve that tongue of *yours*, girl, if you hope to follow his lead. Do you really think silly jokes will frighten us off?"

"No, I think they'll convince you I'm a fool before—"

She charges, dagger out, shouting a war cry. She slashes the first man she reaches, before I rush to her side, wielding my sword. Jacko lets out his own battle cry and jumps on another man, who yowls as the jackalope digs in claws and teeth. Malric roars and leaps at Geraint. Then there's a blur of black as the juvenile rushes in, shrieking and flapping its wings, one of which smacks into me.

"No!" I say to the dragon. "Back! Get back!"

It doesn't listen, and somewhere deep in the cavern comes the answering cry of the other juvenile. Its mother roars, clearly conveying the same message I had to its sibling, but it listens just as well, and soon we have two small dragons in the passage, coughing and flapping their wings and baring their teeth.

They fill the side passage, smacking into me and Alianor and Malric—and stepping on Jacko. The jackalope hisses and chatters at them, and they actually seem to understand that far more than my shouts. They stop trying to attack . . . and in the chaos, one of the men throws a rope halter over the first juvenile's neck.

I swing my sword, cutting the rope lead in his hand. Another leaps forward to grab the halter itself, but Jacko scrambles onto the man's head. As the jackalope rakes the man's scalp with his claws, the man screams, and Alianor says, "I always knew that head-riding thing would come in handy."

I give a grim smile as I free the young dragon from the halter. Then I slash the rope and throw it aside, and nudge the young dragon behind me. We face off. Geraint's men are still in the main tunnel, and we're at the mouth of the side passage. With powerful legs, Jacko kicks his quarry's head as he leaps off him. Malric has a man on the floor. Another ventured too far down the main tunnel and lies unconscious. Only two remain, Alianor and I each holding weapons on them as they brandish theirs.

Geraint is gone. He must have escaped in the melee—footsteps echo down the corridor.

I raise my sword. "Your leader has fled. He knows you are outnumbered. Run now, or we will make you run, and we will not stop these baby dragons if they mistake that for a hunting lesson."

It's not quite as dramatic as Alianor's threats, but it's the best I can do, especially when I *would* stop the young dragons . . . out of fear the poachers would capture them.

The man Jacko had attacked is already fleeing, as he blinks through streaming blood. The one at the end of my sword glances at him, as if considering doing the same.

"Just leave," I say. "Leave, and get out of Tamarel, and we will not pursue you. Your leader has forsaken—"

A roar. Until now, the dragon had been silent. She must have seen her babies being shouldered back and known they were safe. Now she roars again, and there is more than concern in her voice. There is fear and rage.

That's when I hear the footfalls. Coming from inside the cavern. I dart to the main tunnel and look down to the end. The dragon's head no longer fills the opening. Instead, it is blocked by her flank. Her head faces the side cavern, the one where she cannot fit, the one her youngsters use.

As I turn, Geraint appears at the end of the side passage with an egg under each arm.

I lunge into his path, sword raised. As I do, the man I'd been facing off with takes advantage and strikes at me. Malric's there, though. He releases his quarry, leaps between me and my would-be attacker and snarls at both men. Alianor holds off the third. That leaves me with Geraint.

"Put the eggs down," I say.

"Drop them?" he says, his grin growing. "Did you tell me to drop them, your highness?"

I grit my teeth. "Put them on the ground. Carefully."

"I'm a subject of Dorwynne. I'm not under the command—"

"While you are on our land, you are under our command."

He purses his lips. "Are you sure? I'm not some rabble camping within your borders, princess. I work for the king of Dorwynne himself. He entrusted me with his son, whom you have taken. He also entrusted me to bring him these eggs. You might want to consult your mother before you threaten me."

"No."

His brows shoot up. "No? Are you queen now, little girl?"

"I am the royal monster hunter. I am aware of every matter concerning monsters. If you are suggesting my mother sanctioned this, you obviously think me a fool."

"I said nothing of the sort. I simply suggested this could be a diplomatic error on your part. A serious one."

"All right, then," I say. "I was never very good at politics. We'll need to consult my mother. Return the eggs, and I'll take you to her."

The dragon has stopped roaring. She hears conversation. She knows her eggs are still in her caves. She also knows she cannot get to them. So she waits, assessing and considering.

She will not wait forever. If Geraint takes these eggs, she'll fly out to try to stop him on the ground. She'll kill any human in her way . . . or any human she *thinks* is in her way.

"Put down the eggs," I repeat. "You cannot fight while you hold them. Only three of your men remain, and none of those are in any position to help you."

I jerk my head toward the men, who are in the main tunnel, held back by Alianor and Malric, with Jacko watching. The two juvenile dragons wander about, sniffing everyone, as if we're guests come to call. When one of Malric's targets slides a rope from his shoulder, though, a juvenile snaps at him, wings twitching.

"Choose," Geraint says.

"What?"

He nods toward the juveniles. "The king of Dorwynne expects a dragon. I can take one of those two or I can take both eggs."

"Both eggs?" Alianor says. "You said he expects *a* dragon."

"The young ones are alive and healthy. The eggs are unlikely to both hatch. I'd likely only get one viable baby. The eggs or one young dragon. You choose, princess."

"I'm not the one you need to worry about," I say. "My mother isn't the one you need to worry about. I'm not protecting the dragon. I'm protecting my country *from* the dragon. From what she will do if you take her baby. She's already sent the monsters fleeing toward Tamarel, because she felt threatened. What will she do when she's lost two more eggs? Or a baby dragon?"

His smile returns, showing his teeth. "I believe that's *your* problem."

My hands clench around my sword. I want to . . . not *kill* him. I couldn't do that. But I want to stop him in any way I can, and I fear that if I lose my temper, I might lash out worse than I intend to.

"One egg," Alianor says.

I turn on her, but she meets my gaze with a steady look. She isn't really telling him he can have an egg. She intends for us to get it back.

I'm not sure what good that will do. We've already played this particular game—Geraint gets an egg, we steal it, the dragon takes it, Geraint comes back and takes two.

Alianor is trying to buy us time. I understand that. But I also understand that the dragon will not put up with another round of this game.

"Fine," Geraint says. "One egg. Now catch."

He tosses one egg, and I lunge, dropping to one knee and then falling backward when it smacks me in the chest. I manage to catch it, though, arms wrapped around it as I sit on the ground, sword awkwardly half-clutched in one hand. I realize my mistake and go to fix my grip on the sword, but before I can, there is a dagger at my throat. Geraint's dagger. Malric snarls and Alianor shouts, but Geraint only digs in the dagger tip, until they quiet.

"Such a child." He sneers at me as I let my sword drop and clutch the egg instead. "You couldn't help falling for that one, could you? Now I will take both eggs and both of these young dragons you've helpfully calmed for me."

He waves at his three men. "Lead those two off. Take this egg." He motions to the one still under his arm. "When you are safely outside, shout and I'll release the princess. Everyone else—"

Geraint falls back with a howl as Alianor dives to catch the egg before it falls. I'm on my feet, my own dagger in hand. Blood runs from his leg where I stabbed him.

CHAPTER THIRTY-ONE

"**D**id you really think I'd drop my only weapon?" I say. "That I'd give up so easily?"

I lunge at Geraint and slash his side. His eyes widen in such shock that you'd think I'd driven my blade into his heart.

We're in the side cavern now—the juveniles' bedroom—and I can see Dain near the cave mouth. He's still fast asleep with Dez on his chest. Geraint lifts his dagger, but Jacko leaps onto his leg and sinks his teeth into the spot I'd stabbed.

My blade slams up, broadside, against Geraint's wrist and his dagger clangs to the floor. When he scrambles for it, I kick him. He stumbles, and I bend and roll the egg aside, freeing both of my hands.

I'm about to deliver another slash when one of the young dragons barrels past me. It hits Geraint with its broad head and sends him into the wall. Then the dragon grabs him by the leg and drags him, screaming, along the floor. The young dragon snuffles at Geraint's injuries.

"It's the blood," Alianor says. "He smells blood."

The dragon chomps down, right on the leg I cut. Geraint screams, and the mother dragon roars, and the baby is about to back off in surprise when I leap in and pretend to haul the young beast off the poacher. By then, its sibling is there, black tongue darting out as it samples the air and picks up the taste of blood.

Geraint scrambles to his feet.

"They're going to eat you," Alianor says. "And we won't stop them."

The second juvenile faces off with Geraint, tongue flicking. The first has already lost interest, but I pretend that I'm holding the beast back. It thinks that's a fine game, and it snaps and hisses in play.

"Go!" I say to Geraint. "Get out of here now!"

Geraint darts past the first juvenile and he tears into the side passage. At the last second, he reaches down to grab the egg I'd put on the floor, but Alianor's there, grabbing his tunic and shoving him along. Then Malric is between Geraint and the egg. The poacher snaps a command to his men ... but the tunnel is empty.

"Yeah, they're gone," Alianor says. "They took off when it looked like you were about to be dragon chow."

"Go," I say. "This is your last chance—"

Geraint still tries to feint around Malric to get the egg, but the warg knocks him to the floor. A brief struggle ensues before Malric has Geraint securely pinned.

"Are the others really gone?" I ask Alianor.

She nods. "For now." She hoists up both eggs, one under each arm. Then she walks toward me. "Trade you these for babysitting duty? I think Mom wants them—now."

The dragon roars, and Alianor stumbles back, nearly losing her footing. Jacko trumpets his alert cry as I dive in to steady Alianor. Then we both look up to see the head of a dragon, less than five feet away. She's shoved her body forward as far as it will go and snaked her head into the side cavern. Behind her shoulder, I see Dain, still sleeping.

He's still sleeping, and the dragon is between us . . . and we're holding her eggs and standing with her two youngsters, as if we're about to run off with all four.

The mother roars again, and as her jaws widen, her breath takes on that smell I know well.

"Don't inhale!" I say to Alianor. "Get back."

"The eggs—"

"Just get back."

We both back away as far as we can, well out of her reach. She roars her fury and shakes her head. The one juvenile nudges my shoulder, completely unconcerned and wanting to resume play. The other bends its head to sniff Jacko.

"We'll roll the eggs toward her," I say. "Give me one."

She does. We bend and roll the eggs. They don't reach the mother dragon, who strains to get them.

"I'm sorry," I say. "We don't dare come any closer. But we aren't holding them anymore. If you'll back up—"

She roars, the sound deafening.

"I think that's a no," Alianor murmurs.

"Count of three, hold your breath, run forward and give your egg another push."

As soon as we come closer, the dragon breathes again. We each shove an egg, as quickly as we can. Then, as we back away, I stumble over Jacko, who's standing in place, blinking. He must have been coming to help me and inhaled some of the sedative. When I stumble, I accidentally breathe in. I clamp my mouth shut, grab Jacko and back away.

The poison hits me like getting slammed in the head, a sudden dizziness that rocks me off balance. I manage to brace against a wall, clutching Jacko, who's now fully asleep, as the two young dragons sniff us. Across the cavern, the dragon has one egg in her mouth. She places it behind her and does the same for the second. Then she eyes her two youngsters and roars.

"Playtime's over, guys," Alianor says. "Mom wants you home."

When they ignore her, I set the sleeping jackalope down and give one juvenile a shove. Momma Dragon roars, and I back away, hands raised.

"I'm not hurting them," I say. "Not taking them. They're just . . ."

"Making friends with the royal monster hunter," Alianor says. "As all young monsters do. Now we just need Dain to wake up and tell us you're not—absolutely not—taking these guys home."

I glance at Dain. He's still unconscious . . . and still on the other side of the dragon. I need her to retreat so I can slip him away, and I'd rather he *didn't* wake up before that.

"Hey, Dain!" Alianor begins, but I frantically shush her. She figures out why and nods. If he startles awake—or Dez does—it'll remind the dragon they're there.

"We need to lead these guys down the main tunnel," I say. "Get them back to Momma that way."

"And get her away from Dain."

"Right. I'm going to try leading them. Will you wait here?"

She nods. "Wait here and wake Dain when it's safe."

"If you can. Don't take any chances, though. Please."

"I'm Clan Bellamy. We only take chances if there's coin involved. Just don't offer me a new jeweled hair clip if I save him."

I smile and shake my head. "I'll offer you a jeweled hair clip if you *don't* take unnecessary chances. How's that?"

"Mmm, we'll see." She waves me away. "Take your babies and go."

The next part is tougher than it seemed. While the juveniles are curious and happy to follow me, it enrages their mother. I can't tell her what I'm doing. She only sees me touching her babies and herding them into the side passage, out of her sight. She roars and slams into the walls, and the whole cavern shudders with her rage and fear.

I lead the two juveniles into the main tunnel, where Malric still has Geraint pinned. The warg growls at me, telling me he does not like this plan. Or I presume that lip quiver is a growl. I can't hear anything over the bellows of an enraged mother dragon.

And then things get even tougher. There's a warg and the bleeding Geraint on the floor, and the young dragons want to check that out. There's also a sleeping man, one of the poachers. One juvenile lowers its head to examine him and flicks its tongue over his face, and he wakes. He sees a dragon's face hovering over his, and screams, flailing.

The juvenile squeals in surprise, and Momma's hearing must be attuned to that sound, because she manages to hear it over her own cries. She jams her head into the main tunnel, reaching in as far as she can.

Her jaws open, and I hold my breath, but she snaps instead, those sword-sized teeth bared as she snarls and whips her head back and forth. The young dragon only paws at the screaming man, and its sibling idly examines the man's boot before taking the end in its teeth and giving a tentative tug.

"You do realize your mother is freaking out twenty feet away, right?" I say to them. "She's going to have her hands—well, talons—full with you two. Now I know how my mother feels."

I get behind one and push. "Go! Get home! See, Momma Dragon? I'm shoving them in *your* direction."

I'm joking—half-panicked, half-exasperated—but the dragon does stop roaring. She even pulls back a little to eye us as I shove the juvenile from behind, its tail smacking me with every step. Finally, I give one last push, and the juvenile is within her reach . . . and immediately twists around and tries to dive back toward me. She grabs her baby and hauls it to her side, hissing and snapping as the young one rumbles in its chest like a grumbling child.

She shoulders that one aside and then waits as I propel its sibling her way. At the last moment, the second juvenile realizes its fate and tries to scramble away, but it's within Momma's reach now, too. I give a tremendous shove, and the baby grabs my arm in its talons, and we both go tumbling. My head strikes rock, and I black out for a heartbeat and then open my eyes . . .

The mother dragon is above me. Just like the first time. She's looking down at me, her massive head poised over me. My heart stops.

She eyes me. Her jaws open, and all I see is teeth and the black hole of her throat. Then her jaws shut and she sniffs me. Her golden eye comes so close I can see flecks of black shimmering in it. She blinks and snorts ... and then she raises her head, moving away.

"I'm sorry," I say as I sit up. Across the cavern, I see a broken egg. The one Geraint's men purposely broke. My heart cracks a little. "I'm very sorry. I—"

One young dragon tackles me. Clearly, I am sitting on the ground waiting for that. It leaps on me with a chirp of joy. I fend it off, waiting for its mother to roar. She doesn't. Nor does she help. She just watches for a moment and then begins licking one of the stolen eggs, cleaning our human smell from it.

"You are not taking that home," croaks a voice, and I manage to shove the young dragon aside enough to see Dain rising unsteadily, Alianor helping him, Dez still asleep on Dain's chest.

That's when the other juvenile joins in and jumps on me. Dain shakes his head as I sputter and fight my way from under the two dragons, as their nips get harder than I'd like.

"What is it with you invading monster nurseries?" Dain says, his voice still crackling. "The gryphons weren't enough. You had to find yourself a dragon den."

Alianor chuckles. "Monsters are going to be circulating Rowan's picture everywhere. Beware this human. She comes into your nurseries and plays with your babies."

"I'm not—" I push one dragon's snout aside. "Not

trying—" I push the other's tail away. "Not trying to play. Momma Dragon? Help me out here?"

She only looks over and then returns to cleaning her eggs.

"I think she's saying you're hired," Alianor says as she tries to extricate me from the youngsters. "Your new job. Dragon nanny."

"Just help me out of here. Please. I don't want to overstay our welcome."

Alianor helps . . . which only makes the young dragons think she's joining the game. Dain heads over, unsteady on his feet, the sleeping dropbear still clinging to him. One juvenile lunges at him, and he staggers back, but the beast only knocks him down and licks his face, like an oversized puppy. That wakes Dez up . . . and she freaks out, but then Jacko comes running and jumps on the juvenile's back in play, and Dez realizes it's a game and . . .

Well, I'm sure later on, we'll look back and marvel at this moment—"playing" with young dragons as their mother watches—but right now, we're very aware of that mother dragon, and the fact that we need to get out of here before her mood changes. Also, baby dragons bite *hard*.

It's Malric who breaks it up, prowling in and dragging me away, all the while glowering like I'm goofing off and he's forced to be the adult here.

"I wasn't—" I say, but he's already gone, diving in to get Jacko next. "Hey, wait! What about Geraint?"

"Covered!" a voice calls from the tunnel.

I take Jacko from Malric and head back into the tunnel as Malric rescues the others. There, I find Trysten holding a dagger to Geraint's throat.

Trysten grins. "I kinda like this. Feels very satisfying." Before I can respond, he says, "Wilmot sent me in. Doscach showed me the way. Wilmot and I were both coming when Geraint's men started appearing out of the water, ranting about killer baby dragons." He peers down the tunnel. "I see what they mean."

"Is Wilmot okay? Sunniva?"

"She's with him. And he's with a troop of your mother's men, led by Kaylein and the captain of your mother's guard."

I grin. "Berinon!"

"Yep, Kaylein brought help, and a couple of your hunters tracked us from where we left her and Cedany. They have the poachers. We just need to get this one out." He glances over my shoulder at Dain and his grin grows. "You're okay."

Dain nods and sneaks a look at me. "Thank you for coming after me."

"Did you really think she wouldn't?" Alianor comes up behind him, panting with exertion. "She *ran* all the way here. Took off the second she saw you grabbed by the dragon."

I call for Malric, saving Dain from a response. The warg backs into the tunnel, growling at the young dragons as they try to follow.

"Hey!" Alianor says. "You took a trophy."

She snatches at something that's stuck in my belt. It's a baby tooth from the dragons. She puts it into my hand. Then she glances toward the smaller cavern.

"I saw a few more in there. They must be teething. Mind if I grab some?"

"Quickly," I say. "And you have to share."

She takes off, and I look down at Geraint.

— 302 —

"On your feet and walk," I say. "I'll let Trysten do the honors. I have a feeling he'd be more than happy to put a few extra holes in you."

And so we tramp down the tunnel with our hostage, Alianor catching up in a few moments, Malric holding off the baby dragons until their mother intercedes and keeps them back. Then the warg catches up, and we continue on, leaving a family of contented dragons behind.

CHAPTER THIRTY-TWO

Just over a week has passed. It took nearly that long to get home to the castle. We went on ahead while Berinon and his men escorted the prisoners. We kept to the riverbed this time, which made a quicker journey. Then it was home to tell our story.

This morning, I'm telling that tale to a group of schoolchildren. I'm in the castle town—the one that sits outside our walls. The children there are accustomed to hearing monster stories, but this one is different. This one has everyone in the kingdom talking, and when the teacher invited me to speak, Mom thought I should go.

Eventually, adventure stories like ours will be turned into bard songs that exaggerate our deeds, but in the earliest days, they're more likely to become twisted into rumor, by fear and worry. Mom's already dealing with a stream of messengers from mayors and lords, all concerned about how the dragon family might endanger Tamarel.

I'm in the village school, which is jammed so tight it's a wonder anyone can breathe. Apparently, all the parents decided *this* was the day they wanted to sit in on their children's lessons.

Dain is with me. I kind of dragged him along. He's a monster hunter, and he needs to take credit for his feats, even if he complains that his "feat" was being snatched by a dragon and rescued by a princess. As I point out, though, he's the one who heroically offered to be taken by the poachers and then snatched the egg from under their noses.

Malric is with me, as always. Jacko, too. Dain brought Dez . . . or Dez came along, attached to Dain. I'd invited Sunniva, since she rescued me from the dragon den the first time. She ignored my request . . . until she flew overhead and saw the children fawning over Doscach. That's where we are now, out-of-doors, with the children greeting Sunniva and Doscach as I speak to the village teacher.

"You must come back," she says. "You are a gifted storyteller, your highness." She nods to Dain. "And you too, Sir Dain."

"I'm not a sir," he says. "Just a regular boy."

"All the more reason to come back. There are many children who do not think they can aspire to things like monster hunting because they are 'just a regular' boy or girl. You are a role model for them."

He mumbles something unintelligible.

An older man shoulders his way in. "I don't suppose you'd part with your dragon's tooth, lad," he says to Dain. "It would fetch a small fortune in Roiva. I'm off there with an envoy tomorrow." He smiles. "I do believe I'll dine all month on the story of the dragons in Tamarel."

Dain frowns, and the teacher explains that the trader means he'll be invited to dinner by those who'll want to hear the dragon story. I only half listen as I realize something I need to tell my mother.

Kaylein escorts Dain and me back to the castle. Cedany had been in town, treating a villager, but she joins us for the walk back.

Just inside the castle gates, we find Berinon speaking to his soldiers. I tell him I need to see my mother—urgently— and he escorts me in while telling Kaylein to take the rest of the afternoon off with Cedany. Kaylein protests, naturally, but not very hard. Cedany will need to go home soon to make sure the workers repair her cabin properly.

I burst into the council chambers to find Mom and Rhydd locked in a meeting with Trysten and the council, where they're discussing what to do about Dorwynne, how to find out whether Geraint was right that the king is trying to buy dragons.

"Did you notice the door was closed?" Heward asks dryly.

"I let her in," Berinon says, his voice a deep rumble. "She says she has news about the dragon."

"About the dragon story," I say. "A problem."

I tell them about the trader and what he said.

"He's going to take this story to other countries," I say.

"And he won't be the only one. This story will not stay in Tamarel. We can't make it stay in Tamarel. People will head into the mountains to see her—or try poaching an egg or baby. Then there are the other kingdoms, and how they'll react. Wilmot said dragons could be used for war. What if they think that's what we're planning to do with them? We need to consider all this and make plans and . . ." I look from Mom to Rhydd. "And you've already thought of this."

"I have," Mom says. "Since it concerned a monster, I should have brought you into the discussions. I planned to do that soon. For now, I wanted you to rest. You've had a very difficult two weeks and . . ." Now she's the one catching my look. She sighs. "And I made a mistake."

Heward clears his throat.

"Yes, I'm admitting to my child that I made a mistake," she snaps at him. "I have my way of parenting, and you have yours. As the royal monster hunter—"

"Elect," Heward says. "Rowan is the royal monster hunter *elect* until she passes her trials."

Mom continues what she'd been saying before he interrupted. "As the royal monster hunter, Rowan should have been told what was under discussion. As for her trials, she has already been to the mountains. Twice, if you include the gryphon's lair."

"That was the foothills," Heward says.

"Either way, I believe she has fulfilled the spirit of her trials, if not the exact requirements. Yes, Heward, she was supposed to go alone. But she went into a dragon's den. Twice. She survived multiple encounters with monsters, all made more dangerous by their panic over the dragon."

"Rompos," Berinon says with a grin. "She was attacked by rompos. I believe that's a first for any monster hunter."

"Proving, I believe, that she has endured more than would have been expected of her in any trial, and therefore should be recognized as the royal monster hunter."

"No," Heward says.

I swear Mom's teeth grind as she turns to him. Even Berinon's eyes blaze, belying his stone-faced expression.

"She has not fulfilled—" Heward begins.

"Fine," Mom says, throwing up her hands. "Fine. In the midst of this dragon crisis, we'll send our royal monster hunter on a solo *camping* trip to the mountains. She can lounge by the campfire and enjoy the peace and quiet, now that all the monsters have been scared out of the area. That is a perfect use of our resources."

"Mariela is right," says a voice. It's Liliath, my great-aunt. "Sending Rowan off on what will now be a simple mission is not the proper use of our royal monster hunter, not while we have this diplomatic issue *involving* a monster."

"Then Rowan can wait until another year—" Heward tries again.

"No," Liliath says. "We need our royal monster hunter. I propose that we strike down two birds with this one stone. We send an envoy across the mountains to explain the situation. Rowan will join the expedition. As the person who has seen the dragons, she can argue most eloquently on their behalf. Rhydd will also go, as his first diplomatic mission."

Mom tenses but doesn't object.

"That will be Rowan's trial," Liliath says. "Escorting the envoy through the mountains and helping convince our neighbors they are in no immediate danger from 'our' dragons."

Liliath turns to the council. "Shall we vote?"

They do, and they agree. Rhydd and I are going across the mountains. Together.

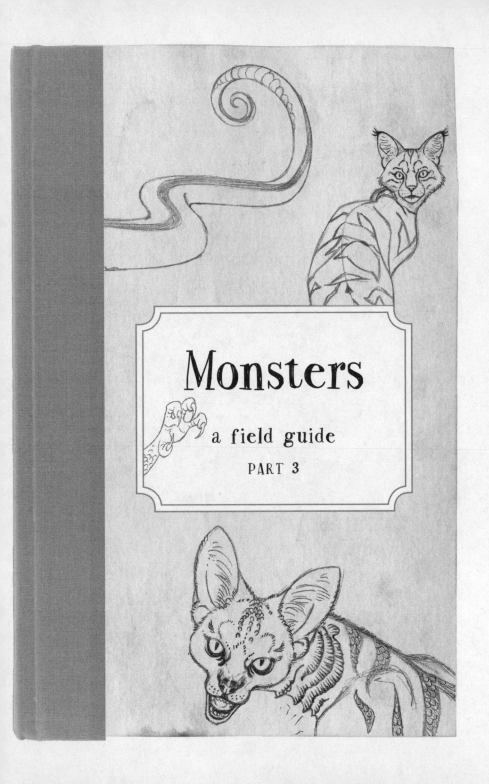

Monsters

a field guide

PART 3

Colocolo

Colocolos are one of the more common monsters in Tamarel, and they're often the first ones people see in the wild. They can be found in barns, where they're considered pests. While farmers are encouraged to relocate colocolos, they're usually killed in the mistaken belief that they live in house walls and drink saliva from sleeping humans.

CROSS-FERTILIZATION?

For most monsters who seem to be a cross between two animals, legends say that one kind of animal fell in love with another kind and had babies. Unless the animals are the same species—like dogs and wolves—that's actually impossible. For colocolos, it's even weirder. People say they're born when snakes and rats fertilize chicken eggs, which is not how fertilization works at all!

Harpy

Unlike other monsters, harpies will come after people for no reason at all. According to legend, it all goes back to the very first harpy. She'd been a human woman whose husband left her for someone else. She jumped off a cliff, and instead of dying, she grew wings and talons and killed her husband.

I don't think harpies actually hate humans. Their scrunched-up simian faces and red eyes make them look angry. They're definitely dangerous, though, so if people avoid them, that's for the best.

bony face and red eyes make the harpy one of the creepiest-looking monsters

swallow-like wings for easy aerial maneuvering

prehensile tail

bird talons allow harpies to carry prey

Dragon

The mountains that separate Tamarel from the rest of the land used to be home to dozens of dragons. History books say that our people lived in harmony with them. Jannah always said that was an oversimplification. We just avoided them by using passages through the mountains that steered clear of their caves. Dragons still attacked us sometimes, and we sometimes attacked them, but mostly we learned to live together.

END OF AN ERA

People across the mountains did not leave the dragons alone. They pillaged their caves for eggs and bones. That led to dragon attacks on villages, which in turn led to people outside Tamarel declaring dragons a menace. Eventually, the dragons decided this wasn't a safe place to raise their young, and they left for lands beyond the ocean.

DRAGON BONES

Dragon bone is supposed to be one of
the strongest materials in the world.

There are hidden places known as dragon burial grounds,
where old dragons went to die. Most of those were emptied
long ago, but my grandfather discovered one before I was
born and only the royal family knows where it is.

Rompo

Legend says that rompos used to be predators, but they were so frightened of prey animals that they starved, and that's why they're so thin. It's also supposedly why they switched to scavenging. Even then, they've been known to creep up on dead prey, circling several times, as if it might still leap up and attack.

CORPSE-EATERS

Another name for rompos is corpse-eaters. It's said that they have a taste for humans and dig up graves. I'd like to believe that's just a legend but . . . well, the first place I ever saw one was in a cemetery, where it was dragging away a body that'd been covered in stones until the ground thawed. Jannah said the part about having a taste for human flesh is nonsense. It's just that rompos have learned that we leave bodies aboveground in winter or don't bury them very deep (rompos are excellent diggers), so we make an easy meal.

Cath Palug

The first ballad I ever memorized was "Larkin and the Cath Palug." Larkin was one of the greatest Clan Dacre monster hunters, and this was the epic tale of his battle with the great cath palug that terrorized the waterways of Tamarel. Then Jannah brought a stuffed cath palug to our monster lessons, and I was certain she'd misidentified the beast. Surely this creature—no bigger than a hunting dog and lacking any special defenses—couldn't be the cath palug of the song. It is. Apparently, the song is meant to be funny. I prefer to think cath palugs were just a lot bigger in the old days.

gills for underwater breathing

webbed feet aid swimming

stripes are actually fish-like scales

Nekomata

A TALE OF TWO TAILS

I've always been fascinated by the nekomata's double tail.
Adaptations always serve an evolutionary purpose, and I don't
understand this one. That led me to research the purpose
of a cat's tail. I know they're used for communication, but
apparently, they're also used for balance. Does having two
tails mean nekomatas are even more agile than regular cats?
I'd need one for study, but considering they're one of the
most dangerous feline monsters, I don't think that'll
happen anytime soon.

EXPERT CAMOUFLAGE

I'd also love to study a nekomata's skin and fur.
What causes its skin to lighten and darken
with its surroundings? Is it blood flow? Is it
a conscious change or an automatic
one? I'd also like to see whether its
fur is different from other cats' or
if the fur seems to change color
because it's so short and the skin
shows through. So many questions.
So few answers. The nekomata
might not be an actual ghost
cat, but it's definitely a
creature of mystery.

Tatzelwurm

BABY DRAGONS?

Jannah says that at least 10 percent of a monster hunter's job is investigating claims of monsters that turn out to be regular animals. Back when dragons lived in the mountains, travelers sometimes claimed to see baby ones running through tunnels and hiding in caves. The monsters they reported, though, weren't much bigger than house cats, and dragons are only that size when they're newly hatched.

For years, monster hunters dismissed these "baby dragon" stories as lizard sightings. This seemed obvious when reports continued long after dragons had abandoned our lands. It was my great-grandmother Tatzel who discovered the truth. While on her monster hunter trials, she stayed in a cave that was also home to a cat-headed lizard beast. She ended up taming it to bring home and prove the existence of the creatures now known as tatzelwurms.

cute kitty-cat face

serpent-like body can coil like a snake

entire body only two feet long, often mistaken for baby dragons

hind legs smaller than front

Property of

Rowan